Eulie's Song

A NOVEL BY

Kathy Lauren Miller

First Edition 2020

ISBN-13: 978-1-7354988-0-5 (print)
ISBN-13: 978-1-7355988-1-2 (e-book)

Book Cover Design by Kathy Lauren Miller
Interior Book Design by Maureen Cutajar

KathyLaurenMiller.com

Blue Cadence Press

Acknowledgements

If we don't remember our history,
we may well find ourselves repeating it.
~ As noted by Edmund Burke, an 18th century Irish philosopher

The attributed sources listed have been an invaluable help in the writing of this novel. Of special interest is the Gullah vernacular, Geechee. It is the English based creole spoken by African Americans who live along the seaboard of South Carolina and Georgia. During slavery in the 18th century, the diversity of African languages the enslaved spoke made communication between the slaves and speakers of colonial English nearly impossible. The enslaved, who toiled in the rice fields of South Carolina and Georgia, appropriated English as a common language which they modified, and which was then influenced by the diverse African languages they spoke.

Gullah Folk Tales from the Georgia Coast, by Charles Colcock Jones, Jr.

Glossary of Gullah Words from Gullah Tours, 1922

Enslaved People's Work on Sugar Plantations of the Caribbean, The Saint Lauretia Project

A New and Accurate Description of the Coast of Guinea, Slave Ships, the Middle Passage by William Bosman, 1705

A Special Note of Thanks

To my husband, Jay, for his encouragement during the writing of this novel, and for the endless cups of hot coffee he delivered to me with just the right amount of cream and honey.

To my Beta Readers: Karen Dowdall, Kristen Corbin, Marilyn Green and Carla Baird, for their insightful critiques and friendship.

One

I sacrifice everything to the beauty of the words.
~ Patrick Chamoiseau ~

JUNE 1962 BATEAUX BAY, GEORGIA

If desperation was a color, it would be red. And hot. Leela's cheeks are aflame with her efforts. She eyes her reflection in the mirror. With her tongue pressed between her teeth, she attempts—for the umpteenth time—to sound out her name. Yet her name and every word she's tried gets stuck to the roof of her mouth and stays there. Consonants trip her tongue; she can never get past those before her stutter kicks in. She was relentlessly bullied in elementary school. When she got to middle school, she stopped talking altogether. It didn't stop the bullying though. She was called deaf, dumb and retarded. Years of speech therapy didn't help. Leela will be fifteen soon, and more than anything, she wants to talk. She wants to be like other girls her age. She's desperate for a miracle, and she believes she's found one.

Yesterday, she'd taken her time selecting five stones from the scatter she'd found along the sandy road in front of her grandmother's house. The stones are about the size and shape of marbles. After washing them, she places one stone on her tongue. It has a salty, bitter taste. Quickly, before her gag reflex can overwhelm her, she places the other four stones in her mouth. She leans over the old fashion pedestal sink eyeing her reflection in the grainy waves of her grandmother's antique mirror. Her cheeks are puffed out. She breathes through her nose, holding back a cough when a stone slides to the back of her throat. Thoughts of choking cluster like pin pricks crowding out reason and need. Still, she is desperate and willing to believe in ancient miracles.

Saliva gathers in her mouth. Fear precludes the option of swallowing. The stones shift with the movement of her tongue. If she chokes now, she will blame it on the Greeks. In ancient times, she'd read, the great orators improved their speaking skills by practicing with stones in their mouths. She believes this to be true because it was written in italics in her ninth-grade history text. In her mind, anything written in italics is a bona fide truth.

Her first word—hello—sounds muffled, unintelligible, yet she presses on gaining some control over the stones. She tries her own name, which was always difficult because of the back to back consonants. Her tongue seldom got past the first consonant, and if it did, it was waylaid by the second one which resulted in the inevitable onslaught of stuttering. Once begun, there was no stopping it.

She'd been named after her maternal great grandmother, Laura Lee. It was her mother, Sable, a lover of words, who had combined the two words into a linguistic blend, a portmanteau.

Leela would most definitely have preferred a simpler vowel-consonant blend. A palindrome like Ava or Eve would have given her tongue a reprieve.

After several more words, all muffled, she finds she does not stutter. She moves on to a simple sentence. Her words are garbled, sounding as foreign as a dead language in an airless tomb. After a series of words and sentences, the stones, slick with saliva, begin to slide to the back of her throat. She can no longer suppress the overwhelming urge to swallow.

Leela bends over the sink. The stones tumble from her mouth. She catches them in her waiting palms before wrapping them in a washcloth. Leela has wished for a miracle and she is not disappointed. She sends up a prayer to those ancient Greeks and relishes what she now knows: She does not stutter with stones in her mouth. Hope rises in her heart.

Her stammering came on suddenly when she was six years old. Before that, she'd been as talkative as any kid her age. Then one day, her words came out wrong, and stayed wrong. Leela stumbled through elementary school with as few utterances as was necessary. That was until the day Mrs. Laskowski required the entire fifth grade to read their book reports orally and in the most terrifying place of all—the auditorium. When it was Leela's turn at the podium, her heart thundering in her ears, she stumbled through the title—omitting the consonants. When it came to the author's name, the first consonant stuck to the roof of her mouth. She tried with all her might to get past that consonant. Her valiant effort resulted in utterances sounding more like a braying lamb then human language. Her peers snorted. The snorts became guffaws and the guffaws became howls of laughter.

The book was White Fang. The author was Jack London.

She wanted to tell her mom what happened. She couldn't get the words out. That was the day she decided not to force her tongue to do what it could not. She refused to speak. Her parents went to Mrs. Laskowski for answers. But the teacher, who was usually talkative, pleaded ignorance. Days passed, then weeks. Still, Leela would only shake her head when asked to speak. Her father, Dale, banged the table in anger. Her mother, Sable, pleaded with Leela. Her speech therapist raised her arms in defeat. Leela came to rely on a notepad and sign language for her needs.

A girl without words is a solitary girl. Leela prefers this solitude over being the object of cruel laughter. She has her books, her writing—notebooks full of her poetry, and before her life took an unexpected turn, she had the birds. Her backyard at the time was small, bordered with a white fence and dotted with a combination of birdhouses and birdfeeders. There were the morning singers and those who sang at twilight. Doves cooed in their nests beneath the eaves. She learned to be statue-still—suet, seeds or grub worms in the palms of her hands. When she whistled their call notes they'd come, picking at the free meals she offered.

Now, Leela will not only be entering the tenth grade, she will be entering a new school in this new town far away from everything she has ever known.

Leela rinses the vestiges of brine from her mouth and wipes away the beads of perspiration which have formed across her brow. The narrow bathroom, even with its high ceiling, is stifling. The June sun in Georgia is too merciless to be considered benign sunshine. It permeates the limestone aquifer beneath the topsoil begetting waves of super-heated humidity. A fine layer of damp descends on furniture, clothes and skin. Milk spoils in the icebox, vegetables wilt in the sink. The air, tinged with salt from the bay below the escarpment that falls sharply from their front yard, smells of dead fish. Granny Vernell said the red tide had come early this year, but Leela's mother, fan blowing two inches from her face, said it smelled like the old fishing bay it had always been.

Leela is no longer content with her silent mouth. She is no longer content with herself. There is too much and too little of everything. She stands naked, bathwater puddling at her feet. She steps back from the dressing mirror, considers her body and decides there is too little to like. Her breasts are mere buds, her body, shapeless as a boy's. There are too many freckles on her face, and her chin is too pointed. Her mouth is too wide. The damp, humid air has turned her nut-brown hair into a nest of unmanageable curls.

The one saving grace to offset her discontent are her eyes. They are almond-shaped, fringed with thick, dark lashes. Her eyebrows arch like wings over eyes that are of an unusual color—some would say—strange. Her mother insists they are violet, but Leela sees eyes that are always changing color, like the chameleons that flit across porch railings. She can count on her eyes to be any color on any given day or time of day, but she can't count on much else, except her own self-imposed vow of silence. An unlikely talent, this vow of silence Leela has perfected, and which serves to shroud her like a cocoon. In her dreams, it is not a smothering cocoon, but a chrysalis and she is the butterfly inside waiting with quivering wings.

Downstairs the whir of her grandmother's treadle sewing machine reverberates along heart of pine floors, shimmies up the front hall staircase—canted by time and use beyond its normal curve—and settles to a fine hum beneath Leela's bare feet. It's late morning and her daily schedule has already formed an implacable routine.

Twelve days ago, Leela and her mother arrived with their suitcases and sad faces to live with granny Vernell. Over dressed for the heat, and still queasy from the Greyhound's diesel fumes, they had stood on the buckled steps of granny Vernell's wide front porch looking like the poor relatives they now were.

They'd travel by train and then by bus to reach their destination. The train ride, Leela's first, should have been an adventure, but present circumstances eclipsed any pretense of that. The *Southern Coastal Special*, an aging streamliner, belied its name. The cramped coach section, with its soiled upholstery, was littered with forgotten food wrappers and smelled vaguely of baby poop and spoiled oranges. There was no money for first class, let alone a berth in one of the Pullman sleepers. Leela's usually talkative mother became more silent and morose with every passing mile that drew them farther from Albany, New York. Farther from the husband and father who had left them.

It was angry voices, slammed doors and sneered accusations that set Leela and her mother on a course as far from their familiar landscape as the earth was to the moon. The night Leela's father left with his garment bag slung casually over his shoulder, Leela knew where to put the blame. The words business trip oozed from his lips like black oil. Her mother, slamming kitchen door cabinets at the time, stopped long enough to call out: "And don't ever come back."

Dale Hawkins, short in stature, but high on self-perceived importance, was a person of few words and even fewer gestures of affection. When Leela was little, she did everything she could to get his attention. Followed him around like a yapping puppy he would shush with a wave of his hand. In the evenings, she sat at his feet, a pat on the head her reward, a bone of attention tossed her way while he watched Walter Cronkite do the news.

When her father left that night, she stood in the driveway watching the taillights of the DeSoto fad into tiny red orbs. Before he left, he placed his palm on the top of her head, telling her to be a good girl. His hand had stayed there long enough to make her feel like a new disciple of Oral Roberts. Salvation was the last thing on her mind. Instead, it was about *his* betrayal. The stones in the driveway pinched her bare feet. With vengeance beating in her young chest, she grabbed a handful, drew back her arm and threw them at his retreating car.

Two

❧ WHISTLING DIXIE ❧

I never saw a wild thing feel sorry for itself.
~ D H Lawrence ~

The gas jets on her grandmother's old Chambers range hiss like snakes. This is Leela's third attempt to light the burners. Escaped fumes sting her nose. The lit matchstick dances in her nervous fingers.

"Good Lawd child, has your mother taught you nothin'." Granny Vernell's heavy steps shake the kitchen's red linoleum floor. Vernell thrusts Leela's fingers close to the burner, orange flames erupt. Leela jumps back, but not before the flames singe the tips of her fingers.

"Ma, Leela isn't used to a gas stove." Sable sits hunched over her morning coffee at the breakfast table. She's been there all morning gazing through the window as though mesmerized by the palm fronds that slice a miniature view of the bay. She's taken up residence in a flowered housecoat which bears the stains of picked over meals.

9

"I can't find what she is used to. She don't cook, don't sew and I ain't ever knowed a child that won't talk," Vernell declares. She fills a blue speckled graniteware pot with water and grits, slams it on the newly lit burner. She hands Leela a long wooden spoon and makes stirring gestures with her hand.

"She's not deaf, Ma."

"Are you sure 'bout that? She don't listen too well."

"Yes, Ma." Sable rubs a spot between her eyes, "I'm sure. Leela doesn't like to talk, that's all. She can whistle any tune you're likely to hear on the radio. And wait till you hear her bird calls. She's so good you'll think you're hearing the bird itself."

"Is that so," Vernell shifts her stance to Leela. Vernell is a large woman, solid with stocky legs and capable hands. Her girth makes the narrow kitchen seem smaller than it is. "I got me a favorite song. It's by them Kingston brothers, Tom Dooley. Reckon you can whistle that, Leela?"

Leela, tired and groggy from lack of sleep, dips her chin. She'd had another nightmare last night. She woke with her heart pounding. Sleep was always impossible afterwards. To please her grandmother, Leela hums a few bars to get the pitch before pursing her lips. Her whistling is pitch perfect, though she doesn't like the song because it is about a poor boy bound to die.

"Well I'll be, if that ain't somethin' special, I don't know what is," Vernell slaps her generous thigh and taps her foot to the melody.

When Leela whistles the last mournful note, her grandmother pats her on the head and declares it was the prettiest thing she'd ever heard. She tells Leela her grandpa—God rest his soul—was a mighty fine whistler too.

Leela mimics her grandmother's smile, though her lips slant down when she turns to the grit pot now bubbling on the stove.

The pat on her head reminds her of her father. She doesn't like being patted on the head, not anymore. She wants to say that she's not a dog, but the words as always do not leave her lips.

Vernell rinses a cup from the drain board, pours herself some coffee and pulls out a chair to sit with her daughter.

"Sable, honey, it won't do to have you sittin' around the house all day long in your housecoat. Ain't nothin' good ever come from feelin' sorry for yourself." She takes Sable's pale, smooth hand into her own work worn hands; the veins stand out like knotted rivers, the tips of her fingers rough from years of needle pricks.

"I know Ma, I know. I just need a few more days to get my head on straight." Sable stirs her coffee until the grounds swirl to the top.

"Thinkin' 'bout things ain't gonna fill our bellies, honey. Social Security don't pay me much and what I earn from sewing pays for the electric bill and gas for the stove. Times are hard around here. The bay's about been fished out and the oyster beds have gone bad, what with the red tide. You know your daddy, and I don't mean to speak ill of the dead, but he didn't leave me much except this big old house, and it leakin' by the seams. It's all I can do to keep it standing upright."

"Ma, can we talk about this later. My head's fuzzy with a headache," Sable rubs her forehead to prove the point. Her coppery-brown hair, unwashed for days, frame the soft curves of her face.

"We got to get out of this house today," Vernell declares. She slaps the table, setting the dishes to rattling. "Some fresh air will do you good. And we're doin' it right after breakfast before it gets hotter than Hades. You get yourself cleaned up. You still as pretty as the day you left here."

11

Leela has stirred the grits until they are too thick to stir. A burning smell rises, catching Vernell's attention.

"Lawd have mercy, child. You've about burned them grits."

Three

❧ THE MURAL ☙

Wanderer, there is no path, the path is made by walking.
~ Antonio Machado ~

After their breakfast of slightly burned grits and day-old corn fritters, and after much cajoling by Vernell, Sable finally relents. Leela gets washed and dressed in a flash, excited to be going somewhere, to see this new place. She's waits on the front porch, which granny Vernell calls the veranda. The enormous front door, its dark wood fossilized from untold years of salt spray, has a multitude of fine cracks running through it. Above the door is a curved fanlight bordered with intricate scrolls. Four white columns support a ceiling that looks to have once been blue. Paint is peeling from every surface like sunburned skin.

Leela decides to like the old house; its imperfections appeal to her. She likes the nooks and crannies and the way the worn floors slant every which way. What she finds strange is that none of the six upstairs bedrooms have closets. Instead, there are large

13

wardrobes granny Vernell said were called chiffoniers. Her mother's childhood bedroom is situated at the end of a long hallway at the back of the upstairs. Granny sleeps downstairs in what had once been a ladies' parlor. Said she'd turned it into a sleeping room because it is cool in the summer and warm in the winter. Said that Leela would understand when she grew to be an old lady.

Leela had been given the choice of any of the other five bedrooms. Thrilled by the prospect, Leela had taken her time. She investigated each room thoroughly. She tested the mattresses of each bed to feel their comfort. The beds were built high up from the floor. Some had white canopies and skirts that puddled the floor. She traced the outlines of the antique beds and furniture with her fingers and studied the direction of sunlight through the tall casement windows. There were no rugs of any kind anywhere in the house. Granny didn't believe in rugs. Said that rugs were just an accident waiting to happen, the way they slip right under a person's feet.

When Leela chose the lone bedroom on the third floor near the attic, the one with a long bank of windows and a view of the bay, her grandmother shook her head. Said that Leela didn't know nothin' about weather. Said the afternoon sun set the room to boiling in the summer, and in the winter, the winds off the bay blow through the sills leaving the room damp and cold. Said that no one ever stayed in that room long—not even when she'd taken in folks to board during the Great Depression. Said it wasn't even a real bedroom, just fixed up like one. That it had once been a sewing room because of the light, and after that a school room for the young ones, but that had been long ago, long before Leela's grandpa had married her and brought her here from her family's farm in Dothan, Alabama. Which wasn't a farm anymore, but a subdivision now.

Despite Vernell's admonition, Leela had moved her few belongings into the room that had once served other purposes. There was a pine chiffonier on one wall and a bed with a wrought iron headboard pushed up against the back wall. Leela had chosen the room because of the view, and that alone would have been enough. It was the painted mural that caused her to suck in her breath. It was enormous, taking up the better part of one entire wall. Even pocked marked with water stains, it still looked fresh, as if it had been recently painted. It depicted a series of scenes, from an island with tall, waving grasses, to a schooner on the ocean and to a town and a harbor moored with tall masted ships.

Leela had marveled at the way the waves seemed to shimmer and lap on island shores; and how white sails billowed on schooners while flashes of lightening erupted from roiling clouds. There was a mist shrouded mountain and within the valley below it, thatched huts were set in a circle. Leela had puzzled over the mural. How did this room, and none of the others, come to have such a painting? And who had painted it?

When Sable and Vernell come out to the porch, Leela is rocking in one of the two old, creaky rockers. She tears off a page from her ever-present notepad and hands it to granny Vernell.

"What's this?" Vernell arches a quizzical eyebrow.

"Just read it Ma. Leela's got a question for you."

"Good Lawd, Sable, is this how she's gonna' talk to me? Why, I never heard of such a thing."

"Ma, it's the only way, unless you want to take up sign language. Leela's going to talk again someday, aren't you, honey."

15

Sable puts her arm around her daughter. Leela dips her chin, her face pinking with a blush. She thinks of the stones she's hidden in the painted bedroom. Last night she'd dreamt of stones, white and perfectly round with glints of mica.

"Well, I hope so. I'd get mighty tired of having to scratch down everything I ever wanted to say." With a pinched expression, Vernell reads the note.

"No child, I got no idea. That mural's always been there, even in your great-grandpa's time and before. Your grandpa didn't know, nor any of his kinfolks, God rest their souls, and most of them passed on before I came here. An old colored nanny used to sit out here, passing the time in one of these rockers tellin all kind of stories about this place. No one paid her much mind, her being in her nineties and senile. There's an old family Bible in the front parlor with names and writin' in it. Some pictures too. And there's an album in the rolltop desk. Maybe that'll tell you somethin'. The attic is full of all manner of what nots, but it's not safe. Floorboards are old and rotten. A person might fall clean through. Come on now, we got to get goin' before the sun heats up the blacktop. Gets so hot the tar about melts the soles right of your shoes."

Leela looks to her mother, but Sable has already crossed the yard to the unpaved road. Vernell adjusts the wide-brimmed straw hat she calls her *walkin-hat* and gives Leela a quick hug. They head down the sand and crushed oyster shell path toward the paved road. Vernell, with her short, powerful strides, leads the way.

Four

❧ THE BIRD MAN ❧

The great art of life is sensation, to feel that we exist, even in pain.
~ Lord Byron ~

A few minutes later, Leela wishes she'd chosen her thick-soled saddle shoes, scuff marks and all, instead of the delicate sandals that gather sand and grit with every step. In short order, she's kicked off the sandals, looping them through her fingers, deciding to go barefoot until they get to the paved road. Leela tugs at the sundress granny Vernell had made for her. Said it was too hot and humid for the twill pants and long sleeve blouses Leela had brought. Vernell had gone right to work altering a cast-off sundress which had not pleased its previous owner. Leela was inclined to agree with the previous owner. Made of polished cotton, the dress had bright splashes of red hibiscus flowers throughout with lime green piping at the neck, sleeves and hem. Leela couldn't decide if she looked like a Christmas tree or a hula dancer. Not wanting to offend her granny, who seemed thoroughly pleased, Leela smiled her thanks.

At least, she thinks, trailing after her granny and mother, she doesn't know anyone here. Back home she always wore clothing that didn't attract attention. Being non-descript and unassuming allowed Leela to slip through middle school with ghost-like precision. She liked it that way. She'd become a keen observer of her fellow classmates who—when they weren't bullying her—ignored her.

Leela hurries to keep pace with her mother and granny Vernell. The narrow road is bordered by palm trees, palmettos and flowering shrubs with bright blossoms. Their tropical scents are powerful and fill Leela with a sense of longing, a sense of being in a place time has forgotten. When they reach the blacktop road, they pass century old homes set back in wide, well-manicured yards. Some are elaborate structures with gabled roofs and ornate scrolls of woodwork over deep porches.

After they pass over railroad tracks, she sees houses overgrown with kudzu, their porch railings split like broken bones. Shutters tilt loose on rusted hinges. Leela tries to imagine who might have lived in these abandoned houses. One such house stands out, time worn like the others, but intact. It has a low-slung roof and a wide porch. The front lawn is immaculate, but what causes her to gasp is the garden. Surrounding the house are masses of flowers, a profusion of colors and scents that takes her breath away. To Leela, it looks magical, like a place in a fairytale. Suddenly, a figure emerges from the porch. Startled, Leela stumbles, her mouth agape, she loses her balance and nearly trips over her sandals. The man, whose skin is the color of caramel, is tall and painfully thin. He doesn't move the way normal people do. His steps are jerky, his arms in constant motion, like a bird with broken wings. His head moves back and forth, the way a bird pecks at the ground.

Vernell raises her hand, warding him away, "Get on back now, ya hear." She grabs Leela's arm, pulling her roughly along until they are well past the offending house and man. Vernell's face is flushed red, her lips set in a thin line. Sable, her face drained of color, puts a gentle hand on Vernell's arm.

"Ma let him be. He doesn't mean any harm, you know."

"I won't have it, ya hear. Him comin' out starin' at me every time I pass this way. I've a mind to put the sheriff on him," Vernell says, her voice rising in anger.

Leela is taken aback by her grandmother's reaction. The poor man is obviously impaired in the most grotesque way. Leela has never seen a person move the way he did. She hadn't felt threatened, just curious and a bit remorseful for having stared at him with her mouth open. His dark eyes had a gentle look about them, yet there was defiance there too. She is lucky, she supposes, her own handicap is not visible to the naked eye. It is easily hidden behind a smile, or a frown. It's a coward's way really, and she feels shame bite at her. The *Birdman*—the moniker had come instantly to her mind—challenged the world with his affliction. She marvels at his courage.

"Leela, watch out." Her mother's sharp call interrupts her musings. Leela looks up, skidding to a stop mere inches from a decidedly forbidding bush. Vernell grabs her arm, jerking her away. "Honey, that's a Spanish Bayonet, child. Those pointed ends are as sharp as knives, cut clean through your skin they will," Vernell says, her is voice terse, but the anger seems gone. The Birdman is apparently forgotten, done with like a period at the end of a bad sentence. Leela can't turn that page so easily; his image remains.

Leela has lost count of the cross streets they've passed. The sun marks high noon and bears down on them. Waves of humidity rise like steam beneath their feet. Everything is old here, she thinks, a world away from the ranch houses where she'd lived. In her subdivision, the houses were set end to end like dominoes, their matchbox front yards bearing identical crew-cuts.

Memories of home flood her thoughts. She is distracted; her view of the world around her turns inward, away from the presence of grand homes faded with age, of tropical scents, of dangerous bushes and of a man with broken wings. She thinks of her father, how the smell of his aftershave made her feel giddy, how the tip of his mustache tickled her cheek when he bent to kiss her cheek. How he lied and smiled at the same time. He said he would always love her, but she no longer believes him. Hate has replaced her love. But she finds to no relief in hating. The pain in her heart has taken on a life of its own.

Her grandmother's voice buzzes wasp-like in her ear. "Stop that day dreamin', child. The two of you about to worry me to an early grave, what with your mom down in the dumps and you starin' at nothing all day. I swear, if the two of you aren't miserable company. Buck up now, put behind whatever is ailin' you and move on."

"All right Ma, that's enough." Sable takes Leela's hand. "How about a nice cold root beer float? Sable turns to Vernell, "Does McCrory's still make those great floats, Ma?"

Vernell is quick to smile, adding, "Best you'll ever get." With that they go around a corner bringing into full view the town square, and beyond, a street with narrow sidewalks and rows of shops.

Five

❧ ROOT BEER FLOATS ☙

The best way out is always through.
~ Robert Frost ~

The square is bordered by huge live oaks, their twisted branches hanging low, almost touching the ground. Spanish Moss drapes from their limbs, giving the trees a ghostly appearance. A large white gazebo is centered in the middle of the square and is surrounded by mounds of blooming azaleas. On one side, a bronze statue captures the likeness of some Civil War hero. Black wrought iron benches rest in quiet corners. It is a place of eternal repose, unchanging, and as still as death. The part of Leela's brain that considers poetry the ultimate form of expression, is stimulated. She imagines herself there amid the azaleas and live oaks, soaking up the atmosphere while writing line after line of remarkable poetry.

They walk on, passing windowed store fronts, a Woolworth's 5 & 10, and finally McCrory's Pharmacy. Once inside, they take seats at the soda fountain's counter. The tall, metal topped stools swivel back and forth. A group of teens huddle at the end of the counter. The boys stand with puffed out chests; the girls whisper and giggle behind manicured nails painted a rainbow of colors. Upon seeing the new faces of Sable and Leela, their voices hush as if they have become one entity, like a gaggle of geese moments before flight.

It is Leela who garners their stares. Red faced and flustered, she hides behind Vernell whose large form becomes a refuge from prying eyes. She is sure it's the Christmas sundress that makes them ogle her. She pats down her hair, sure it has gone all frizzy in the heat. She sinks into herself. She is not ready for this, for them.

"Why Sable Stone are my old eyes deceivin' me? How long you been back?" A man with a white apron tied around his narrow waist stands behind the counter. Wisps of thin, gray hair have been meticulously combed over a perfectly round bald spot.

"Mister McCrory, nice to see you. And its Hawkins now, don't you remember?" Sable slides onto her stool, her back ramrod straight, her red lips set in a grim smile—as if the whole town hadn't known she'd come back, husbandless. Word spreads fast in a small town.

"Oh, that's right. My old brain ain't what it used to be. Getting old, ain't we Vernell."

Vernell harrumphs at that. Leela sees her grandmother isn't pleased with the comparison. "Why Otis, you old fool, don't be pretendin' I'm as old as you. Just get on with you now and fix us three of your Root Beer floats."

"Vernell Stone, you're as sharped tongued as ever. You want one scoop of vanilla or two?"

"Two and you know I do," Vernell snaps at him.

"And what's your name, little lady?" He waits, head cocked for Leela's reply. She freezes, looks to her mother. She feels like a mouse with her tiny paw inches away from the mouse trap.

"Mister McCrory, this is my daughter, Leela. Can we get those root beers now?" Sable says, her voice sweet, her smile a placating one. Leela apes her mother's smile.

"Sure thing, comin' right up."

Leela and her mother share a glance of conspiracy. Leela signs, thank you, the tips of her fingers just brushing her lips. In public places, they have learned to keep their signing under the radar of inquisitive eyes. Back when Leela decided to forego speech, she searched the public library for a book on signing, found she was adept and taught her mother. Now it has evolved into slights of hand, a flicker of fingers, as much nuance as substance.

Leela, hunched low between her mother and grandmother, could not resist a furtive glance at the teens. The girls, deeply tanned, wear crisp white blouses and brightly colored Bermuda shorts. The boys, sporting a mix of ducktails and crew cuts, are more subdued in kakis, jeans and t-shirts. To Leela they are the image of summer, of carefree days, of riding in cars with the radio at full blast with no destination in mind. None of which she's ever experienced.

Back home in Albany the middle school she'd attended was large and filled to brimming with a diversity of groups. It was easy to become anonymous, to slide through classrooms with a barely a flicker of recognition. There was no expectation of speech on her part. There were many other voices to do that. Whenever possible, she'd hidden in the safety of their countless numbers. Still, when she had no other choice but to speak, smirks twisted the faces of her peers. Bullies found their target.

Here in this small town there would be few options. Here she would be transported back in time to Mrs. Laskowski's fifth-grade class faced, once again, with the insurmountable task of an oral book report, no doubt. Apprehension, solid as stone, settles in Leela's stomach. The promise of a root beer float loses its appeal. Instead, burgeoning dread, palpable as a heartbeat, serves itself up to her.

"Sable, you here for the summer? I know Vernell must be happy as a clam to see her pretty granddaughter." Mr. McCrory slides the root beers across the counter. Coffee colored foam splashes from the glass rims forming tiny beads on the highly polished wood surface.

"Oh, I'm not sure really. Perhaps through the fall, or maybe longer." Sable concentrates on the float.

"Now, don't you go pesterin' her with a pot full of questions. I reckon Sable will stay as long as she needs to," Vernell waves his queries away with a flip of her hand.

"Vernell, don't go getting all fired up. You sure are testy today. Must be the heat and all," McCrory says, before turning to Sable. "Mighty glad to have your pretty face back in town, Sable, mighty glad."

Sable nods, smiling at him, then samples the ice cream on the tip of her spoon. Vernell has attacked her float with relish. Leela stares at her float as if it has suddenly become curdled milk. All she wants right now is a glass of water and a one-way ticket back to Albany, father or no father.

Vernell nudges Leela's shoulder. "Come on, eat up, child. We need to stop by the Grille. Miss Ina has some altering for me to pick-up. Then to the A&P to get some fresh peaches. I've a mind to make us a cobbler. The way its heatin' up means we're in for a storm soon. They roll off the bay about every afternoon when the heat is high. Let's get a move on or we'll get soaked to the bone on the way home."

"Ma, Leela looks a bit pale. She's not used to this heat and humidity. She might get sick to her stomach. Just let her be." Sable asks Mr. McCrory for a glass of water and fresh napkins.

Leela, rescued from the offending float, is patting her face with a damp napkin when she becomes acutely aware of movement directly behind her. Accompanying the teens hushed voices are their scents, a co-mingling of tanning lotion, hairspray and perfume. One scent stands out among the others, the sweet, cloying scent of White Shoulders. Leela knows her perfumes; her father was a prodigious giver of perfumes. Every birthday, every holiday, her mother received perfumes, gift wrapped and labeled with an indifferent pen. Her mother had a drawer full of perfumes.

The wearer of White Shoulders wedges herself between Vernell and Leela. Her crisp white shirt is a stark contrast against her golden tan.

"Miss Vernell," White Shoulders says, "My mother wants to know if you've finished sewing my new dress? You know, the one for the Fourth of July celebration." She says this while staring pointedly at Leela.

"Take a picture, Darla, why don't cha'," says a boy standing behind her. He appears older than the others. He's tall, olive-skinned and undeniably good looking. He puts his hand on the girl's arm with familiar ease. His dark hair, slicked back in a duck-tail, glistens under the florescent lights.

25

"Oh hush, Finn," Darla slaps his hand lightly, turning away from Leela without so much as nod, as if Leela failed to be worthy of further perusal. "You *can* have it ready, can't you Miss Vernell?" Darla purrs.

Vernell nods, "Tell your mama I'll be there tomorrow 'bout one o'clock."

Darla tugs at Finn's arm; he brushes it off, shifting his gaze to Leela.

"Hi, I'm Finn Connell, nice to meet you," he says, smiling broadly at her. His teeth flash bright white against his dark tan.

Leela feels a deep flush rising from her neck to blaze shamefully across her cheeks. She can do nothing but return his smile—there is nothing else she can do except to offer him a limp hand in exchange. He takes her hand in both of his waiting for her reply while a quizzical look forms around his eyes. Leela feels as if she is falling, falling ever deeper into a dark well.

"Finn, this is my granddaughter, Leela Hawkins and my daughter, Sable.

"Leela. That's a pretty name. Well, see you around," he says flashing another smile before Darla pulls him away to the exit.

Vernell harrumphs, "Now if that ain't a pure shame, me havin' to up and speak for you, Leela. You got to git over whatever is troubling you. Finn's a good boy, from good people. Still, I don't want you messin around with Darla. Her mama and your mama have hard feelings for each other, so stay clear of her and that crowd, ya hear?"

Leela shrugs, signs: *They wouldn't want me anyway.*

"What was all that," Vernell demands of Sable.

"She said not to worry, Ma."

Six

ॐ THE CATFISH BAR & GRILLE ॐ

I dwell in possibility.
~ Emily Dickinson ~

B y the time they leave McCrory's, the sky has turned from searing blue to gray haze. Shimmers of heat rise from the sidewalk as they head toward the Catfish Bar and Grille.

"Leela," Vernell says, pointing to the sky. "See them fluffy clouds building up and looking like they have flat anvils at the top?"

Leela nods, finger spells the words cumulus clouds.

"What'd she say?" Vernell asks Sable.

"She said, cumulus clouds, Ma."

"Cumu…what? Anyway, see the way they look dark and heavy at the bottom, that means we're in for a thunderstorm, and by the looks of it, a big one." Vernell plows speedily ahead with Sable and Leela stretching their legs to catch up. They pass boat docks and wharves where corrugated buildings, rust weathered, line the marina. Shrimp boats, their black nets hanging like widows' veils from their riggings, are moored to creosote pilings. Leela, who has always been moored to the land, stares wide-eyed, crinkling her nose at the fishy odors.

The Catfish Bar and Grille is a turn of the century two storied building with multiple gables. A wraparound porch is centered by two narrow doors inset with etched glass. They swing open as patrons exit. Leela hangs back while Sable acknowledges old friends and introduces Leela.

Inside, her mother repeats the same litany regarding her return to one patron after another. Leela's cheeks are sore from so many perfunctory smiles. Finally, they settle at the bar and wait for Miss Ina to finish at the cash register. A waitress strides through a pair of galley doors cradling serving dishes on both arms. Behind her, the pungent smells of fried fish and corn fritters waft from the kitchen. She is a large woman; the buttons on her pink uniform look ready to pop from their buttonholes. Wisps of unnaturally red hair have escaped her hair net and match her penciled-on arched brows.

The waitress comes to a halt.

"Sable Stone, my God, is it really you?" With that said, she slaps the plates down in front of two startled patrons and turns to Sable in one swift movement. She wraps Sable in a full body hug.

"Loretta Tucker," Sable says, pulling back and smiling the first true smile Leela has seen on her mother's face since their arrival.

"Sable Stone, you still as pretty as the day you was crowned Homecoming Queen. Now, I can't say the same for myself. Put on a pound or twenty since you last seen me."

"You look just fine. How is Ray? Still fishing?" Sable asks.

"Lawd have mercy, no. Didn't Vernell tell you? I'm divorced

now. Ray ran off down to Mobile with Justine Witherspoon a couple of years back. Got me two kids, as you know. And they are the two best kids ever. I got daddy's house and me still taking care of him as usual. So not much has changed. They still roll up the sidewalks here at sundown."

"Oh, Loretta, I'm so sorry to hear about you and Ray. I mean, you were high school sweethearts. I can't believe he would leave you."

"Well, it's done and over now. Wouldn't have him back if I could. What about you Sable? Vernell never said a word 'bout you comin' home," she stares at Vernell with narrowed eyes as if she's been terribly slighted. Vernell shrugs.

Sable looks down at her hands. "Dale and I are taking a break for the summer, maybe longer. We'll see."

"Well, I'm sure Vernell could use some help with her sewin' and such," Loretta plops her wide bottom down on the stool beside Sable's.

"I won't be much help. I'm all thumbs when it comes to a needle and thread. Though I am looking to do something to bring in a little extra cash," Sable's voice is lowered to a whisper. Her pale cheeks have bloomed pink.

Leela's eyes widen at this; an icy-cold nugget settles itself in the pit of her stomach. She is more than aware their circumstances have changed, but her mother needing to work? This then is the crevice into which her father has allowed them to fall. No, she thinks, he's pushed them. Her mother has never held a job, ever. What skills does her mom have? She doesn't know how to type, has never worked a cash register, and as far as Leela knows, has never sewn anything more difficult than a hem.

"Well, Sable, I don't know what to tell you. Ain't much

happening around here these days, except the fishing. And even that has slowed. It's mostly the tourists that keep businesses open. We do need an extra hand in the kitchen, mostly washin' dishes, but I don't think that's for you, Sable," Loretta says, lifting her ample shoulders in a shrug.

Leela, sitting behind Vernell, raises her hand the way she never did when sitting in a classroom.

"Why, Vernell, who is that pretty gal sittin' so quiet like behind you?"

"This is Sable's daughter, Leela, and you know it." Vernell says, getting up from her stool and going over to the cash register to see Miss Ina.

"Leela, that sure is a pretty name. I knew your great-grandma, Laura Lee, God bless her soul. Nice to finally meet you," Loretta grabs for Leela's hand still poised in mid-air, shakes it and waits for her to reply.

Leela looks to her mother, signs she wants to wash dishes. Sable shakes her head no.

"Whoa now, did I miss something? What was that hand stuff?" Loretta arches her penciled-on eyebrows, wiggling her fingers in imitation.

In hushed tones, Sable explains about Leela's stuttering and her refusal to speak. Loretta leans back, nodding. Comprehension spreads across her broad face the way butter melts on toast. She smiles, winks at Leela as if they share a secret.

"Seems to me that washing dishes is something you don't need talkin' to do. Talkin' just slows down the process. It pays fifty cents an hour. Good money for a teenager." Loretta slips off her stool, adjusts her skirt which had risen to her ample thighs and goes over to Leela.

Sable shakes her head, presses her lips into a thin line.

"Come on now, Sable. This young lady needs something to do over the summer. Wouldn't hurt her to learn about making a livin' and I'll be here most every day."

Leela gives her mother a pleading look, signs, *please, please I can do this mother.*"

Seconds tick by and to Leela it feels like an eternity before her mother, her face set in indecision, speaks. "I don't, well, maybe. But only during the day, not at night, is that clear?" Sable shakes her head as if she can't believe she's allowing this. Leela jumps up, throws her arms around her mother.

"Well now, Sable, that settles it," Loretta claps once, sealing the deal. "I'll speak to Miss Ina and she'll be right glad to have some help for Izzy and Ham. Our cook, Maribel, will be pleased to have an extra pair of hands. With that Loretta heads over to the register where Vernell and Miss Ina have their heads together as they look over a length of material.

Moments later, Loretta waves Sable and Leela over to speak to Miss Ina, who eyes Leela with a speculative look, before turning to Sable. "Welcome back, Sable. Vernell tells me you might be here for a spell. You too Leela, glad to have you here." Leela offers up a trembling smile. Miss Ina, she observes, seems to be about her grandmother's age, but unlike her grandmother, Miss Ina is reed thin and has a face wrinkled as a bed sheet.

"It's good to be back," Sable says. 'Loretta said you might need some help in the kitchen this summer. But you need to know this will be Leela's first job." Sable has a death grip on Leela's hand as though Leela were a small child who is set to wander into traffic at any moment.

"Quit worrying, Sable. Leela will be just fine, won't she Miss

Ina." Loretta brushes away Sable's misgivings with a wave of her hand. The grey heads of Miss Ina and Vernell nod in unison.

Miss Ina levels her be-speckled gaze on Leela. "Leela, you'll need to be here early. We start serving at seven o'clock in the morning. You'll get a late morning break and a lunch break. Your shift ends at three o'clock."

Leela, tugging her hand from her mother's grip, bobs her head repeatedly. Her stomach is aflutter. She takes a deep breath, feeling suddenly taller, older, as if a mantle of adulthood has suddenly been placed upon her shoulders. Pride swells her chest.

While the women exchange small talk, Leela studies the restaurant, from the black and white tile floor to the tin ceiling punched with a pattern of star-like designs. Two porthole glass windows are set into the swinging doors. The wood has been oiled to a lustrous shine. She is about to venture a peek through one of the portholes, when the swinging doors open throwing her off balance. She is caught, saved from an embarrassing tumble by two heavily muscled arms. Leela finds herself staring into the bluest eyes she's ever seen.

"Watch your step there, little lady," Blue Eyes says, setting her gently, but firmly on her feet as if she were as weightless as a paper doll. A smile forms at the corners of his lips and then stops short when he sees Sable and Vernell.

"Brick, you're back. I didn't expect to see you for a couple more hours." Miss Ina's face light's up.

Leela, standing next to him, cranes her head back to see his face. He's especially tall; his chest and neck are developed like that of a football player or a prize fighter. Leela watches a subtle change move across his face, settling into something flat and unwelcoming.

"We had to cut the trip short, Ma. We didn't have enough ice to pack what we'd caught. He walks over to the bar, steps behind the counter, takes a beer glass from the cooler and pulls a draft until the foam flows over the rim.

"How are you Brick?" Sable asks, her voice carries a tremble.

"Good, and you?" He sips his beer, turning his back on Sable to speak to a bearded man sitting at the end of the bar.

"Good," Sable says to the back of his blue denim shirt. She walks over to Leela, grabs her hand. "We're going to head back now, Ma. Are you coming?" Sable's voice is devoid of inflection. Leela has heard this tone many times before; it heralds one of her mom's headaches. Sable doesn't wait for Vernell to answer. She pushes through the entrance door, pulling Leela behind her. The sidewalk shows sprinkles of rain. The clouds billow high in the sky, their undersides the color of gun metal.

"Wait up, Sable," Loretta says, holding the door open for Vernell. It's my break, so I'm driving y'all home. Looks like the bottom's gonna drop out any minute."

Sable open's her mouth to say no, but Vernell cuts her short. "That'd be nice of you, Loretta," she says, giving Sable an arched look. Vernell holds a bundle of material close to her chest as they follow Loretta up the street to where her car is parked. The pale blue Rambler sedan has countless dings and dents and has serious rust issues. Worn brakes squeal as Loretta shifts out of park into drive. Loretta keeps up a stream of chatter. Sable is quiet, her face turned to the window which bears the imprints of little fingers.

By the time they reach home, the rain is coming down in silver sheets. Loretta waves them off as they make a mad dash for the porch. Sable continues her silence, going directly to her bedroom upstairs. Leela has no clue as to what caused her mother's head-ache, but she knows better than to interfere. Vernell tells Leela to check all the windows and goes to her workroom.

After checking all the windows—she hadn't realized there were so many—Leela is left to her own devices. She goes to her bedroom, flops on the high bed and contemplates everything that happened in town. She sighs, remembering how the boy, Finn, had held her hand and smiled at her.

While she muses, her gaze travels around the room. Shadows move over the walls and the mural. She wonders again about the artist who'd painted it. It must have taken countless hours, so intricate are the details. Waves seem to lap the shore and the sailing ship seems to dip in and out of the sea. The room itself takes on a cocoon like aura, warm and humid as though the room is an island separate from the rest of the house. Lulled by the sounds of rain against the windows, Leela drifts off into dreams of trees shrouded by fog. Her bare feet grip tiny grains of sand as waves lap the shore. There are others, people hidden by the trees. she can hear their whispers. The rain comes down heavier and heavier until it sounds like music, ethereal and insistent. Her name is in the music, like a song. It comes from far away, then closer and closer until it pounds against her head like drumbeats.

Leela wakes startled by what she thinks is thunder. Someone is banging on her door. Her grandmother's voice splits the air. "Leela, don't you hear me calling you? Don't be locking your door, you hear. Come on down, dinner's ready."

Leela goes to the door; she didn't remember having locked it. It opens easily. Granny Vernell, her arms akimbo, her lips pressed into a stern line, shakes her head before she turns on her heels and heads down the hall.

Leela rubs the sleep from her eyes. Her head is fuzzy, as if she's slept too hard. Vague memories of her dream dissolve into nothingness, leaving a disjointed stream of images: rain, fog, trees. In the past, she has written some of her best poetry upon waking. She grabs her notebook. The words flow as if they've already been written:

> *This rainy day, the finality of fog*
> *on trees that weep the melody of songs,*
> *songs that are no longer sung.*

Leela hears her grandmother's insistent voice calling out to her. She closes her notebook, goes to the bathroom, splashes her face with tepid water, then hurries downstairs to the kitchen.

Her mother is back in the flowered housecoat again.

Seven

 IZZY AND HAM

Friendship has splendors that love knows not.
~ Mariama Ba ~

The next morning, at the crack of dawn, her grandmother is shaking Leela awake. She opens her eyes to slivers of pinkish light filtering through the bank of windows. She'd tossed and turned all night, not only from her nerves about the job, but from troubling dreams that slip from her mind like wisps of smoke. Still, her heart jumps at the thought of beginning her first day of work. She hops out of bed, dresses in the clothing she'd laid out last night, a white tee shirt, a loose denim jumper and sneakers. In the bathroom, she splashes her face with tepid water, brushes her teeth and pulls her brown curls into a tight ponytail. That done, she skips downstairs. The smell of eggs and bacon perk up her appetite, overriding her nervous stomach.

Her mom is not up, though Granny Vernell has set out a plate for her. The cup of coffee by her plate is a surprise. Her mom

37

doesn't let her drink coffee. She takes a sip. It's heavily laced with cream and sugar and tastes delicious.

"Figured you could use a kick start, seeing those tired eyes of yours," Vernell says. "You're old enough to have a cup now that you're a working girl, right?"

Leela bobs her head, offering her granny a conspiratorial smile.

"I'll be walking with you, but just for today. I've my own work to do and lord knows your mom isn't an early riser, never has been. We'll be expecting you back thirty minutes or so after your shift ends, so don't tarry as your mom will fret."

Leela nods, gives her grandmother a thumbs up.

"Just do whatever Miss Mirabel says. Izzy and Ham are colored kids. They know their place. You'll get along with them just fine."

Leela gulps down her food. She's filled with a mixture of excitement and anxiety. The excitement because this is her first job ever, but anxious, wondering how they will handle her silence. She pats the jumper pocket to make sure her note pad and pencil are there. Granny Vernell points to the clock. She's ready to go and so is Leela. She's more than ready.

The walk goes faster than yesterday. The morning is mild. The sun is just peeking through early clouds. When they pass the house of flowers, as Leela thinks of it, the Birdman does not make an appearance.

Vernell takes her hand, stopping her. "Listen to me, Leela. If that colored man comes out, you just keep on walkin'. Don't pay him no mind, you hear me? If he bothers you, you let me know straight away."

Leela nods, not daring even a glance at the flowers.

When they arrive, Loretta is at the entrance of the Catfish Grille, keys jangling at her fingertips.

"Mornin' Vernell, Leela," Loretta calls out. She opens the door and they step inside where it's cool and dark. The tang of vinegar and fried fish linger in the air. Loretta flips a light switch and Leela blinks against the sudden glare of florescent lights.

Loretta is all business, taking Leela's hand and leading her to the swinging doors. "This won't take but a minute, Vernell. You can head on home or stay for a cup of coffee." She doesn't wait for an answer as the doors swing closed behind them. The kitchen is bright and busy. Bacon sizzles, dishes clatter and two apron clad teens turn in unison toward them.

"Izzy, Ham, stop what you're doing and come on over here. This is Leela Hawkins, our new helper." The two share a wide-eyed glance between them before moving out from behind the counter. The boy flashes a smile, showing teeth as white and as perfectly even as a row of Chiclet gum. His hair is dark and dense and clipped close to his head. His skin is so dark it glistens like onyx. His eyes are as brown as chestnuts. The girl is taller than the boy, but Leela thinks they are both about her age. The girl wears an air of authority, but her smile is as bright as the boy's. Leela tries not to stare at the girl, at her eyes which are a startling blue, made even more startling by her brown complexion. Her hair, lighter than the boy's, is pulled back into a bun. The two come forward as a pair.

"Leela, this is Isabel Banner, her mom is Miss Mirabel, our day cook. This," Loretta nods to the boy, "is Abraham Jones. These two will show you the ropes. And don't be bothering Miss Mirabel while she's cookin, ain't that right, Mirabel?" The cook turns from the large range, nodding as she moves from the stove to the long metal counter. She's a heavy woman, built large like granny Vernell. A white apron is tied around her thick waist. A black-hair net covers her dark curls.

"Okay, y'all get to work. I'll be in and out as usual." Loretta winks at Leela. The swinging doors close behind her.

The two teens stand gawking at Leela. Her heart pounds, her hands have become clammy. Do they expect her to say something? Hadn't Loretta told them? The boy steps forward, his brown eyes are soft and gentle.

"Hi, Leela," he says as his hands move upward. His finger spells her name. Leela's mouth drops open. She quickly signs back, *you sign?"*

"I know some signs," he says, "My cousin is deaf. She goes to a special school. She's taught me some signs and the alphabet. "I sure would like to learn more, though. Will you teach me?".

Leela nods, blinking against the burn of tears in her eyes. Her relief is so great she's close to bursting into sobs. She signs, mouths, *Thank you.*

"Hey, me too," says the girl. "I wanna learn because if signing will stop Ham's constant yapping, it'll be a blessing. You can call me Izzy. Everyone does. He's Ham, but most everyone calls him Hambone because he's so full of himself thinking about how smart he is with all his book readin'."

"Ha, I am not full of myself, Leela, I'm an armchair philosopher, there's a difference. Some things just need saying, is all. Have you read the teachings of Socrates or Plato?"

Leela shakes her head. She'd heard of them, of course.

"Y'all stop yapping and show Leela what needs doing. Order's will be coming in shortly," Miss Mirabel calls out, but she smiles at Leela, softening her reproach.

Izzy goes to the metal table and brings out a long white piece of material that turns into an apron. She slips it over Leela's neck, double wrapping long ties at Leela's waist. The apron falls well below her knees.

"First," Izzy says, "you scrape the food off here," she points to two large trash bins, "and then the plates go into this here sink, and you spray them with the sprayer. Then they go onto the conveyor belt, here, where soap and hot water washes and rinses them." Leela nods, following her motions. "Oh, and you gotta turn it on here with this button, okay?"

Ham speaks up. "You gotta wipe them as fast as you can with these drying cloths and put 'em here," he says, pointing to a row of metal shelves at the end of the conveyor belt. "Now here comes the real workin' part, he laughs, "We gotta wash and dry the glasses, cups and flatware by hand. They go on this shelf over here. Once you get fast, it'll free up Izzy so she can start her pie making."

Izzy lifts her chin, "I'm training to be a pastry chef," she says with pride. "Ma is training me. She's the best pie maker around."

I love pie, especially pumpkin pie, Leela signs. Ham signs pie but tells her he doesn't know the other words she signed. Leela finger spells pumpkin for Ham.

"Leela says she likes pumpkin pie," Ham tells Izzy.

"How do you sign pumpkin?" Izzy asks.

Leela signs the letter 'P' with her right hand and thumps the back of her left fist with the 'P' sign.

"That's easy," Izzy laughs, imitating Leela.

Loretta bangs open the swinging doors, shouts out a complicated stream of orders. Miss Mirabel nods. Leela wonders how she can possibly remember all those details.

The morning is a blur of dishes and more dishes and by their break time at ten o'clock—when breakfast serving is over—Leela's hands are wrinkled from hot dishwater and her arms are tired. The restaurant closes for one hour and reopens at eleven for the lunch service. Ham and Izzy order burgers and fries for lunch and take Leela to a corner booth inside the restaurant.

In no time at all, delicious smelling burgers are placed in front of them by Loretta. "I heard you did real good, Leela," she says. "I had a feeling you would." She sets down three glasses of soda pop and leaves them to their lunch."

Leela looks at her lunch, her stomach growling as Izzy and Ham dig in.

I don't have money to pay for this. I didn't bring any money, she signs. Ham translates, and Izzy shares a grin with him. "You don't pay, Leela, it comes with the job. We get a free lunch so eat up, times wasting.' Leela returns her grin and bites into the best hamburger she's ever had. The threesome eat, talk and sign as if they've been the best of friends forever. That's how Leela thinks of them. Her best friends, ever. Well, her only friends ever.

Leela's taking a sip of her soda pop when she feels as if she's being stared at. She looks over to a table on the opposite side of the restaurant and sees a pretty woman staring at her. The woman's pale blonde hair is done up in one of those fancy French twists set with pearl combs that match the pearls at her neck and the studs at her ears. Her dress is frilly and as soft a pink as her glossy lipstick.

Leela quickly lowers her gaze. She feels heat coming up to her cheeks.

"Don't mind her, Leela. She's nobody important," Izzy says loud enough for the woman to hear.

"Hush now, don't be saying things like that, Izzy. You'll be getting us into trouble," Ham whispers. "That's Luanne Devlin and she's about as important as any of us are likely to meet. Her father is Judge Clayton.

"You know Brick doesn't keep any of his girl friends around for long, Ham."

"That's Brick's business, not ours. So, zip it," Ham tells her, making a zipping motion with his fingers.

Leela signs, *you mean Mister Brick Beaufort, Miss Ina's son?*
Ham translates for Izzy.

"The one and only and he owns this place and a shrimp boat, plus his charter boats. Mister Brick's done all right for himself." Izzy smiles proudly, "I heard Miss Loretta say…"

Ham claps his hand over her mouth. "You stop that gossiping right now. Granme´ Delia says gossip don't do a body a bit of good. It'll come back at you is what she says."

Is she your grandmother? Leela signs.

"Sort of. I mean, she's a grandmother to all us colored folks around here," Ham pauses and in a whispery voice says, "She's a *quimboiseur*, a storyteller. Maybe she'll invite you to a Gathering soon. I think she would like you, Leela."

A storyteller? I love stories, Leela signs.

Ham translates for Izzy, and turns to Leela, adding, "Granme´ Delia is a special storyteller."

Izzy scoots close to Leela, whispering, "What he means, Leela, is that she's a secret storyteller. She's a keeper of memories. She tells about Africa, and well, about us, us colored folks and our history. Your family too. All of us here in Bateaux Bay. If you are ever invited to a Gathering you must promise to never tell anyone, not even your mom or Miss Vernell," Izzy says, her

43

bright blue eyes narrowing, her mouth set in a prim line. She holds out her pinky, "Do you swear to keep our secret?

Leela bobs her head.

"Cross you heart and hope to die if you break it." Izzy intones.

Leela curls her pinky around Izzy's. *I swear,* she mouths, crossing her heart with her other hand. Her heart swelling, she is astounded at what the day has brought. She has friends and a secret.

The three of them are clearing the table, hands full of plates and glasses, when Brick comes in. When he sees them, he comes over, his gaze directed at Leela.

"So, Leela Hawkins, welcome to the Grille," he says, holding out his hand for her to shake.

Leela stares at it until Izzy nudges her. Setting her plate and glass down, she thrusts out her right hand and he takes it in his big, warm one. "I heard you did a good job this morning. I'm sure Izzy and Ham appreciate the help," he tells her. Leela attempts a wobbly smile. He smiles in return, though Leela sees a certain look round his eyes, as if he's suffered a loss that pains him still.

The lady who'd so rudely stared at Leela glides over, her steps measured and elegant as if she were a princess or a queen. She stands possessively by Brick's side eyeing Izzy and Ham with a finely arched brow, her glossy lips pinched in a disapproving frown.

"I didn't know *they* ate in the restaurant itself, Brick. Whatever will your customers think?"

He smiles, leveling her with a dark look, "Why, I think they'll be glad they get their food hot off the grille."

"Brick, really," she snaps, "don't be so obtuse. Never mind, we need to get going. My father's a stickler for being on time to these fund raisers.

To Leela, Izzy and Ham, he says, "Keep up the good work, kids. Bye Leela. Nice to have you here."

Izzy takes control, pushing Leela in front of her toward the swinging doors to the kitchen. Ham takes up the rear. Leela takes a furtive look back at Brick and the blonde woman, Luanne Devlin. The woman is staring at her with hard, glittering eyes. Leela gasps, ducking her head. A chill goes down her spine. She hopes never to see that woman and her evil eyes again.

The afternoon work is as fast and furious as the morning was and by the end, Leela is bone tired but happy. Her arms are sore, and she feels muscles she never knew she had. By the time they've cleaned up the kitchen and readied it for the evening shift, it's three o'clock.

Leela signs, *I've had a busy, but wonderful day thanks to the two of you.* Izzy and Ham return her smile. Ham starts to translate, but Izzy stops him, "I get what she said. I feel the same way, Leela. Having you here sure took a load off us. Thank you."

"Ditto," Ham flashes his signature smile.

Leela heads for the swinging doors, thinking they're right behind her, but when she presses the door open, they're at the kitchen's back door.

She looks back at them, her palms up in a question.

"Ham and I can't go through the restaurant when patrons are there," Izzy says.

Leela looks to Ham, signing, *but why not?*

"It's just the way it is, Leela. But you go on ahead. It's okay for you."

45

Leela shakes her head. *I go where you go*, she signs, moving toward them.

"I had a feeling you'd see it that way. Come on, then," Ham flashes her a grin.

The late afternoon sun slants down, hot and humid. A trifle of the bay's breeze cools the perspiration on their brows as the walk.

"Loretta told us you moved here from Albany. What's it like up north." Ham asks her.

"*It's crowded and cooler, a lot cooler*, Leela signs, laughing. *But I like it here, now that I've met you two. It will be nice to have friends when school starts.*

Ham tells Izzy, who shakes her head, saying, "Oh, we don't attend Bateaux High. We go to Washington High, it's our school."

Leela signs, *I didn't know there were two high schools. I'll tell my mom I want to go to your high school.*

Ham translates for Izzy. They share a quizzical look. "Leela," Ham says, "You, ah, you can't go to our high school any more than we can go to yours."

But why not? I don't understand.

"You're south of the Mason-Dixon line now, Leela," Ham tells her. Schools here are segregated. It's always been that way, far back as I know. It's just the way it is."

But it shouldn't be that way. It's not fair.

"It's Jim Crow's law, Leela," Izzy says. "We don't mind much. We like being with our own kind too."

But I am your kind, aren't I? Leela signs, her chest tightening.

"Of course, you are," Ham and Izzy say in unison. Izzy grabs Leela's hand.

"You're the best kind," Ham says softly. "Things are different here. But we'll still be friends, even after school starts. That's a promise."

The trio part ways at the railroad tracks, with handshakes and a see you tomorrow goodbye. But Leela's happy day has been tainted by what they've told her. She doesn't like Jim Crow, whoever he is.

When she gets to the house of flowers, she pauses there, taking in the scent and sight of so many flowers in bloom. A shadow moves behind the porch railings. She wonders if it's the Birdman. She lifts her hand in a wave. The shadow moves into the afternoon light. The Birdman comes to the steps and stops. He raises his hand in a wave. Leela smiles, waves back. He watches her as she passes. He has a nice face, she thinks, a face that would be considered handsome if it weren't for the twitches that mar it.

When she gets home, her mom is pacing the sandy front yard.

"Where have you been," Sable demands. "I was at the grille waiting for you, but you never came out. They said you'd already left.

Mom, Leela signs, *I went out the back with Izzy and Ham. I didn't know you'd be there, okay?"*

"Izzy and Ham? You mean the two-colored kids, the kitchen helpers?

Yes, Mom, they're my age and they were so nice to me. Ham even signs. It was so busy, but fun too, Leela signs.

"I'm glad you're back safe and sound, and I'm glad you did a good job. Loretta told me. So, are you going to walk with them every day?" Sable says, her eyes pinched, worried.

Yes, Mom, they're my friends now.

"I'm proud of you, you know that, right?"

47

Leela lifts her shoulders, nods.

Sable takes Leela hands in her own, but she is looking pass Leela, her eyes focusing on something distant. Her eyes close, but not before a tear slips along her high cheekbone.

"*Mom,* Leela wipes the tear away and pulls at her mother's hands until Sable looks at her, *It's okay. Mom. I'm okay. I like what I'm doing. Please don't be sad.*

"This isn't, I mean, this is not what I'd planned, I'd hoped, you know, for something better for you, Leela, something better than here."

Mom, it's great here. I love this big old house and I have friends, real friends.

"Yes, that's all well and good, honey, but you'll have other friends when school starts. Friends who go to the same school."

I know Mom, they told me, but it doesn't matter. I wouldn't care if Izzy and Ham were striped like zebras. It's hearts that count, not color. Right?

Yes, yes, of course. I, I just don't want—Leela, it's different here. Some things are different here.

Well, maybe it's time some things changed, Leela signs, her eyes, her mouth set in anger.

"All right, but just socialize with them at the restaurant and walking home. No other activities. Not without my or Loretta or your granny's supervision. Okay?"

When do I ever have activities, Mom? And, who is this Jim Crow? I don't like him at all.

"What? Jim who?" Sable asks, surprised.

Jim Crow. He's the one who makes kids go to separate schools.

"I, I don't actually know. It's just the law, Leela."

Well, it's a bad law. Somebody needs to change it.

Eight

Art makes visible, the invisible
~ Delia Dubois ~

Leela follows her mother up the veranda's steps and into the house. The hum of granny Vernell's sewing machine vibrates the air. Sweet and savory scents drift from the kitchen. Leela notices her mother's hair is clean and styled. And that her mother has an apron on. She stops, pulling at her mother's arm

Mom, are you cooking? She signs.

"Yes, I figured it's time I do something. I guess you could say we're celebrating not only your job, but mine too.

Mom, a job? You have a job?

"Yes, I do have a job. I know, I've never worked before, but there's a first time for everything, right? With you at the Grille and granny Vernell busy sewing, I decided to walk to the public library, the Clayton Memorial Library. It's not far and I used to go all the time when I lived here. Rachel McFadden, a friend

49

from my high school days, is now the head librarian and well, we got to talking and she asked if I'd like a part-time position and that it might go full time later. The hours are fair, but it means I won't be here when you get home. I'll have to work some evenings too. But your grandmother will be here, so I said yes."

Barely able to contain her excitement, Leela follows her mom into the kitchen.

Mom, we're going to be okay. I'm so happy, she signs and claps her hands.

"Honey, all this is just for now. We still haven't heard from dad and, until then…"

Dad? Leela frowns. *But he left us, Mom. He left us for…* She can't bring herself to sign the woman's name.

"Leela, there are things in a marriage you are not old enough to understand. People work things out sometimes."

But he hurt you mom. He hurt us. I hate him. I don't ever want to see him again.

"You don't mean that, Leela. I know you're disappointed in him, I am too. Let's talk about this later, okay? Go get cleaned up and I'll set the table. Granny Vernell made a peach cobbler."

Leela stills her hands, letting them drop to her sides. Disappointed in him? That does not begin to describe how she feels. She trudges up the kitchen's narrow backstairs to her bedroom. The anger she feels is a red-hot coal burning inside her chest. How her mother can forgive him baffles her. She will never, ever forgive him. But then, her mother had not seen what Leela had seen. She had seen *that* woman in the car with her father. A shade of a memory comes to her, dark and foreboding, turning her stomach, making her hands go all clammy. It's like the same recurring dream that troubles her sleep, the one that always slips away upon awakening. Wiping her hands on her jumper, she closes her eyes until the bad feeling passes.

Closing her bedroom door behind her, she is, as usual, drawn to the bank of windows and its shimmering view of the bay and the town beyond. She smiles to see the seeds she'd scattered along the sills have been picked over. Who are you, she wonders? Are you a songbird? She'd read about the southern mockingbirds and how they mimicked what they heard. Leela purses her lips, whistling a favorite tune. She waits, whistles again. With a sigh, she's backing away from the window when suddenly she hears a faint return whistle. It's her tune followed by a call note, a *tchack, tchack*. It's a mockingbird, for sure, she claps her hands in glee. She'd read about their distinctive calls. Oh, you'll want more than seeds, Leela smiles. She'll need to get some berries and dig up some mealworms too. A flutter of wings zip past her windows leaving an impression of soft gray with white tips.

Her heart lightened by this discovery Leela shakes off her dark mood. In a sudden moment of clarity, it dawns on Leela she doesn't have to go back to her father, if it comes to that. She can stay here with her grandmother. She belongs here. Her history is here. If her mother wants to go back to him, fine, let her. She is done with her father, done with his false promises and his betrayal. Done with being displaced every year, sometimes even twice in a year. Done with new schools, new subdivisions and their box-like homes. In her mind, it's settled. This house, this town is where she belongs. She feels this to her core. She is determined to make it happen.

Stepping away from windows, Leela flops down her bed and brings her notebook to her chest. Writing verses has always been her outlet. With pencil to the paper, she closes her eyes, waiting for inspiration to strike. A shaft of sunlight falls across the mural. Leela studies it, eyeing the details the sun has highlighted. She will write about the shimmering waves and the rocky shoreline, she decides. She flips off the bed and goes to the mural. She trails her fingers over the vivid, life-like scenes. The more she views it, the more she realizes the painting is more than just pretty, random scenes linked together. It's more like a sequence of events, like a story in pictures. A story? Leela's imagination is galvanized by this realization.

First there is the island with its mist shrouded mountains and the thatched huts surrounded by tall bamboo-like grasses. Beyond the huts are structures with plumes of gray smoke rising. Behind one of the structures is a towering windmill. Set back from these is a white house on a hill. A man on horse-back wears a broad-brimmed hat. The whip he carries seems to snap at the air. Within the waves of the towering grasses are dark skinned people, their long, curved knives slash at the grasses. One figure stands out among the others, a girl. She is young, a teenager like Leela. She is surprisingly fair skinned. Not white, exactly, but close with her creamy toned skin. She and the other girls and women wear bright cloths wrapped around their heads. The boys and men wear conical hats woven of grass. The girl's eyes are violet and are set in a perfectly oval face. She wears a sleeveless, drab colored shift that is pulled up between her long, tanned legs and tied to a cord around her waist. There's no mistaking the look of contempt in her eyes. She doesn't look at her surroundings but seems to stare at the world outside of the mural. Leela glides her fingers over the girl. She is about to pull away when her fingers slide over deep indentations beneath the smooth surface of the girl's shift. Leela focuses her gaze on that spot, but all she sees is the girl's shift. Puzzled, she traces a finger over each indentation noting how symmetrical and evenly spaced they are. It's probably nothing, just a quirk of the paint or the wall behind it, she thinks. But still—her imagination having already been piqued—she decides to do a rubbing like she'd done in art class. They'd used tracing papers and pencils to make rubbings of leaves in order to see nature's beautiful patterns.

Leela digs through her writing supplies. At the bottom of the box is a single piece of tracing paper leftover from school. With pencil and paper in hand, she slides her fingers over the girl's shift until she finds the indentations. Placing the paper over that area, Leela gently rubs the tip of the pencil there. First one letter and then another is exposed. By the time she's finished, three words are revealed. Leela sits back on her heels. Words, there are words, Leela is stunned by it.

The simple sentence reads: I am Eulie.

Eulie. Was she the artist? Or was she a model for the artist? When was it painted and why in this room and not in the parlor or formal dining room? Are there more hidden markings? More words to discover. With excitement building in her chest, Leela glides her fingers over other portions of the painting. Her fingers still when she feels a series of markings. She keeps going until finds yet another series of markings. So many she loses count.

She'll need to buy more tracing paper, lots of it. What a story she'll have for Izzy and Ham tomorrow.

Granny Vernell's shrill voice quivers the air.

"Leela, we're waitin' on you. Come on down, supper's gettin' cold," Vernell hollers up the stairs. Leela is about to take the tracing paper with her, but stops, thinking better of it. It's her secret. She's not ready to share it with her mom or granny

Vernell. She slips the paper into her notebook and heads downstairs.

At supper, stifling yawn after yawn despite the delicious smelling chowder, Leela's head bobs again and again.

"Leela," Granny Vernell nudges her, "your head is about ready to fall into your bowl. Go on upstairs now and get to bed. You've an early start again tomorrow. Your momma and I'll clean up the kitchen."

She smiles her thanks and heads up the backstairs. She slips into her shorty pajamas and flops down on her bed. Yawning, her eyelids drooping, she is fast asleep in an instant. Her dreams involve tall grasses and a violet-eyed girl in a drab shift.

Nine

❧ EULIE ❧

Not all riches are gold. There is memory.
~ Konte' Kre'yol, a creole storyteller ~

THE ISLAND OF MARTINIQUE, JUNE 1848

Eulie had long given up any pretense of modesty. The thread-
bare muslin shift revealed more than it covered when it
rained, and it rained most days. It was raining now, sluicing
down the faces and bodies of the female cane field workers. The
men fared no better in their ragged breeches and bakoua hats.
Neither rain nor boiling sun deterred the workers as their billhooks rose and fell among the sugarcane fields. The swish and
crack of the sharp, curved knives against the stalks was like the
sound of bones being broken.

"You, girl," a boy called out.

She angled her body toward the speaker, her arms cradling
cut stalks ready for the cart. It was Ozee, a boy about her age.
She'd felt his black eyes on her all morning, though he would
never seek to look her in the eyes. Nor would anyone besides the

very young who knew no better, and the whites, the *bekes* who ran the plantation. Even those of low caste, the mixed *chabines* like her, refused set their sight on her eyes.

Ozee was handsome, his skin the blackest of blacks. He was desired by many girls. Yet she'd often felt his gaze upon her. If not for the color of her eyes, he might think to take her hand, lead her to the cover of the forest beyond the beach, despite her being among the lowest of castes. He might think it, but Eulie knew he would never act on it. There are some lines that can never be crossed.

"I am Eulie," she said, lowering her gaze the way a modest girl should, though catching his countenance through her lashes.

"I know who you are, girl" he said, not unkindly. Of course, he knew, but to say her name was to see it.

"You are Ozee," she said.

Casting his gaze away from her, he smiled a crooked smile at her attempt to engage him. He was cunning, but so was she. She returned his crooked smile. It was a game that had no good end.

"This cart is full. Take it to the mill house now, he said, slapping the mule's hind quarters with the flat of his machete."

"Oh, so it is," she answered, grabbing the yoke as the mule jumped forward. Arching her neck, she pressed her lips together and whistled the call of a mating dove. She stifled a giggle to see the startled look on his face.

She had dallied, and he knew it. Her days at the field would soon end. No longer a young child, she would be trained for the mill and even for the boiling house. Dread of those murderous places welled up in her as she made a pretense of guiding the mule along the rutted path. Her mother had died in the mill house when her hands had been caught and crushed by the iron rollers that pressed the juice from the cane. Her arms had been sliced clean through by a worker with an axe. It was his sole purpose for being there, so frequent were the incidents. Her mother had not survived. Most did not.

She closed her eyes, letting the mule lead for he knew the way as well as she. Her mother's face swam in her vision, but with the passage of seasons, the vision had blurred. Her name had been Serafina. She'd had violet eyes, eyes that changed color in the light, as did the eyes of the ancient deadly serpent, Basilisk. Serafina had passed those eyes to Eulie. And her gaze was no less frightening.

The next morning, Eulie stirred on her pallet of woven grass as the sky sent slivers of pink dawn through the hut. Birds sung out their morning chorus. Eulie had learned to mimic their calls, especially the high call notes of the red throated gray warbler. So close was her mimicry, the birds paused their calls to listen. The children, a hub around her, slumbered on, their bodies curled in like grub worms. She was the eldest orphan now that Malaika was gone, a maroon, a runaway. Eulie crossed her heart, praying the girl had found the mountain lair of the fugitive slaves. If anyone could, it would be Malaika. She was known to be *djok*, strong of spirit. Massa Stone had sent the plantation's overseer and the other whites, the *bekes* to hunt her down. Yet even with their braying hounds, they had failed. The many she left behind, the enslaved, would suffer for her crime. Food, just enough to keep body and soul together, was shorted. No matter the heavy toil of sugar cane harvest was upon them. The *bekes* called it honey cane, but those who harvested it called it death cane for the brutal work and danger it posed.

Those who were known to consort with Malaika, were whipped. Eulie had been dragged to the post, but Massa Stone had stayed the overseer's hand. Eulie knew not why but said a host of Hail Mary's for her deliverance and gave thanks for the priest who had saved her soul.

The next morning, Eulie rubbed sleep from her tired eyes. Every muscle sore from yesterday's planting of the cane shoots. Her stomach growled with hunger and was echoed by the stomachs of the young who slept around her. Eulie had scavenged for prickly cucumbers and crickets and had rolled them in *bonano* leaves, roasting them in hot embers as Malaika had done during the lean times. It filled their bellies but left them still wanting. Malaika had been their protector, she with the fierce golden eyes and proud bearing had been one of them, one of the young slaves without *manmans*, mothers to protect them. Malaika's mother, it was said, had been of royalty. She had been kidnapped from a village and taken with a chain of others to the Guinea coast. She had been beautiful, it was said, a queen who railed against her enslavement. She never spoke her name. It was after she was delivered of a child sired by a beke, that she snuck away to the cliffs towering over the sea. It was where many leaped to their deaths believing they would return to their home villages reborn and whole.

Eulie shook the sleepers awake. She was nearing her thirteenth season and prayed fervently to Mary, the mother of all, to stay her bleeding. For as long as she stayed a child, she need not fear the bekes. She gathered the sleepy-eyed, the youngest being four seasons and led them to the hogshead barrel to splash their faces. God willing, Agata, the cook from the Massa's house would take pity and bring the yams to break their fast.

With her bright muslin tigon wrapped around her head, a protection from the sun, Eulie and the children gathered the bagasse, the crushed cane waste from the mill house. They tossed it into a cart pulled by a stubborn mule. The sound of the iron rollers crushing the cane sent chills of terror through Eulie. She was not there to hear her mother's screams that day. But she had heard the screams of others when their hands were caught by crushing rollers and brought to sudden silence as a worker raised his axe to severe the hand from the arm.

When their cart was full, Eulie and the children took the bagasse to the boiling house where it was used for fuel to heat the syrup in the coppers. When the sugar syrup was close to crystallizing, it was poured off in hogshead barrels or clay molds. Eulie and the children carted the sugar filled clay molds to the curing house. Massa Hector, the overseer, was there eyeing her with his devil-blue eyes. His thumbs were crooked, a *pamoise*. Those who had crooked thumbs had evil hearts, it was said. Massa Hector had been watching her of late, waiting for her to bleed, a wanting in his eyes. First, he would beat her. She had seen it in the clench of his fists. Then he would drag her, as he had others, and take her behind the rocks at the black sand beach and give her pain. The pain might swell her belly as it had other girls he'd taken.

Eulie, wily as the iguana and as swift of foot, was determined to avoid such a fate. She knew the hiding places. The forests, the stone outcroppings, the storage buildings and even the windmill house had hidey holes for one as small as she to seek refuge in. Her last resort, should he find her, were the cliffs that towered over the ocean. She would fling herself into the deep even though her soul would not go to the before land to be reborn.

She was born here. She did not want to return. The priest promised she would go to heaven. She prayed he'd spoke the truth.

Late in the evenings, when the moon's glow cast its shimmer on the cane stalks, she and the children would often huddle behind tall grasses to watch the dancers. The enslaved danced to the music of the singing wood, their bare feet tapping out rhythms on the ground. They sang the songs of *Madinina*, the island of flowers.

On the day of her first bleeding, the women came to her hut. Their heads bowed so as not to catch her glance, they laid red hibiscus and scraps of muslin at her feet. The hibiscus marked her as a woman, the muslin, to stem the flow. Days after her confinement, she kept the children close whenever she ventured out, hoping their presence offered her a measure of protection against the *bekes*.

The men and boys in the village eyed her speculatively. Not that any were bold enough to approach her. So, it came as a profound shock when she found a string of shells formed into a necklace by her hut. A wooden pendant carved into the shape of a star hung from it. The star marked it as coming from Ozee's hut. Each hut belonging to a family was marked in such a way, from star constellations to animal shapes and things of nature. It meant she'd been claimed by a single male in the family. The only single male in this family was Ozee. If she wore it, it meant she excepted his claiming. A claimed female was deemed untouchable by other males, including the *bekes*. Eulie held the pendant to her chest. Why had he done this? Why had he put himself in harm's way on her account. Hector would target him, would lay the lash on his back. Ozee could not marry her; his family would never allow it. She was a chabine, low caste and shunned because of her eyes. Surely his act went beyond pity for there were other girls in need of protection. Eulie's heart swelled. Tears sprang to her eyes. Since her mother's passing, she'd not known another's consideration, save for Malaika's brand of cold indifference. The orphaned young were generally left to scrounge for food and necessities. Families had their own children to feed and clothe.

What did Ozee see in her she did not see in herself? How had she touched his heart? There was no question of her keeping his necklace. He would find it at dawn's light by his hut, wrapped in her tigon. Inside she would place wild lilies. Lilies were a sign of love and chastity. He would know of her heart, of her love and her admiration for his gift. From this point on, she would not tease him with the sway of her hips. She would not seek to find his gaze. She would not put him in harm's way. If Massa Hector came for her, she would run to the cliffs.

Ten

❧ A TASTE OF FEAR ❧

Life shrinks or expands in proportion to one's courage
~ Anais Nin ~

Two weeks pass quickly. Leela is efficient at her job. She loves working with Ham and Izzy. Though today, Leela's hands tremble. She trails nervously behind Loretta. The plates of food she carries are heavy, laden as they are with hamburgers and French fries. Loretta, one hand bandaged from a mishap with a hot frypan, had conscripted her from the kitchen to help serve the customers. It's lunch, the busiest time, and the restaurant is packed with customers. Leela blanches when she sees who she will be serving. It's the White Shoulders' girl, Darla and her gaggle of teens. Oh no, Leela's cheeks flame red. With the group is the boy, Finn, who'd held her hand at McCrory's.

"Leela," Finn greets her with a broad smile, eyes widening in surprise. "What're you, I mean, I didn't know you worked here."

Darla, who'd been deep in conversation with the girl next to her, swivels her head around, her blonde hair flipping over her shoulder. "Who? Oh, that one," she smirks, eyeing Leela dispassionately. "Finn," she reaches across the table and grabs his hand, "Mom said we need to be at the parade stand early next Saturday. We should dress alike. You know, all red, white and blue for the Fourth."

"Uh huh," he says, brushing away her hand as Loretta directs Leela, pointing to who gets which plate.

"Will you be at the parade, Leela?" Finn reaches over, takes a plate from her and shoves it toward Darla.

"Leela will be there, most everyone will, Finn," Loretta quips. "We'll be back with the rest of y'all's order in a jiffy."

Leela backs away, attempting a smile which is near impossible because her lips are trembling. With a sinking heart, she follows Loretta back to the kitchen. How is she ever going to survive here? If she stutters, they will laugh. If she writes notes, they will make fun of her. If she signs, they'll call her a retard. It's all happened before. She needs to practice every day, every night with the stones. And then—maybe there will be a miracle.

Back in the kitchen, Loretta turns to Leela. "Honey, you did just fine. Smile and do as I say, okay? I really need your help for a few days until this hand gets better. Can you do this for me? And pay no mind to Darla's snippy ways. None of us do."

Leela bobs her head, straightens her spine, though her stomach heaves. She swallows hard.

Ham and Izzy, busy chopping lettuce at the metal table, stop what they're doing and give her a thumb's up. "You got this, Leela," Ham offers up his bright white Chiclet smile.

Taking a deep breath through trembling lips, Leela takes two plates from the warming tray.

"Leela, don't you fret now, the rest of the customers will be a piece of cake," Loretta says while placing drinks on a tray.

Darla has changed seats, having scooted next to Finn so she's near the servers. Finn's lips are pressed into a frown. Darla's eyes narrow into blue slits as Leela approaches. The other teens, who hadn't paid any attention before, stare hard at Leela. She blinks, stunned by the hostility directed at her. With trembling hands, Leela sets the plates down; they clatter on the table. Loretta places the drinks while saying, "Five burgers and fries, and five cokes. Ketchup's on the table. Enjoy." Loretta slaps the bill on the table. Leela turns on her heels, follows Loretta's quick pace back to the kitchen. She can feel their stares raking her back. She lets out the breath she hadn't realized she been holding. Why had they stared at her like that?

Later, after the rush, when Ham, Izzy and Leela are cleaning up the kitchen, Leela asks Ham and Izzy if they know who Darla is.

"Darla? As in Darla Devlin? Oh Lordy, don't tell me you had to wait on her?" Ham shakes his head.

"That's Luanne Clayton Devlin's daughter. You remember, the blonde lady who was with Brick," Izzy says. Leela nods, signs *yes*.

"Yep, and that lady's sure trying to get her claws in Brick, but he's too smart for her, and that's a fact," Izzy chortles, wipes her hands on her less than white apron.

But, Leela signs, *isn't she already married?*

"Was," Ham shrugs, "her husband passed away. Heard it was an illness, no one knows."

"More like some kind of poi..."

"You hush, Izzy. Don't be saying things like that or you'll bring evil on yourself. Granme´ Delia says evil words beget evil."

Leela nods, in full agreement with Granme´ Delia, whoever she is. A shiver spools down her spine as she recalls the way the Devlin woman had looked at her. Her daughter had done the same. But why? She'd never done anything to either. She didn't even know them.

"Leela," Izzy is quick to move on, "tell us more about the painted wall and the words. I've never heard the name Eulie before. We should ask Granme´ Delia.

"Yes, and she speaks in different languages too," Ham whispers, a knowing look in his eyes. Most of us don't understand all her words, but it's funny how we all seem to know what she's saying."

"It's because she tells the stories with her hands. Sort of like you, Leela," Izzy says. You speak with your hands, just like Granme´ Delia.

She's like me?

Izzy shakes her head. "Oh no, she has a wonderful voice, but she uses her hands like you do, but it's not in place of speaking. Anyway, you'll see when you come to the Gathering.

Ham, smiling one of his I've-got-a-secret-smiles, says, "and you've been invited!"

Izzy chirps in, "It's next Saturday. We don't go to the parade or picnic, none of us coloreds do. We have our own celebration. Everyone brings food and there's marimba music and Granme´ Delia tells a story. Do you think you can come?"

Leela's eyes light with surprise, though her lips pull into a frown, signing, *I'm supposed to go with granny Vernell and my mom to the parade and picnic, but I'd rather to go to the gathering with you.*

Ham translates for Izzy.

Izzy's smile fades. "That's okay, Leela. There'll be other times.

I'll try to find a way, Leela signs to Ham. *Where does Granmé Delia live?*

Ham shakes his head, "Oh, it not at her house. It's held in a special place. But you've seen her house, I'm sure. You pass it on the way here.

I don't know her house, Leela signs, shaking her head.

"You can't miss it, Leela. It's the house with all the flowers," Izzy says.

Flowers? Where the Birdman lives? Leela signs.

"The birdman?" Ham looks to Izzy, puzzled, as he tells her what Leela signed.

Leela pantomimes the way the Birdman moves.

Ham and Izzy share a glance and burst out laughing at her antics.

"That has to be Ishmael, Granmé Delia's grandson," Izzy says.

"Never thought of him that way," Ham nods, "but that's a darn good imitation."

It wasn't to make fun of him, really. I would never, it's just what I thought when I saw him. I think he's nice, I do, really," Leela signs quickly, her cheeks flushing in embarrassment.

Ham translates. Turns to Leela. "Leela, it's okay. He'd laugh if he saw you imitate him. Ishmael's got a great sense of humor."

Please don't tell him I called him Birdman. Leela signs.

Seeing Leela's distress, Ham grabs her hands, "We won't say a word, I promise. We weren't laughing at you or Ishmael. It's just that you really got him, the way he moves. And that's not an easy thing to do. I bet you could tell stories the way Granmé Delia does."

"Hey, here's an idea," Izzy says, "if you can sneak away at four o'clock on Saturday, we'll meet you here and take you to the Gathering. It's not an easy place to get to and its sort of a secret place, okay. We'll wait for a bit, if you don't come, we'll know you couldn't get away. Deal?"

Leela ponders this. Sneak away? Could she? Why not? She'd only stay for a little while. Her mother will be busy talking to her old friends and granny Vernell will be helping to serve food. With all the goings on and the crowd, she probably wouldn't even be missed.

She squeezes Izzy's hands, nodding, then turns to Ham, signing, *I think I might be able to sneak away. I'll try, you know I will."*

Ham claps his hands together, "Yes! But remember, you can't tell anyone, not even your mom or your granny. The Gathering is secret and where it's held is secret too.

Leela nods, crosses her heart and zips her lips.

Izzy, ever the pragmatist, says, "Okay, let's get this kitchen ready for the next shift and skedaddle outa here!"

It's late afternoon when the three friends make their way home. They are tired but excited about the Gathering and the dollar bill given to each by Loretta. They'd worked hard during the rush. The unaccustomed tip had surprised all three. It's the first money Leela has ever made. She's a wage earner now, incredible as it seems to her. A lightness fills her as never before. She'd always felt more of a liability because of her stuttering. She'd never babysat like other girls her age. Who'd hire someone to look after their kids who couldn't talk? But now she has a job and the best friends ever. Her smile spreads from ear to ear. Her cheeks hurt from so much smiling, though it's a good hurt.

They'd come to the railroad tracks, ready to go their separate ways, when a red pickup truck zooms up beside them, screeching to a stop. Loud music and raucous laughter spills out. It's loaded with teens waving Confederate flags

Darla's in the passenger seat of the cab. She points to Leela, "There she is."

Several of the boys hop out of the bed of the truck, shouting, "Hey, we got us a couple picaninnies

"Nah, those ain't no picaninnies, they be coons," said one of the boys, sniggering.

More boys and girls hop of the truck's bed.

Leela's heard the word nigger before, but never the others. She looks at Izzy whose eyes are wide with fright. Ham moves in front of Izzy and Leela in a defensive position, smiling a big tooth grin. "Hey y'all, we be walking home from the Grille. We work there, y'all know we do."

Two of the boys, their hands fisting as they swagger close, snigger: "That's so, huh, well git on home then if you know what's good. Now git, niggers. We got some talkin' to do with that gal behind you, ain't that so, Darla," one of them says, glancing back at the cab.

"You know what to do, Rusty," she calls out from the cab. She smirks at Leela, her blue eyes narrowed with menace. "Fix her up so Finn won't take another look at her."

"Sure Boss, we're leavin'," Ham replies, turning as if he's going to walk away, but says through clenched teeth, "Run, both of you, run!"

Izzy shakes her head. Leela is too stunned to move. Why do they want to talk to her? Darla said fix her up. What does that mean?

Ham turns back, offers up a shrug to the boy called, Rusty.

The boys look to each other, laughing. One of them, the tallest, unbuckles his belt and slips it out, snapping the air with it. "Boy, you lookin' for an ass whoopin'?"

Leela's breath catches in her throat, her heart makes one violent quake before lunging into a gallop. She wants to scream at them to stop, but the word freezes on her tongue. She jumps forward, pushing Ham and Izzy back. She puts up her hands, envisioning the stones, feeling their weight on her tongue: "N...nooo." She hears the word, her mouth in an O. Was that her? Had she said that?

"Hey y'all, looks like we got us a nigger lover here," the boy Rusty sneers, snapping his belt near Leela's face.

"Do it, Rusty. Mark her up," Darla demands.

Rusty raises the belt, again snapping it toward Leela's face, but Izzy and Ham shove her behind them, their bodies shielding her. The belt lashes against Ham's raised arm, barely missing his face.

Rusty bares his teeth in an evil grin. Holding the belt high, he's ready to lash out again, when a squeal of brakes from behind the pickup truck freezes his arm. All the kids stop their cat calls as Brick and Finn hop out of a truck.

"What's going on here," Brick says in a cool, calm voice, but his expression is thunderous.

"Nothin, just having some fun, Brick," Rusty has the belt looped around his forearm.

Brick looks over at the cab. "Is that so, Darla?"

"Brick," Darla simpers, fluttering her lashes, "it was those coloreds and her, that white girl, she was calling me nasty names. Rusty was just scaring them into taking it back."

Izzy and Ham each have an arm around Leela. She's chalk pale and trembling. All three stare hard at Brick and Finn.

Finn, his gate stiff with outrage but full of purpose, stalks to the cab. He bangs his fist against the cab's door. "What the hell, Darla? You lost your mind or somethin'?"

Brick holds up his hand before any of them can deny what he's seen. "Fun's over, y'all get home before I tell your parents what you've been up to. Go on home now. I don't want to see your faces the rest of the evening. And you, Russell Fowler, if I ever see that belt of yours outa your pants again, I'll be whooping *you* with it, understood?"

Finn rushes over to Leela, his back to the cab. Darla's eyes have narrowed to glittering slits. Those slits are honed on Leela.

After the kids have piled up in the bed of the pickup truck, the driver shoves the gears into a grinding first and the truck takes off; tires burn against the pavement as they speed away.

Finn has his arm around Leela, giving Izzy and Ham leave to do some trembling of their own.

"Leela, are you hurt? Izzy, Ham?" Brick looks them over, sees the purple bruise rising on Ham's forearm. What the hell?" Brick's face goes dark. "Come on, let's get you all home."

"Leela, her face going from chalk white to an embarrassed pink, signs to Ham, *Ask Brick not to tell my mom. She'll make me quit work.*

Brick takes Leela's hands gently into his, "Leela, I know you sign and why. It's okay, Loretta told me. She said you'll talk when you're ready, isn't that right?" He looks to Ham, "Can you teach me some signs? I've been meaning to learn as my great gram is going deaf. She's doing some signing at the nursing home."

71

"Sure will, be glad to. Oh, and don't tell Leela's mom about what just happened. Leela says her mom will make her quit work at the grille."

"Well, we can't have that, can we? You have my word."

"Mine too," Finn nods at Leela, "Ah, you don't, I mean, you don't talk at all?"

With her heart heavy as a stone in her chest, Leela slowly shakes her head. She digs into her pants pocket, pulling out her note pad and pencil.

I stammer, but I'm practicing how not to, she writes, tears off the page, handing it to him

"Oh," he smiles, "I used to stammer, like when I was a kid. I could, you know, help you practice. If you'd like?" His green eyes are so clear, so honest that Leela finds herself nodding. His answering smile dazzles her.

"Okay, y'all hop in the back," Brick gestures to Finn, Izzy and Ham. "Leela, you ride in the cab with me."

"You know," Brick says, after they've settled in the cab, "you take after your mom. You have her hair and her eyes. Back in the day, your mom was the prettiest girl in town. But you know what? I believe you've got her beat by a mile."

Leela blushes, shakes her head.

"Are you friends with Finn?

Leela shrugs, shakes her head.

"Well, Finn's a good boy. None better around these parts. He works for me when I need an extra hand on the Miss Ina. After the tourist season slacks off, you should come. Ever been on a fishing boat, Leela?"

She shakes her head.

"Well then, would you like to?"

She dips her chin, offering up her brightest smile.

His eyes widen like he's seeing something that startles him. He looks away and that same sadness she's seen in him shows in the downturn of his mouth. "So much like your mother," he says in a soft, whispery voice.

Questions bubble up in her mind. How well did he know her mom? Had they been friends? More than friends? She grits her teeth. How she hates being wordless. Her hands clench. She will cure herself. Somehow, someway, she will.

Brick drives her home first. He pats her hand, saying, "if those kids and Darla give you a hard time again, you let me know, okay? Leela nods, smiling her thanks.

After she gets out, she hurries to the bed of the truck, signs goodbye to Izzy and Ham. When her gaze shifts to Finn, she offers him a shy smile.

"See ya, Leela," he says, showing a dimple in his cheek.

A dimple, Leela sighs, waving bye.

Eleven

൚ LEELA AND FINN ൙

True love is rare, true friendship, rarer still
~ Anonymous ~

The next day, after their shift has ended, Leela, Izzy and Ham slip out the kitchen's back door. Ham's in the middle of explaining something about reasoning and paradoxes when all three stop and stare. Finn Connell is standing at the bottom of the steps, arms crossed and grinning.

"Hey y'all. I'm off my shift from the Miss Ina," Finn says. "Thought I'd walk with y'all today. Brick usually gives me a ride, but I don't live far, so…"

The three exchange glances, relief lighting their faces, "That'd be just fine," Ham says. Izzy bobs her head. Leela's face has flushed pink. Finn's all genial smiles, though his green-eyed gaze is totally focused on her. He'd offered to help her with her stammering, but if he keeps looking at her in that way, she's bound to stammer twice as much. Does he mean to help her today? Or is

75

he here because of what happened yesterday?

Whatever the reason, relief fills her chest. The three of them had not talked about the incident with Darla. Still, it had been on their minds. Ham had been more talkative than usual, and Izzy had been markedly subdued. But they'd gone on with their day, worried but resolved. What choice did they have? Well, Izzy and Ham could take an alternate route, if they had a mind to, but Leela didn't know another way home. As it was, Darla and the others had been after *her*, not them. Leela had been ready to suggest they go on without her before Finn showed up. She didn't want them to be hurt on her account. She couldn't stand that.

Does Finn know something, she wonders. Does he think they are after her still? What she doesn't understand is why? Why is Darla trying to hurt her? After all, she's only laid eyes on Finn twice, and then for just a few minutes. He'd held her hand at the soda shop and talked to her at the grille. Now here he is, and she thinks maybe he shouldn't walk with them. If Darla sees him, well—she might do something even worse than what she and her friends tried yesterday.

Last night, she'd barely slept, the horror of that boy threatening them with his belt engraved on her memory. If Brick and Finn hadn't shown up when they did—she holds back a shudder. And now Finn wants to help her with her stuttering. She's worried about that too. If he's seen with her will those boys turn on him?

Her decision is made for her when Finn takes her by her elbow. The four walk-abreast for a short while before pairing up. Izzy and Ham taking the lead, with Izzy glancing back, a sly grin creasing her cheeks. Happy chatter flies back and forth between

Finn, Ham and Izzy. Leela casts furtive glances at Finn. His dark hair is not slicked back as she has seen before. It is ruffled by the hot wind, straying over his forehead. He pushes it back with a careless hand now and again. His skin is olive, deeply tanned, blemish free. His jaw is square with a shadow of a beard, yet, there is a boyish softness to his cheeks. He is tall, at least a head taller than her. The sleeves of his T-shirt are rolled up high, revealing lean muscles. He smells like the bay, briny with the tang of fish. His hands, salt reddened, are square too with tapering fingers. He walks with long, easy strides. He appears as comfortable in his own skin as she is not in hers.

When they get to the railroad tracks, the event of yesterday on their minds, the group hesitates, each holding a bated breath. They listen for the squeal of brakes, of raucous laughter. There is a collective sigh of relief as minutes tick by with no sign of Darla and her friends, though Finn has a hard look in his eyes.

Leela gives Izzy and Ham a quick hug. They, in turn, say their goodbye to Finn.

"Stay safe," Finn hollers to their departing figures.

Finn turns to Leela, his arm sliding close to hers. They walk in silence for a bit, but Leela can't stop the blush rising to her cheeks every time Finn flicks a glance at her.

He breaks the silence. "I'm really sorry about what happened to you yesterday. I don't know what's got into them, doing something like that. Darla, she, well, she's always had her way.

Leela lifts one shoulder in a shrug.

"I've seen her temper, but what she started yesterday, well, I'm not going to let her get away with it."

Leela stops, she puts her hand on his arm. Pulling out her note pad, she scribbles few words.

He reads what she's written, shaking his head, "No, Leela, it's not okay. But if you really don't want me to handle this, okay. But if she bothers you again, well…"

Shaking her head, Leela puts a hand on his arm.

They walk on in silence. To Leela it's natural, her silence. She's been voiceless for so long, it's part of her now. She wonders if Finn truly understands what he's getting into with his offer of helping her with her stammer. Longing and fear of failure tighten her chest. As they walk, their hands meet. As if it is a natural thing, Finn's hand slips into hers. It feels rough and very warm. She feels the warmth travel up her arm and through her body. Her breath hitches. So, this is what it's like to hold a boy's hand. And not just any boy's hand. Finn's hand.

When they reach the Birdman's house—she can't help but think of him that way—she pauses to see if he has come out to the porch. He's done so every time when she's passed his house. Finn gives her a quizzical look.

"Do you know Granmeˊ Delia?" Finn asks.

Leela shakes her head just as Ishmael comes to the porch steps, as if he'd been waiting for her. She smiles, waves to him.

"This is Ishmael, Granmeˊ Delia's grandson," he says, raising his hand in greeting. "Hey Ishmael," Finn calls out."

In his way, Ishmael waves back. But this time, instead of sliding back into the porch's shadows, he comes forward, going down the steps, making his way along the stone path to them. His body moves against gravity as though someone else is pulling the strings, like a marionette. It's almost painful to watch, but at the same time, Leela thinks it is the bravest thing she's ever seen.

Ishmael reaches out to Finn, his hand jerking in air as he

attempts to shake hands. Finn, smiling, grabs hold of Ishmael's hand and they shake.

"Ishmael, this is Leela Hawkins, Miss Vernell Stone's grand-daughter."

Ishmael jerks his head in a nod, his lips twisting into a smile. His mouth moves slowly, saying, "H-Hi, L-Lee-la."

Leela offers up a bright, trembling smile, thrusting her hand out for him to shake. He latches on, pumping her hand. His lopsided grin spreads, brown eyes crinkling at the corners. He bobs his head with enthusiasm.

"Tell Granme´ Delia hi for me," Finn says, waving their goodbye, as he and Leela move away from the stone path.

When they've gone some distance, Finn says, "It's a shame he's so afflicted."

Leela's heart constricts, remembering how similar words had been directed at her over the years. She'd been referred to as deaf and dumb more than once, even by her own grandmother. She thinks of Ishmael and his courage. She is acutely ashamed of her own cowardice. Her own *affliction* is nothing, nothing at all compared to his. Yet he faces the world with his, regardless. What if she isn't ever able to speak without that awful braying? Will Finn think of her as afflicted too? A nameless dread wells up, she swallows hard, her tongue suddenly feels too big for her mouth.

Just moments ago, she'd felt almost normal, like a regular girl. A girl whose hand was being held by a boy. The thought of Finn thinking of her as anything but normal, makes her stomach twist.

"Leela," Finn says, startling her. They'd come to the sandy front yard of her house and she hadn't even noticed. "I've always liked this house" he says, admiring it. "It's beautiful. I bet it was really something back in the old days."

She views the house, as if seeing it for the first time through his eyes. It was shabby, no doubt, but it still had a bit of grandeur even so with its wide veranda and high windows. The wings on each side of the veranda give the structure an elegant look. She could feel pride in this, at least. He follows her up the slanting porch steps and onto the porch. She digs out her notepad, writes that she needs to tell granny Vernell they have company. Handing him the note, she slips inside.

A short time later, Leela comes out with Vernell who carries a tray with two glasses of ice-tea and a plate of brownies. Finn is sitting in one of the rockers, though when he sees Vernell, he's quick to stand.

"Finn Connell," granny Vernell says, "you're lookin' more like your daddy every day. How's your momma doing? And your sister, Anna? She still at college?"

"We're all doing fine, thank you, Ma'am, and yes, Anna's still in college, but for the summer she's helping my mom at the hair salon," Finn says politely, taking the tray from granny Vernell.

"That's good, real good to hear. Now, y'all just take your time. It's a pretty afternoon for sittin' on the porch. Nice for Leela to have some company for a change. Y'all need anything, just give me a holler. I'll be gettin' supper ready," she says, wiping her hands on her apron.

"Yes, Ma'am, thank you," Finn dips his head, smiling at her.

Granny Vernell flicks a glance at Leela, her brow arched, her lips working on a satisfied grin. She'd been beside herself when Leela gave her the note about Finn visiting. She'd hustled up the tea and brownies in a wink, telling Leela about Finn's people, good, hard-working family. "You done good for yourself, Leela. Don't know how you done it though, you not talkin' one bit, but I reckon a pretty face does the trick."

When Vernell's back is turned, Leela rolls her eyes. By now, she's used to granny Vernell's back-handed compliments. Granny Vernell refused to learn the simplest of signs and har-rumphed every time Leela handed her a note.

The aged, fossilized door closes behind Vernell with a thud. To Leela, it sounds like the closing of a tomb. Her mouth is dry, her tongue, grown thick and unwieldly.

Finn puts the tray on the rattan table which is set between two rockers. Leela sips her tea, her gaze flickering between the palm fronds which shade the porch to Finn. Finn offers her a brownie, but she shakes her head. When she glances back after a prolonged perusal of the fronds, there is one brownie left. She arches a brow, pressing her lips together to keep from laughing.

Finn flushes, making his tan even deeper.

"I, ah, your granny sure makes good brownies," he grins. "How about we start practicing," he continues, wiping his hands on his jeans. He stares at her, waiting, as if she is the one who should say something first.

She stares back, lifts her shoulders and with a shake of her head, takes out her note pad. This is when her heart begins a rapid beat, fluttering in her chest. She squeezes her hands to stop their tremble, writing, *Consonants are hard for me. Say words that begin with vowels.*

"Oh, right. Well, um, here's an easy one, egg."

Leela gathers what little spit she has and swallowing hard, nods. She'd been working with the stones daily, but her voice, the sound of isn't pleasant; it's raspy like the squeaky hinge of a door.

"Ae-ae-ga-gah." Leela covers her mouth. Ugly, she thinks, her voice is so ugly.

Finn's gaze flicks away for a second. He clears his throat. "Okay, how about, hum, *ear*," he points to his ear.

She narrows her eyes, giving him a scorching stare."

"Right, sorry. Listen, how about we move on to the alphabet. Is that okay? Would that work better?"

Leela blows out a breath of relief, nodding.

"Okay, you repeat after me and let's not stop even if you stutter some. That's how my therapist did it with me, okay?"

And she did stutter, with nearly every letter. But each subsequent utterance became easier as she relaxed. They went through the entire alphabet twice. Each time she opened her mouth and repeated a letter, Finn's eyes glowed, as if what she was doing was the most remarkable thing. He's inched closer to her, their knees touching, his hands folded over hers. Leela, lost in the emerald green of his eyes, did not hear or even care if she stuttered.

"That was easy as pie. Let's try one more thing. A simple sentence, okay. But you have to say it quickly. Say, *I like Finn*."

She laughs at him. Her laughter comes easily, as does her whistling. She swallows again and tries to focus on those three simple words.

"I-I-la-la-la-ik Fa-fa-fa-in." Her hands fly up to her lips, her eyes round as saucers. She is on fire with humiliation. She has failed, miserably. She's brayed like a mule.

"Hey, Leela, it's okay. It's a start."

She nods, looking everywhere but at him. She can't bear to see his expression.

"Listen, I have to go," Finn stands. My mom will be expecting me."

He takes her hand, leading her down the steps. "I'll walk y'all home on the days Brick lets me go early. We can practice some more, if you'd like?"

As per her usual habit, Leela nods, though in her mind she's thinking, not a chance. She won't humiliate herself again.

"Wait, I can't tomorrow. It's the Fourth, remember? I'm in the parade. I'll be the one on a float," he laughs. "Brick always closes the Grille on the Fourth. The whole town closes-up shop. There's a picnic and dance at the Gazebo after the parade. It's a big deal. So, ah, see ya tomorrow, Leela."

She returns his wave. She'd gone from feeling as if her whole body was on fire to icy cold and trembling.

She watches until he's out of sight.

Vernell, who'd been listening through the raised kitchen window, meets her at the door. "Well, it could have gone worse. He'll be back. You mark my words."

Leela studies her feet, not wanting her grandmother to see her humiliation. No, she won't let him come back. She'll find a way to avoid him. He might offer to help her out of pity, but she will not humiliate herself in that way ever again. If she learns to speak without stuttering, it will be by her own doing. Her own doing and the stones.

After supper, Leela cleans up the kitchen and goes to her bedroom. Granny Vernell had chatted on about her sewing and about the Fourth of July celebration. Leela, of course, was silent. She'd nibbled at her food. Her appetite had left with Finn. Before bed, she locks her bathroom door, unwraps the stones, placing each one with infinite care on her tongue. She practices until her mouth is sore from the movement of the stones. She vows to practice every minute she can.

Later, she tries to write poetry, but she can't stop envisioning how she'd humiliated herself. Her face flames remembering the look on his face when she brayed horribly. Tossing the writing pad on her bed, she goes to the mural. Sliding her fingers over the raised markings, she decides to occupy her mind with finding more words, more about this girl, Eulie. She grabs her pencil and the tracing papers she'd had her mom buy.

She starts with the girl, Eulie, in the cane field. There are wide paths trodden in the grasses. One path leads to the big white house above the cane fields. Leela follows that path with her fingers until she comes to the white house. It has a slanted roof with a wide porch and tall shuttered windows. Here she finds a slew of markings. She traces lightly over them until the words reveal entire sentences.

> *Agata bid me come. I am to be a house girl.*
> *Massa Stone asks if I have bled. I say yes.*
> *He asks if I have lain with a boy. I say no.*
> *He smiles.*
> *I do not like his smile.*
> *He asks if I believe in Jesus*
> *I say yes.*

Leela sits back. Her eyes wide with shock. Stone? His name was Stone. It means, it must mean she and her family are the descendants of a slave owner. Holy cow, she thinks. Slaves must have lived here. Eulie must have been a slave. Leela's stomach twists. She is sickened by this discovery. Slavery here in this house, in this family? Leela runs her fingers softly over Eulie's slight form. What kind of life had she endured, this young girl who'd been a slave?

She's about to trace more markings when she hears a vehicle brake to a stop in the front yard. Leela goes to the window. Who could that be? No one, besides Loretta and Brick, have driven to this house since she's lived here. The risen moon shines a spotlight on the front yard, revealing a truck. It looks like Brick's truck, Leela thinks. She stands at the window. After a few minutes, Brick gets out and goes to the side of the truck. He opens the cab's door and her mother gets out. Her mother and Brick? Leela looks at the clock on her nightstand. It's late. Almost ten o'clock. Leela opens her door and goes to the first landing of the staircase. Granny Vernell is in her night clothes unlocking the door. Leela hears words she can't make out. Then granny says, "I was startin' to worry, Sable. Next time you call, you hear?"

"Ma, I was walking home, Brick just offered me a ride. I stayed late to finish shelving."

Vernell waves to Brick as he drives off, then turns to Sable, "Ain't that the second time Brick's given you a ride home this week?"

"Yes, Ma. He drives past the library every day on his way home from the Grill, okay. Nothing to it."

"Uh huh, so you say," granny mumbles on her way back to bed.

Leela slips back into her room. So, her mom and Brick, they were, or are friends, she thinks, smiling. She likes Brick. He's nice and good looking too. Better looking than her lying, cheating father. Way more good looking. With a satisfied grin, Leela goes back to the mural, placing the paper where she'd left off, and begins again, rubbing the tip of the pencil over the markings. Letters form words and the words form sentences.

Massa Stone, he says, show me your hands.

Twelve

This is my world. I must endure.
~ Eulie ~

THE ISLAND OF MARTINIQUE, JULY 1848

Eulie stood next to Agata, her heart trilling, her hands clasped at her waist to stem their tremble. She kept her head bowed beneath Massa Stone's perusal. Heat raced up her throat, flaming her cheeks. His gaze, dark as pond water, chilled her soul. He was a tall man, built thick with hands capable of crushing her with ease. His black boots, polished to a high shine, cast her reflection back at her.

"Show me your hands, girl," he quipped harshly.

Without lifting her gaze, Eulie unclasped her hands, showing her palms.

"What are these stains?"

"It is dye, Massa," said Agata. "This girl makes dye from flowers to paint the *tigons*." Agata pointed to Eulie's head wrap which had colorful flower designs, then to her own head which

87

was wrapped in swirling layers of Madras cloth. Silver loops dangled from her ears.

"No more dye, he barked, clean her hands, make sure she's bathed and properly attired."

"Yes, Massa Stone," Agata said.

"She'll do," he said. She will serve with Joshua at Friday's supper."

Agata, her expression one of forbearance, inclined her head, though she flicked a worried glance at Eulie. Massa Stone turned on his heel, going into the room opposite them, leaving them alone in the wide hall. Male voices filtered from the room.

The hall, open from one end to the other end of the house, drew in cool breezes. Eulie lifted her gaze, her heart plummeting upon hearing his words about the dye on her hands. Eulie bit down on her lip in despair. To become a house slave was one thing, but to be denied her sole source of trade was another. From the crushed petals of hibiscus, rose and frangipani she made dye and painted the tigons for the female slaves. She infused their soaps of ash and lye with the essence. She traded her skill to provide whatever food or cloth the other slaves might offer. How was she to feed and clothe the children now?

Agata took her by the arm, her fingers pinching Eulie's skin as she guided her down the hall. She took her into a narrow room lit by a single high window.

"These shelves," Agata pointed to row upon row of shelving, "hold the china from which you will serve the place settings. China is easy to crack. Break one, you will be punished. You will find the cutlery in these drawers," she continued, pulling open several more.

Eulie nodded, staring dumbfounded at these marvels. She'd seen carved wooden bowls and spoons, though she'd never eaten from them. She and the children ate with their fingers from the bonano leaves as did most of the other slaves.

Eulie followed Agata's swishing skirts.

"This is the drawing room," Agata said, going about the room naming the furniture. Said Eulie was to dust and polish the wood. She was never to sit on any piece ever. When they entered another room, Eulie's eyes grew round. She felt she'd stepped into a magical place. A long wall was covered with scenes of the island. There were leafy trees, palms, flowers and all manner of birds and animals. She knew these plants, these creatures. Her fingers itched to touch them. The birds looked ready to take flight; the iguanas to arch their backs, hissing. Oh, she thought, that one day she might paint a scene such as this.

"Here is where Massa and the overseers break their morning fast and are served their supper. This cupboard is the linen press. You will set the places and help Joshua serve the meals. You have much to learn Eulie. You are known to be a chaste girl. For your sake, let's hope you are a smart one. You were chosen because you speak the English tongue well enough. As did Serafina, your mother. She was once a house girl, but she was too pretty for her own good. She smiled too much. She looked them in the eyes. You must keep your head down and your smiles to yourself or shame will fall upon you. Unless otherwise bid, you will only enter the rooms I've shown you."

Eulie, startled by this revelation, stared at her bare feet to hide her confusion. Her mother, a house girl? Her mother had served here. What had happened to her? Why had she been sent back to the fields? Eulie's heart quaked with the realization she had much to learn and even more to fear.

In her heart, Eulie wanted to fail, to be sent back to the fields and the children. She hated to be in the presence of the *bekes*. She cringed at the thought of being under the scrutiny of the male overseers, visitors, and the Massa himself. And had it not been for Joshua, she would undoubtedly have failed. Joshua was Massa Stone's elderly manservant. He was like no other slave she'd ever known. Over the course of days and weeks, Joshua made the unbearable, bearable. Most unbearable of all was the kitchen.

The kitchen, separate and set back from the house, was a hot place that never cooled. The walls, made of stone, absorbed the heat from the brick ovens. Eulie's pallet, woven of bagasse and filled with dried grass, did little to slake the heat from her body. At first, she'd taken to leaving the shutters open at night for the air, but Agata had bade her close and bar them along with the hatched door. The Massa's overseers, she'd said, who were often in their cups, might seek her out. This news struck fear in Eulie's chest. She had no need to wonder which overseer had in his mind to do more than lay a whip to her back.

Agata's words came to pass for late in the evenings there would often come a banging on the kitchen's door and a rattling of the shutters. On those nights, huddled on her pallet, her eyes grown accustomed to the dark lit only by the ovens' embers and by the slivers of moonlight piercing the roof's slats, Eulie's heart pounded in fear, her gut twisted with loathing.

The kitchen's heat was a thing of continual misery for her. Every evening, prior to barring the doors and shutters, Eulie dipped a wooden bucket into the hogshead rain barrel outside the kitchen. She rarely slept through the night without sluicing water over her body. With her night shift soaked through, she found a few hours of rest.

Each morning, after she set the loaves to rise—their wondrous rising was a thing of magic as was the foul-smelling fungi Agata called yeast—Eulie set about chopping yams, onions and vegetables from the garden. On occasion, Agata gave her a taste of the bread—she'd hold it on her tongue, savoring the flavor, but most often Agata gave her the burnt crusts. Hard biscuit bread was her usual fare with pot leftovers. Still, it was the best food she'd ever had. She hoarded leftovers for the children she'd left behind.

After her kitchen work was finished, Eulie brought food to the children. She tended their needs as best she could. Tanni, the eldest at nine seasons, had taken over Eulie's role. The children followed her like the baby chicks they were. The children were not the only reason she made a daily trek to the fields. Ozee and his family had a hut nearby. When he came in from the cane fields, she made a show of walking with the children. Often, when she felt his gaze upon her person, her heart would flutter. She would cast her gaze away, dipping her head, and allowing a shy smile to form on her lips as her thanks. He'd set a claim on her, making it known to all his intent to protect her. A claim she'd had to reject, for his sake. She knew he would never have acted on his claim by taking her to the forest as he would have another girl. There are some lines that can never be crossed. He would not dishonor his family in that way.

One day, when she went to her old hut to gather the children for their walk, the children excitedly pointed to a small bundle of tightly wrapped bonano leaves. The shape of a star was drawn in charcoal ash on the leaves. With fingers atremble, she slowly peeled back the leaves to reveal the carved wooden shape of a bird. He'd painted it pale gray, no doubt from ash, and beneath its throat was a smear of red. She recognized the scent of hibiscus. In great detail, he had carved the red throated gray warbler, her favorite bird. The children danced their excitement, pursing their lips for her to whistle. Suddenly, her heart felt too large for her chest. Blinking back the flow of her tears, and with the bird in her hands, Eulie stepped from the hut. Ozee stood on the path mere feet from her. She raised her face to him. For the first time, he met her gaze. She raised the bird, holding it up to the sky and whistled the cooing, sweet sounds of the gray warbler. In the days and months that followed, here they would meet. He, mere feet from her, as they spoke of simple things, of his work and hers.

Agata, with little patience and much forbearance, had spent her days training Eulie in her duties as a house slave. Eulie scrubbed the hardwood floors, polished the mahogany furniture with beeswax and lemon, and carried slop buckets to the outdoor privy. She boiled water for the wash tub, scrubbing the Massa's breeches and fine shirt linens with soap the like of which she'd never seen. Agata said it came from a place called London. It smelled of the foreign place it had come from. Those in the Massa's house paused their work, keening their ears to the bird songs she whistled.

Slender and strong from years of planting cane stalks, Eulie took easily to these tasks. It was serving at the china laden table in the dining room that caused her stomach to go queasy and her hands clumsy. Ship captains and men from the town, as well as the overseers, regularly took their suppers with Massa Stone. The flicker of many tapers set in silver sconces and candelabras set the room ablaze. The men, their male stench strong in her nose, made her uneasy as did their bold stares though she was layered from neck to bare toes in shift, gown and smock. She had never in her life worn more than a coarse hemp shift. She was hot and sweaty beneath the layers. Sweat puddled between her breasts, slight as they were, and trickled down to her belly.

She followed Joshua's lead as they ladled soup from large tureens, forked meat and fish from massive platters along with the garden vegetables she'd chopped and prepared. It was Joshua who calmed her nerves each evening. He was as black as Ozee, but with grayish hair pulled into a short cue and tied with a black ribbon. He was finely dressed in tan breeches, a waistcoat and a white linen shirt. He wore tanned leather shoes with sliver buckles. Joshua kept his head bent forward in proper deference, though his back was ramrod straight. He served with measured ease and elegance. She had only to return his gaze to feel her heart slow its rapid pace. It was Joshua's staid presence more than the Massa's that stayed the men's hands from her person.

When the men lingered over their spirits, their words slurring, Joshua bade her remove platters and dishes from the sideboard. These she carried to the washroom where she scraped the china plates clean and dipped each piece with utmost care into the porcelain basin, washing and wiping them with soft linen cloths. By the time she returned the china to the pantry, the tapers had been snuffed out and the men gone to the veranda for smokes. Only then would she return to the dining room to help Joshua remove the remains of the meal.

Eulie took to old Joshua and he to her. He was kind and patient. He did not mind her eyes the way Agata did. The other house slaves cast their glances away every time she passed them. Joshua, as Massa's manservant, held a privileged position in the household. Massa Stone had been a close friend of Joshua's former, now deceased master who had, in turn, willed Joshua to Massa Stone. It is the way of things, Joshua told her. He had not minded. Had he desired manumission the Massa would have granted it. He'd been beyond his prime and had grown comfortable as a manservant. He had never married, though he had once loved a woman he told Eulie. She had been wise, schooled in the old ways. She saw to it that no issue resulted from their coupling. They had both wished it so. Neither had wanted a babe born into servitude.

Joshua entranced her with his stories of the *Before Land*, of Africa. When he was a young boy, he said, he lived in a small village with his parents and siblings. The elder women held sway; they invoked the law, presided over the marriages. Women owned the land they tilled. They married or cast away men of their own choosing. Cowie shells strung around necks and arms displayed their wealth as well as beaten gold bangles and earrings. Both sexes wore long pieces of calico or muslin wrapped loosely around their bodies. The cloths, spun and woven by the women, were usually dyed blue, a color favored by all. It was extracted from a berry which, Joshua told her, made their cloths brighter and bluer than of the English cloths. Their land, he said, was fruitful with all manner of fruits, vegetables and spices. His people, he said, were a village of dancers, musicians and poets. Celebrations were held often with songs and dances amid the rhythmic beat of drums.

But war had come to his village and many, those who had not escaped, were taken as slaves. He and others from his village, the young and able, had been sold to the Guinea men, the white slavers. Chained at wrist and hobbled at ankles, they had walked for weeks to the coast before being put into the dank, poisonous hold of a schooner.

With wide eyes, Eulie had listened. She often dreamt of his village and its wonders and wept for Joshua's loss.

Months turned into a year and then another year. Eulie became adept at serving and at evading the attentions of *bekes*. She mimicked Joshua's manners and speech until her bearing and her English tongue equaled and often rivaled those of the men she served. Joshua was her friend, her protector and her teacher. Joshua's old master had educated him. He taught Eulie. It was their shared secret, for it was against the law for any slave to be educated. Massa Stone held Joshua in such high esteem, no male, not even the dreaded overseer Hector dared make advances toward her.

Then one day, Joshua drew her aside.

"This news will come to be known soon enough, Eulie. It is not my wish to be parted from you, but I must go where my master leads. The Massa is set to depart the island with crew and cargo before the spring squalls set in. We return to his home in the Americas to a city called Savannah."

His news struck her with the force of a blow. Breath left her. She was speechless, her eyes filled with stinging tears.

"Now, calm yourself, Eulie," he bade her, grasping her trembling hands. "Set your mind at ease, at least for the moment. It is my hope you will accompany us, but I cannot say it will come to pass. Should it not, Agata will be here looking to the master's household until we return. You will be safe here under her protection; besides, a certain overseer will be voyaging on the *Eastern Wind* with us. He is Massa Stone's purser."

Still, Eulie did not sleep that night or for many nights thereafter. Even though she was relieved Hector would be gone, it was Joshua's leaving that broke her heart.

Yet, there came a day under the searing noon sun, when fear once again bit at her. Her hair, unbound from her tigon and damp from the wash, flowed past her shoulders as it dried in the sun. She had her mother's hair, a soft brown, glinted copper in the sun. She was sitting on a stool fingering her hair to hasten it's drying when Massa Stone and a man she'd never laid eyes on came to the kitchen's door. She stood so abruptly the stool tumbled to her bare feet. Clasping her hands at her waist, head bowed, she waited, grateful her hair had fallen forward to cover the heat in her cheeks. Mortified and feeling exposed in her thin shift as it was still damp and near transparent in places. Her smock hung on a hook by the door, but to reach for it meant revealing even more of herself. Massa Stone grabbed her smock, shoving toward her.

"Cover yourself, girl," he spat. She did so with quick, sure motions, relief easing her tight throat. She held still as words passed between the men. A hand brushed at her hair. She shivered, drawing her clasped hands closer to her breast.

Finally, Massa bade her to lift her head. She did so reluctantly.

"Oh, yes I see. She is a fine quadroon. I've a mind to make an offer, the man said eagerly, his sour breath wafting over her.

"You may not," the Massa said, appraising Eulie from the top of her unbound hair to her bare feet. I have decided to make a gift of her to my wife and children."

"Ah," said the man, "indeed, Silas."

Thirteen

☙ THE FOURTH OF JULY ❧

A person's opinion of the world is also a confession of their character
~ Ralph Waldo Emerson ~

There'd been no cooling breezes off the bay for several nights. Leela, sweat soaked and irritable from lack of sleep, kicks at the sheets tangled around her legs. Granny Vernell had been right about the scorching heat in the room, though Leela would never admit it to her. Yet the heat wasn't the real reason she'd barely slept. It was the coming day; it was the parade and the picnic that set her heart thrumming. How would people react when she didn't reply to their comments, there questions? Could she get away with pretending to have laryngitis as she had when she'd served customers at the Grille?

And Finn will be there. After yesterday's humiliation, he's the last person she wants to see. Darla and her gang of meanies will be there. Dread swells within her chest, her stomach twists. She could play possum. Pretend to be sick. And if it wasn't for the

Gathering, she would. She's done it before when she'd wanted to get out of something. If she stays home, her mom will insist on staying with her. Then she wouldn't be able to sneak away to meet Ham and Izzy. And she wants to go to the Gathering more than anything.

If only she could speak without stuttering, then she'd be able to standup for herself, talk to anyone, anyone at all; and boy did she have a lot to say. Then she'd tell Darla and the meanies a thing or two. Then Finn wouldn't look at her as if she were afflicted. She was sure he had. The way his eyes, green as grass, had shifted downward. It was a telling thing. A thing she couldn't stand. Pity.

With a heart so sore, it pained her physically, Leela tumbles from bed. Dread builds as she stands beneath the old shower head. What drenches her is water warm enough for a bath. After pulling on blue Bermuda shorts and a white, sleeveless shirt, she plaits her hair into braids to keep it from curling in the heat.

Down in the kitchen, she scrunches her nose at the grits and biscuits laid out on the table.

"Sit down and have a bite, Leela," Granny says, pulling out a chair for her. "It'll be a good while before lunch."

Leela looks to her mom who is pushing grits around her plate. Leela shakes her head, signing it's too hot to eat. Granny hands her a glass of fresh squeezed orange juice which she gladly accepts.

"It's time to go," Sable says, rising from her place at the table. Leela is surprised to see her mom all decked out. Her sundress is a pale pink, cut low in front and softened with lace edging. It fits her narrow waist and hips. Her nut-brown hair shines with coppery glints. Years have slipped away, revealing a vision of the way her mom must've looked when she was a young girl. Leela sucks in a breath, crosses her fingers and sends a silent prayer to the powers that be. Please let us stay here. This is where we're meant to be. This is where her mom is treated with the respect and the admiration she deserves. And this is where she, Leela, will conquer her stuttering, and if not, she'll accept whatever humiliation comes her way. She will do it for her mom.

"*Mom you are so beautiful,*" Leela signs, circling her face with the letter B sign.

"Oh Leela," Sable brushes Leela's words away, her face flushing at the compliment. Granny, who didn't know signs and didn't want to, had seen the admiration on Leela's face; she dips her chin in agreement, saying, "You look pretty as a picture, Sable. And we ain't the only ones who's gonna' notice either."

"Enough, you two. You'll make me self-conscious," Sable turns away, shaking her head. She picks up the wicker basket which holds their lunch and heads for the front door. Leela and her grandmother share a look, a silent communion. They both have an inkling of who will be sitting up and taking notice of Sable. And it wouldn't only be Brick.

As usual, Vernell sets the pace. When they arrive at the park, the crush of people hurriedly stake out their picnic sites before the parade is set to begin. Blankets are spread on tuffs of green grass. Folding chairs pop-up, a garden of clashing vinyl colors. Vernell plunks down their small cooler under a wide oak at the edge of the park. Sable shakes out their picnic blanket and sets down the basket. From her large carryall bag, Vernell pulls out a small battery-operated fan. She clicks it on and holds it near Sable's face, then Leela's.

"Can't have my girls lookin' all sweaty when those floats pass by," she says, winking at Leela. "It'll be here in my bag, Sable. I expect you to use it as often as you need. Got fresh batteries in it for y'all.

They head toward Mainstreet, clearly visible from the park, where people are lining up along sidewalks. Vernell leads the way in a curly-cue fashion through the crowded park. She finds a good viewing spot for them at the corner of Main and Broad. Says they'll get a good look at the band and floats when they turn the corner. Leela, having never attended a parade before, finds herself unexpectedly giddy with excitement.

When Police sirens herald the starting of the parade, Leela jerks, startled by the unexpected sound. Little kids scream, jumping up and down, tugging at their parents' hands. Miniature Dixie and American flags wave through the crowd as the high school band revs up their discordant sounds. Drum majorettes twirl and toss their batons. Cheerleaders prance, calling out cheers to the crowd. A shiny red convertible follows them. Propped up on the back seat sits an older man and a younger woman. They wave to the crowd. Leela recognizes the woman. It's the evil-eyed blonde woman from the Grille, Brick's friend. The driver is Brick. Leela waves to him.

"That's Senator Clayton and his daughter, Luanne," Granny Vernell harrumphs, pursing her lips in distain. She leans into Leela, "That man's been wantin' our property for years. Said it's got the best view of the bay. Heard they want to tear down the house to build something modern. Over my dead and buried body, is what I told him." Leela grabs her grandmother's hand, giving it a squeeze, though her heart pricks with unease. The thought of those people wanting her house makes her stomach feel hollow.

The floats behind the red convertible are festooned with flowers, some are painted to look like pirate ships, and some are draped with Dixie flags. Atop one such float is a raised platform, a dais where the queen and her court are perched. Darla, with a sparkling crown perched on her upswept blonde hair, waves to the crowd. She wears a white sequined gown with red and blue stripes. Next to her is Finn. He matches her with a white suit, blue shirt and red tie. A silver crown tops his black hair. Leela's heart sinks, though she can't look away.

When their float turns the corner, Darla spies Leela. Smirking, she grabs Finn's hand, tugs it to her side before jerking their clasped hands high. Finn follows the line of Darla's death stare to Leela. His eyes widen when he sees her. A smile broadens his face just as Darla leans over planting a kiss on Finn's mouth. Blood rushes to Leela cheeks. She ducks her head as the float passes by. Her joy at seeing a parade evaporates. She stares at her sandaled feet until the parade peters out to kids trailing the last float like gamboling puppies.

Leela doesn't look up until she feels the tug of her grandmother's hand. She and her mother are being pulled through the dispersing crowd. Her mother waves to old friends as they make their way back to the park. Leela is grateful for their place at the far edge of the park. Maybe she can hide there without having to see or engage with anyone until she can sneak away.

When they reach the picnic blanket, Leela plops down, pulling her knees up to her chin. What would it feel like, she wonders, to be the queen up on that dais? With a longing sigh, she conjures images of herself and Finn waving to the crowd. That image morphs into a headline: *Mute Queen signs to the crowd*. Leela grits her teeth. Last night she'd practiced with the stones until her tongue became numb.

"Hey," Granny Vernell says, giving Leela's shoulder a shake.

"Looks like someone's got a dark cloud hangin' over her pretty head." With a soft grunt, she squats down next to Leela

"I saw it too. He didn't kiss her back though, so cheer up, honey. He about broke his neck lookin' back, trying to get your attention."

Leela shakes her head. Pulls her notepad and pencil from her short's pocket. *It doesn't make any difference Granny,* she writes.

"Oh, why's that?"

Leela scribbles quickly, writing, *I don't want to see him or any other boy until I can talk. What would be the point?*

"Well, by the look of him, he sure seemed to want your attention Leela. Maybe you talkin' ain't that important to him. As I recall, boys like to do all the talking anyways," she nudges Leela, winking.

Leela gives her a lukewarm grimace that passes for a smile and grabs for the picnic basket.

"Wasn't that fun, Leela," Sable says, coming up to them. "It brought back so many memories," she says, sliding down and curling her legs neatly beneath the sundress. Her mother is radiant, glowing from all the attention she'd received. Before long there's a gathering of her mother's old classmates around their picnic blanket. "I was remembering when I was the queen," she continues, "What a day that was."

"Uh huh," Vernell says, cutting her eyes to Leela as she digs out a jug of lemonade from the cooler.

"I remember that day like it was yesterday," says a woman with russet colored hair coiffed into a bouffant. "Brick and you, king and queen. We were all so young, so full of ourselves," the woman says, blowing out a dramatic sigh."

Leela looks to her mom. Her eyes widening with surprise. Her mom had been the queen? Why had she never talked about it?

"Yes, well, all that's ancient history now," Sable casts her gaze down.

"Not so long ago that a pair of jealous eyes aren't burning a hole through you right now, Sable," says a woman squatting next to her mom.

"That's so," says another. "Luanne ain't never got over you bein' picked for queen. She had it in her mind to be queen so she could get next to Brick, don't cha know."

"That's true, Sable. She's about fit to be tied, you comin' back here and all," says another.

Sable waves their comments away, ducking her head as her cheeks flush.

The women continue gossiping, talking over one another until Leela's ears buzz. So, she muses, that explains why Luanne hates her family. And why Darla is so evil towards her. It all makes sense now. Leela bites into her ham and cheese sandwich. Her plan is to keep her mouth busy with chewing. A mouth full of food precludes the option of speaking, she figures. Wafting off the women is the nauseating scent of sweat mixed with heavily applied talcum powder. Leela's stomach turns. The sandwich has taken on the flavor of sawdust. She takes a swig of lemonade to clear the taste from her mouth. Caught up in her own wayward thoughts, Leela tunes out the women's chatter until her ears perk up at some alarming gossip.

A heavy-set woman pipes up, "Did y'all see the National Guard driving round in their jeeps?

A woman sitting next to her mom whispers, "It's on account of the protests y'all know, all those goings on up in Birmingham this past May with the coloreds."

"Ya think it might happen here? Oh, Good Lawd. I hope not,"

Granny Vernell shakes her head.

A lady with bouffant hair, her lips twisted into a sneer, says, "Our coloreds know better than to act up. They know what'll happen if they do. And we don't need no Guard to do what needs doing, either. The Klan takes care of that business."

Leela's heart thumps. She'd seen the broadcast of what had happened on television. There had been colored students—hundreds of them—even young children. The newscaster called it the Children's Crusade for Civil Rights. They'd been marching down the street, quiet, polite and peaceful. White folk along the sidewalks had jeered, some had thrown rocks. Police had sprayed them with high-pressure fire hoses, knocking them flat on the street and against buildings. Police dogs had been set on them. It was horrible. Leela had had nightmares about it for weeks. If that were going to happen here, she'd better warn Ham and Izzy. Maybe the Gathering should be called off.

With her gaze lowered, Leela keens her ears to the gossip, hoping to learn more. Her mom and granny are silent on the subject. Leela, still pretending to nibble on her uneaten sandwich, becomes anxious to sneak away. Scanning the park for what she hopes to be an easy escape, she sees Brick and Finn approaching them. She swallows hard, coughing as a piece of potato chip gets stuck in her throat. Her face burns. Finn is staring hard at her. All at once, the women stop talking, while they stare at Brick through lowered lashes. When one eager woman speaks up, the rest join in, vying for his attention.

Brick has eyes only for her mom, though he swivels his head, bobbing his hellos to the other women. Leela attempts to ignore Finn, which becomes quite impossible once he squats down directly in front of her. His white jacket and red tie are gone. His blue shirt sleeves are rolled up to his elbows.

"Hey, Leela. I, ah, I saw you at the parade."

Leela nods, shifting her gaze to avoid his eyes. Her pity radar is on high alert.

"Um, Leela, the band is about ready to start up. The floor at the gazebo is good for dancing. They're gonna play the twist first, you know, Chubby Checker."

Her eyes widen at this. Dance? She's only ever danced in front of her mirror. Frowning, Leela shakes her head.

Finn, ignoring her refusal, says, "Come on, it's fun." He takes her by the hand, pulling her to her feet as the band rev's up.

"Go on now," Granny Vernell gives Leela a firm shove.

Fourteen

꧁ LEELA AND FINN ꧂

Hearts are wild, that's why our ribs are cages
~Anonymous~

Oh no, no, no, no, Leela bemoans to herself as Finn steadily pulls her to the gazebo. She'd been tempted to slap his hand away but making a scene in front of those women would have drawn attention to her. One dance and she'll be off the hook. She knows how to twist. She'd seen it on American Bandstand. He guides her up the steps of the gazebo. It's crowded with gyrating forms both young and old. He's smiling, his green eyes challenging her as he twists away. Okay, so he can dance. He's pretty good, she admits. She'd planned to stand, not moving. She's stubborn that way, but the music travels up her spine and before she knows it her body mirrors his. He bends his knees, twisting low. She follows, giggling. He grabs her hands and they twist together. The band melds into another song, a cha-cha. She goes to move away, but he grabs her hands again.

"Come on, it's easy. Just follow me." And so, she does, laughing when he steps on her toes.

When the band slows into one of her favorite songs, *Love Me Tender*, he pulls her close. His cheek meets hers. He smells of boy sweat, Ivory soap and Old Spice. The cologne reminds her of her dad. She stiffens.

"Hey, you okay?"

She nods, presses her cheek against his shoulder. She listens to the thumping of his heart. It matches hers. "You smell nice," he murmurs against her ear, "like flowers." They sway together, the music lifting her into a heady place.

"Finn!" A strident female voice shatters the moment, causing them to jerk apart. Darla gives Leela a scorching look before inserting herself between them.

"Finn, baby, this is our dance. I know you haven't forgotten how we danced to it at the Spring Fling." She curls her arms around his neck. "We're the king and queen. We stay together."

Finn, his green eyes narrowing, pulls her arms from his neck. "Sure, Darla. I need to walk Leela back to her mom. I'll be back."

Darla's face hardens. "She's not a child, Finn."

"No, *she* isn't," he says, taking Leela's arm, leading her away from the gazebo. "Sorry about that, Leela."

She lifts her shoulders in a shrug, humoring him with a forced smile.

"I, ah, I guess I'll be busy for a while." He looks down at his feet. "I'll come back later, if that's okay. We could, um, walk to the pier together. A good place to catch a breeze, cool off, ya know."

Leela gives him a non-committal shrug. The pier was her plan, her way to sneak away to meet Ham and Izzy at the Grille.

Finn moves in close, whispers in her ear, "It was nice, the dancing. You're nice." Turning on his heels, he glances back, touches his forehead in a salute.

The way he danced with her, looked at, her makes her question her assumptions. Maybe it wasn't out of pity, him paying so much attention to her. She watches him walk away, back to the she-devil. She almost feels sorry for him, imagine that, she muses, her feeling sorry for a boy like Finn. Darla had the look of someone who always gets her way. Finn had said as much. The apple, as they say, doesn't fall far from the tree. Darla's mother, Luanne, had set her sights on Brick. Leela recalled the way the woman behaved at the Grille, as if Brick belonged to her. Granny Vernell had said her mom and Luanne had hard feelings for each other, had been rivals in high school. Leela hadn't understood what she'd meant at the time. Hard feelings, she shakes her head, probably doesn't describe the half of it. She pictures the hard glitter in the eyes of both mother and daughter. It seems to her to be something more than jealousy. It seems like hate. Unaccountably, Leela shivers in the heat.

At the picnic site, Leela finds herself alone. Scanning the groupings of picnickers, she spies granny Vernell with a group of women at a long table, serving up plates of food. Leela looks for the pink dress her mom wore. She sees a flash of pink among the crowd, but it isn't her mom. She checks her watch. It's too early to sneak away from the picnic, she thinks. Though she could go now and leave a note for her mom and granny. They know she likes to be alone to write her poetry. She hates telling them half-truths, and she's been doing that a lot of late. Still, a note would do the trick and let her off the hook of facing them. She writes the note, securing it to granny's picnic bag. Slinging her tote bag over her shoulder, she takes off to the pier. She doesn't believe Finn will show up as he'd said, not with Darla clinging to his arm. But what if he does? What will she do then?

At the pier, she settles down on a park bench near the water. Finn was right. The water is so clear beneath the pier she can see the barnacles attached to the pilings. Minnows and larger fish swirl in the eddies. She lifts her face to the warm breeze wafting off the bay. Closing her eyes, she pictures dancing with Finn and how he'd held her tight. The way he'd looked at her wasn't the way someone did who was doing it out of a sense of obligation, or pity. She wanted to believe he did like her, even with her awful braying. Yet, she couldn't stop herself from questioning his motives. Why would he want to spend time with her when he could be with his friends? Friends who were normal, who carried on actual conversations? Her stomach curled at his perceived kindness to her. Yes, that was it. He was just being kind, wasn't he? Pulling out her notebook and pencil, she pondered what to write. Usually, she wrote about birds and nature, or about how much she hated her father. But now she sought to decipher her mixed feelings, her confusion over Finn.

Sometime later, she's deep in thought and writing furiously, when a voice startles her.

'Hey, looks like you beat me to the pier," Finn quips. "Your mom told be you'd be here doing some writing. I, ah I hope I'm not, um, interrupting?"

You came. Leela hastily scribbled on her notepad while shielding her poetry notebook from his view.

"Yes, um, well, we didn't get to spend much time together, you know, Darla and all."

Oh. So, where is she now? Leela writes.

"Off with her girlfriends, I guess."

Won't she be looking for you?

'Nope." He looks off, holding back a smirk.

Leela scoots over, making room for him on the bench. She had an overwhelming desire to find out about that smirk and what it meant.

"So, um, did you enjoy the parade?" He sits down, moving close to her.

I'd never been to a parade, but I liked it.

"Never?" Finn shakes it his head. "Well, it's no big deal. I got wangled into it. I don't care much for all that stuff. My mom, she was all excited about me being voted king this year. So..."

She looks at him, arching a brow.

"I, ah, I reckon you saw Darla's move on me. She thinks she can get away with stuff like that," he says. Two pink splotches form on his tanned cheeks.

No big deal, right?

Finn nods, "It sure wasn't one for me."

My mom told me you're a grade ahead of me, that you're going to be a junior this year.

"Right, I thought you knew."

She shakes her head, no, writing, *Captain of the football team, no less.* She offers up a crooked smile.

"Yeah, well, I'm hoping for a full ride to UGA on it. I'll be a math major, but what I really want to do is fly planes. You know, for the airlines.

Good, I hope you do, get it I mean. And fly planes.

"What about you?"

A journalist, I hope. Stories for newspapers, that sort of thing.

"Makes sense, you already being a writer," he says, placing his hand over hers.

Leela looks down at their hands before casting her gaze to the waters of the bay. When he threads his fingers into hers, her heart flutters. He's quiet, his gaze on the bay. They sit side by side watching the waves crest on the shimmering bay. She waits for the awkward feeling that always comes when she's with kids or adults who talk. It doesn't come. With Finn, it feels natural and she doesn't know what to make of it.

After a bit, Finn digs into his pants pocket and pulls out a couple of tootsie rolls. "Happy Fourth," he grins, offering her one. Taking it, she smiles back. This is nice, she thinks. They sit in silence, both chewing the sticky chocolate as they take in the view. Clouds scurry across the endless blue of the sky. It's a perfect day, she muses, eyeing his perfect profile from beneath her lashes.

"Leela," he clears this throat nervously, "maybe you could teach me some signs while we work on, the, ah, stuttering? I mean, you know, we'd be helping each other out. Cause, you know, we have deaf people on the Miss Ina sometimes. It would sure make my job easier."

She knits her brows, a kernel of disappointment lodging in her chest. She certainly hadn't expected anything like this. Leela gives him a dubious look. She doesn't quite know how to take his offer. That he's sincere, she believes. What she doesn't believe is that he'd come up with this idea on his own. Had someone, someone with kind intent, suggested this? Brick comes to her mind. It certainly seems like something he would think to do.

She'd already made up her mind to handle her stuttering by herself. Still, she gives both Finn and Brick credit for their effort. And if Finn wants to learn signing, if he truly does, she has no problem with teaching him. With a long sigh, she writes, *Finn, that's a kind offer, but I think it best I work by myself on my stuttering. I'd be happy though to teach you signs. Just tell me what words you'd like to sign, and I'll show you.*

"Oh," he says, looking down at his feet. Then he looks up, confusion mirrored in his eyes. "But why not? I mean, I thought our practice was great." Leela shakes her head, writing, *Let's do some signs. Tell me some words you'd like to learn. It'll be a secret just between you and me.* She's hoping this will lessen his obvious disappointment.

"A secret huh? Just between you and me? I can live with that," he grins. How do you sign secret?"

Leela shows him. He laughs as he makes the sign. He ticks off a list of words. They laugh together as his hands move awkwardly in his effort to imitate her hand movements.

When the sun begins to slant its rays over the bay, Finn looks at his watch. "We better go now," he says, signing, *we go now.* "My mom will wonder where I am.

Leela shakes her head, signing, *you go I write.* She scribbles on her notepad, *poetry.* Shows him the sign for poetry.

Poetry, huh? I like that sign. Well, ah, I'll see you at the park later. He scoots close, his face near hers, pausing as if waiting for her permission. Her lips part slightly in surprise. He must have taken this as permission because he presses his lips against hers. His lips are soft, softer than she'd imagined. And warm, so warm. Heat centers itself in her belly. Her heart races when his lips move against hers. All at once, Finn pulls away, his eyes glazed to a deep, forest green.

"I, ah, should go..." He stumbles back. Leela ducks her head. She tosses off a quick wave as he turns to go. Watching his retreating back, she touches her lips, still warm from his lips. Her first kiss. The scent of tootsie roll on his lips. A handsome, popular boy has just kissed her. What was not to like? And she does like him. She wants to believe in him, trust him. She's afraid she might like him too much. With a shake of her head, she puts these thoughts aside. She has a gathering to attend.

Leela waits until he's out of sight before making her move. Until now, lying and subterfuge hasn't been part of her life skills. And she doesn't feel particularly good about it, especially since Finn had made such an effort to be with her. She could have asked him to go with her, but then, she'd be breaking her vow of secrecy. And that she would never do. She'd promised Izzy and Ham she'd do her best to meet them. And this is her doing her best. Besides, she needs to warn Ham and Izzy about the troops in jeeps.

Fifteen

Will we ever know of what the songbird sings?
~ Choral response to the Storyteller ~

Leela makes her way through back streets, all the while checking over her shoulder. Her deception is a hard rock in the pit of her stomach. She promises herself she won't stay long, certainly not long enough for her mother or granny to miss her. Who knows when she'll have another opportunity?

When she gets to the back entrance of the Grille, Ham and Izzy are waiting as they said they would. Their faces light up when they see her.

I can't be gone very long, she signs to Ham.

We understand, Leela.

Izzy asks, "Are you afraid of cemeteries?"

Surprised, but determined, Leela shrugs. *I don't think so,* she signs.

"Okay then, let's go," Ham says, taking Leela's hand.

Wending through back alleys, the trio is silent. Eventually they pass vacant lots covered with scrub grass and cabbage palms. Crossing over a two-lane road, they head toward a large expanse of thick foliage.

"We're at the cemetery now," Ham turns, giving her an encouraging grin.

Leela can't make out a thing amid the trees and climbing kudzu. Willow trees dip and weep over rusted wrought iron railings. Ham moves aside the willow's branches to uncover a rusted gate tilted on it hinges.

"It's not too much farther, Leela," he says, pulling her through the gate. Izzy follows.

Ahead of them are headstones. Many are cracked, toppling over the graves. No one needs to tell her this place is ancient, more than a hundred years old. The sandy earth beneath her feet buckles, dipping into rectangular shapes. Leela shivers. They pass tumbles of stones; grave markers engulfed by weeds and wild grass; she can only guess where earth becomes grave. It's a dark, forlorn place where names and lives have been lost to time.

"This way," Ham says, moving through a wilderness of pine trees. He is a head of her, pulling her behind him. Izzy has grabbed Leela's free hand. Somehow, unerringly, Ham has found a foot path. Single file, they follow the path deep into the piney woods. To Leela it feels as if the trees have become a door, shutting out the rest of the known world. Their footfalls are muffled, as if the air itself hides this place. After a time, the trees begin to thin, a trickle of sound bounces off tree limbs and trunks. The leaves begin to tremble and sway. Laughter and the rumble of feet shake the path. All at once a clearing, filled with people, opens before them. Rhythmic beats, unlike anything Leela has ever heard, resonates within her chest. She's never seen so many colored people in her life. A few whites mingle with them.

They don't join the melee of dancers; young and old, men, women and children are clapping, stamping to the music. Leela feels the music travel from her chest to her toes.

"Come on, Leela, this way." Ham says. He and Izzy lead her to a weathered building that is more shack than building. It's peaked roof lists to one side. The door, somewhat newer, is open. Inside, there is a nave and the rise of an altar. A painting of colored girls holding flowers is behind the alter. Hand hewn benches take the place of pews.

This is a church? she signs, turning to Ham.

"Yes, as you can see, Leela, but a very old one. Slaves built it and prayed here. Their descendants still do. The few who still live here, at least."

Izzy comes up, grabbing both their hands. "It's time, Granme´ Delia is about ready. Come on, y'all."

Wait, Leela signs. *I want to see the painting by the alter.* It's bold colors and style brought Eulie's painting to her mind. Had Eulie painted this? She had to find out. Waving them away, Leela rushes pass the nave to altar. She stands back to examine the painting. The style is the same, the brilliant colors unfaded by time. It's a rendering of piney woods and a field of flowers. Mixed within are negro girls and women. Their heads are wrapped in colorful cloths. They wear loose gowns or shifts; their hands cradle their rounded bellies. Each hold in their hands the bud, stem and root of a flower, as if having just been plucked from the field. Their faces, plain or pretty, are etched in deep lines of sorrow.

"We gotta go, come on, Leela, let's go now," Izzy says, tugging at Leela.

Leela is pulled away, but she cranes her neck back toward the painting, with a promise to return. She's determined to see if Eulie has marked it as her own.

Outside, everyone has gathered into a circle, swaying to the music which has changed from rhythmic beats to a melodic sound. It seems to come from the earth itself.

What is this music? Leela signs.

Izzy, who's been quick to learn many of Leela signs, answers, "Oh, that's the wood, Leela, the singing wood."

Leela gives her a questioning look.

Ham interjects, "I'll show you." He slings an arm over her shoulders, guiding her pass the swaying people. Two men sit cross-legged on the ground. Between them are several lengths of polished wood placed over a deep depression in the dirt.

"See," Ham says, "the musicians use cloth covered drumsticks to coax the sounds from the wood. The hole in the ground amplifies the sounds.

It's wonderful and so beautiful, Leela signs.

Suddenly, the music stops. The people start chanting words Leela has never heard before.

"Kri, Kri, Kri, Kri."

Soon a single voice answers their calls, "Kra, Kra" The voice is deep, powerful.

What are they chanting, Leela signs.

"These chants are from the old days. The people call out for the storytelling," Izzy tells her, "Granme´ Delia has answered their calls."

Ham, Izzy and Leela move to the circle, others shift, making way for them. On a chair in the center sits a tiny woman. Her skin is the color of milk chocolate. Her hair is wrapped in a bright scarf, beneath it a long white braid reaches to her knees. For the first time, Leela notices how most of the women here also wear the head wrappings. She signs to Izzy, *why are so many wearing headwraps?* Leela circles her head with one hand. Leela had seen the wraps on the women in Eulie's mural and now here.

"They are called tigons. It's tradition," Izzy tells her.

Ham shushes them with a finger to his lips,

Leela scans the crowd. She doesn't recognize any of the coloreds except for Miss Mirabel, the cook from the Grille. Then she spies Ishmael. He smiles at her, his hands clasped together, she assumes, to keep them under his control. She smiles back. Her jaw drops in surprise to see Miss Ina standing next to him. Miss Ina gives her a slow smile.

Then Granme´ Delia begins to speak in a voice clear as a chapel bell.

"*Children of God, sons and daughters of Ham, we are blessed today, for one who has been lost to us has returned.* The crowd murmurs, all casting glances about.

"*Do not seek out the lost, for the lost find their way and will be known to us in time.*"

All nod, murmuring their assent.

Granme´ Delia raises her hands to form the wings of a bird. The wings tremble and the crowd calls out, "Tell us, tell us the story of the songbird who lost her song."

"*She is made of mist, this bird of the island of flowers, though this was not always so. Once she was of sinew, feather and beak, but that was long ago. Once her morning song filled the forest with such beauty, surpassing all other birdsong. But the world, with its terrible secrets, broke her heart and her song was lost to her.*"

"Her heart was broken. Her song was lost," the people echo back to her.

Granme´ Delia's hands move like mist in the air. Leela is transported, lost in the movement of those hands and that voice.

"*As all birds do, this bird of the island of flowers gave birth to an egg, though only this one would ever come from her.*" Granme´ Delia cradles the shape of an egg in her palms. Then her voice lowers into a fearful timber. "*There was danger in the forest. Men, hungry for these eggs, came to take them from the mother birds.*" The crowd groans, echoing her words back to her.

"*This bird of flowers,* Granme´ Delia says, *trembled with fear for she could not bear to lose this egg. She opened her beak, and scooping up the egg, she flew to the highest branches in the forest. Yet, even in those high branches, there was danger. It was where the red-tailed hawks made their nests, as they do to this day. The hawks are fierce birds, the most powerful in the forest. But they are not the most watchful. Arrogant that none can reach their nest, they take flight to forage.*" Granme´ Delia 's hands form the shape of a hawk, winging; its talons rake the air. Her voice is the sound of a screeching hawk.

The crowd trembles, Leela trembles with them, fearing for the small bird and her egg.

"*This bird*" Granme´ Delia says, "*cradled the egg gently in her beak. She perched on the hawk's nest. There was but one hawk egg nestled among the twigs and feathers. A choice was before her. Only one bird was destined to live. Only one bird was destined to fly high above the forest. Her mother's heart broke with her choice, for all birds should live. When the bird of flowers took wing, one egg fell through the branches, tumbling down and down.*" Granme´ Delia's hands tumble, tumble to the ground at her feet.

"Which one, which one?" The crowd calls out, their breaths held in suspense. Leela's own breath is caught in her throat.

Granme´ Delia shakes her head. *"No one knows, for no one was there to see which egg the bird of flowers chose. With her heart so full of sorrow for what she had done, she fell to the earth, breaking her wings."* Granme´ Delia 's hands form the shape of broken wings.

"Her wings were broken," the crowd echoes her words.

"The Lord in his great mercy took pity on this bird of the island of flowers. Healing her wings, he made her a bird of the mist. He gathered the souls of all the lost birds. He bade her to carry them on her wings. To this day, she carries them, searching always to reunite them with their mothers." Granme´ Delia 's hands become wings rising, flying.

"The Lord had mercy. She carries the souls of the lost," the people repeat.

"When you hear the leaves rustle in the forest, know it is her wings that move them. Granme´ Delia's hands flutter as leaves in the wind.

"Her wings rustle the leaves."

"Do not mourn for the bird of flowers, for one day all the lost will be reunited. When that day comes, her song will burst from her soul. It will rise high, high into the ever after. Those of us who are blessed with His words, will hear her beautiful song.

"We who believe, will hear her song."

Granme´ Delia raises her hands, palms out. She scans the faces of those in the circle. Her eyes are such a pale blue as to be almost white. Instantly, there is silence. It's as if the air has been sucked out, a vacuum in which Leela can hear the swish-swish of her own heart mixing with the beats of other hearts.

Granme´ Delia's direct stare lands on Leela. "Come," she calls to Leela, spreading her hands out in welcome.

Leela stands, rooted. Her eyes wide as everyone turns to her.

"Go, go. It's okay. She wants to meet you," Ham nudges her.

All at once, warmth blooms in Leela's chest. The warmth pulls at her until she is stepping forward, moving into the center of the circle.

Granme´ Delia grasps Leela's hands. They are warm hands, supple and strong.

"I knew you would come," she whispers to Leela. "Will you sing with us, Leela?"

Leela lowers her head, shaking it. She wants to sign that she can't sing, that she can only whistle. Granme´ Delia has a firm grip on Leela's hands.

"It is past time, Leela. Your voice is here," Granme´ Delia taps a finger over Leela's heart, then raises her own voice in song: "Oh Canaan, sweet Canaan, I am bound for the land of Canaan."

The melody rings in Leela's ears like a half-remembered song, the words on the tip of her tongue. Suddenly, as if compelled by a will stronger than her own, she hears her own voice rising, joining the chorus of other voices, *"Oh, Canaan, sweet Canaan, I am bound for the land of Canaan. I thought I heard them say, there are lions in the way. Oh Canaan, sweet Canaan. I am bound for the land of Canaan."*

Sixteen

❧ THE MIRACLE ☙

A voice, once let loose, will never still.
~ Granme´ Delia ~

When the last refrain drifts in the air, Granme´ Delia stands, gazing pass the circle to a distant point, as if she could see beyond the pines. She claps her hands twice. All at once, people begin to scatter every which way; moving through the piney forest, they disappear like ghosts.

"Go now Leela, go with Ham and Izzy," Miss Ina calls out to her. She has Ishmael by one hand. Granme´ Delia has his other hand. Soon, they too have disappeared.

With Ham pulling Leela along, they take off, retracing their steps. By the time they reach the cemetery, Leela is breathing hard, her tote bag thumps against her back. She's run through brambles and tripped over fallen tree limbs. She wants to stop, needing to catch her breath, but Ham shakes his head. "We have to get you to the park, Leela."

And they are off again, running across the two-lane road, through alleyways until they reach the street bordering the park. Sirens blare in the distance. They stop, keening their ears. The trio shares worried glances. Ham shrugs, "Probably just the go-ings on down at the gazebo."

"W-w-why did everyone run off like they d-d-did?" Leela asks. Ham and Izzy stare at her as if she's suddenly grown an extra head. Then they are laughing and hugging her.

"W-what?" Leela demands, taking a step back.

"Don't you hear yourself?" Ham says, taking her hands in his.

"I-I-me, t-t-hat was m-me, is me?" Her eyes widen in disbelief.

"Yep, that's you, all you," Izzy quips, her smile beams.

Leela tugs her hands from Ham, starring at them as if they are appendages she'd just discovered.

Shaking her head, she says, "Wh-what ha-happened back there? Why did we-have to run away? I mean, I was having s-so much f-fun singing. I j-just want to sing."

Izzy is giggling. Ham is rolling his eyes, doubling over in heaves of laughter.

Leela stamps her foot, "What is so darn..." She looks down at her hands. They aren't moving, they aren't signing. "Oh, oh, I'm, I'm..." Tears well up in her eyes and suddenly she's sob-bing. Her whole body is wracked with sobs.

Izzy and Ham cough back their laughter. They gather her in their arms. Izzy starts crying first, then a sob crawls up Ham's throat. The stand crying together. After a bit, Leela sniffs, wip-ing her nose against Ham's shirt. She giggles which cause Izzy to giggle. Ham lifts his hands up in the air, "Girls," he moans.

A squeal of tires braking causes them to jump apart.

"Leela," Brick calls out through the open truck window,

"Ham, Izzy, where have you three been? Leela's mom and granny are worried sick. There's a curfew in place."

"What? But why?" Ham asks.

"There's been some trouble. I'll explain later. "You two," Brick nods to Ham and Izzy," hop in the back. Leela, get in the cab. Now."

Leela thinks back to what the ladies had talked about at the picnic, about the protests and the police. She'd forgotten all about warning Ham and Izzy. She gets into the cab, anxiety eclipsing the wonder of her voice.

Brick narrows his eyes at her as he shifts gears. The truck picks up speed. "You, young lady, are in deep trouble. We've been looking everywhere for you, Finn too."

Leela pales, sick at heart for worrying everyone.

Brick blows out a puff of air. He reaches over, smooths down her messy hair. The run through the piney woods had taken a toll, she thinks. There are scratches on her arms and legs. Her shorts and white blouse are rumpled, splotched with grass and dirt.

"You've given us all quite a scare. But you're safe now. Thank God I found you before dark. The State Police and the National Guard are rolling into town. There was a sit-in by a few young colored kids at McCrory's. A peaceful demonstration at the courthouse got out of control. No one knows how it started. There were bricks thrown and fights broke out. Some shop windows were broken and a warehouse by the docks was set on fire."

Brick pats her hand, though his blue eyes light up with concern when he takes in her appearance. "You okay? I mean, you don't look okay."

Leela nods, offering him a weak smile.

Brick pulls to a stop in the sandy driveway of her house. He jumps out, motioning for Ham and Izzy to do the same.

"You two will be staying here for the time being," he nods to Izzy and Ham. "Can't anyone be out on the streets until the curfew is lifted, which probably won't be until tomorrow. We'll call your parents. I'm sure they're wringing their hands over the two of you."

Her mom and granny run toward her. Her mom's eyes are red rimmed, her face drawn into deep lines of worry. Sable throws her arms around Leela, latching on as if she'll never let go. Granny Vernell is all puffed out with fear and anger.

"Child, you deserve a whippin' running off like that," Granny Vernell shouts, even though she's standing two feet from Leela. "About give us a heart attack worrin' over you." She purses her lips at Ham and Izzy. "I shoulda knowed you two would be up to somethin'. Y'all coloreds are nothin but trouble," Granny Vernell spits out, pointing her finger at them.

Indignation flares hot within Leela's chest. Her granny has no right to blame them. Leela moves out of her mother's arms. Her hands bunch into fists at her side when she turns to face her grandmother. "S-stop it. D-don't you blame them. It was my d-doing. I w-wanted to see the old cemetery. It was me, not them." She hears her voice, clear, loud and strident.

Three adult mouths drop open. Granny Vernell mouths soundless words. Sable's knees buckle. "Oh, oh," she says and faints. Brick is there in a second, holding her in his arms. "Somebody go and get a cold washcloth and some water. Now," Brick orders.

Seventeen

A SECRET SHARED

Secrets are sacred
~ Leela ~

It isn't until Sable is settled on the living room couch—a cool washcloth pressed to her forehead, that Leela becomes aware of Ham's absence. Brick and Vernell hover by Sable. She waves a limp hand, insisting she's fine. Leela and Izzy stand at the other end of the couch, looking on.

"Izzy, where's Ham?" Leela whispers.

Izzy shakes her head, "I thought he came inside with us."

"You check outside, I'll check the kitchen and downstairs rooms." Leela tells her. Her worry over Ham eclipses the joy of her voice.

A few minutes later, they meet on the porch, both shaking their heads. Leela feels the first tingling's of alarm. Brick had made it clear no one was allowed out during the curfew.

"D-do you think he went home, Izzy?" Leela asks.

127

"He'd be worried about his family. I'm scared for my family too, Leela."

"We better tell Brick," Leela says, heading inside.

"Jesus, all of the damn, stupid things," Brick groans, getting up from Sable's side. He turns to Izzy, "Call your parents and then check in with Ham's family. And don't you two leave this house, got it? He lowers a hard gaze on Leela and Izzy.

Fully chastened, they stare at their feet.

"I'll have supper on the stove for you when you get back, Brick," Granny Vernell calls out to him.

"And keep this door locked. And don't answer it unless you know who it is," Brick says before shutting the door firmly behind him.

Vernell levels a hard look on Leela and Izzy, shakes her head and turns back to Sable.

"You up to havin' a bit of soup or a cup of coffee, honey?" she says.

"Hot tea, Ma, and an aspirin."

With a last hard look at Leela and Izzy, Vernell heads to the kitchen, calling back, "Supper be ready in a bit. Then y'all are going to bed. And if you don't like that, y'all can just get on up there now with empty bellies."

"Yes ma'am," Izzy is quick to answer. Leela frowns, her heart hardening toward her granny. She goes to her mom.

"Mom, I-I'm so sorry to have worried you."

"You're safe, honey. That's all that matters. But how did, I mean, when did, that is, you're talking.

"I've been practicing, and it sort of just h-happened." Leela says. She's rarely lied to her mom before, not about the important things anyway. And it was, after all, almost the truth.

"It's a miracle. I'm so happy," Sable looks from Leela to Izzy. She holds out her hand to Izzy who is hanging back, shifting her eyes to anywhere but Sable. "Izzy, I'm so glad you've been Leela's friend. Ham too, of course."

"Yes ma'am. We like being her friend," Izzy looks down, wringing her hands, lips trembling.

"Now, don't you worry, Brick will find Ham. Your family and Ham's will be fine. I don't think there's any cause to worry about your people in White Oaks. The guard is here to protect everyone."

"What's White Oaks?" Leela asks, turning to Izzy.

"That's where we live, us coloreds, you know, colored town."

"No, I didn't know. I'm sorry. I t-thought you lived here in Bateaux Bay."

"White Oaks is about five miles north of the Grille. About eight from here."

"Wait, that means…"

"We don't mind walking a bit more. We like hanging out with you.

"But, but that's miles, Izzy."

Izzy shrugs.

Leela holds up her pinky, "Friends forever?"

"Forever," Izzy says, linking her pinky with Leela's.

"Girls, supper's ready." Vernell comes to the living room, a steaming cup of hot tea in her hand for Sable.

"Not hungry," Leela says, turning to Izzy. "Are you?" Izzy shakes her head. Leela stifles a pretend yawn. "We're tired. Going to my room. Night Mom." Leela ignores her grandmother.

"Izzy hangs back. "I need to call my mom. And Ham's too."

Sable sits up, "You go on, I'll call Miss Mirabel and Ham's mom. Don't you worry.

"Thank you, Miss Sable. Um, please let us know about Ham?"

"Of course," Sable smiles warmly at Izzy.

Leela, her hand fasted to Izzy's, leads the way up the curved front staircase. When they get to the landing, Leela tells her to shut her eyes, saying she has a secret to show her. Once in Leela's bedroom, she centers Izzy directly in front of the mural.

"Okay, open your eyes now," Leela can barely keep the excitement from her voice.

Izzy's eyes open and then widen. "Oh, oh, that's, that's like..."

"I know. The painting in the church. Except, there's a story inside this painting. But," Leela puts a finger to Izzy's lips, "you can't tell anyone. Except Ham, of course. It's our secret. Promise?"

Izzy crosses her heart, "Promise and hope to die."

"Place your fingers right here," Leela guides Izzy's fingers over a stretch of the mural. "Feel it?"

"It's just like you told us," Izzy says, her fingers tracing and retracing the indentations.

"Here, do this. It's fun." Leela grabs a tracing paper from her writing box, handing Izzy a pencil. "Trace slowly over it like this," Leela demonstrates. "Now your turn."

Izzy's eyes grow big as words emerge.

"Read it," Leela tells her.

"I am Eulie," Izzy reads.

"And there's more," Leela pulls out a sheaf of papers covered with more tracings. "I'm going to do the entire mural. It's about her life as a slave. Leela shows her the tracing of Massa Stone's name. "He was my great, great, great grandfather. He had slaves

130

right here in this house. Eulie had lived on the island in the painting. He brought her here on a slave ship."

"My great, great grandmother was a slave. My momma told me," Izzy says. "Granme Delia's grandmother was too. Her people have lived in Bateaux Bay since slave days. Her daughter, Monique is Ishmael's mom. But she left years ago."

"I need to find out more about Eulie, Izzy. I need to find out what happened to her. My mom told me there's lots of old stuff in the attic. She said there used to be a library in the room that's now granny's sewing room. Maybe the books and papers that were in there are in the attic now." Leela's violet eyes sparkle with a challenge. "Are you afraid of old, dark places, Izzy?" Leela arches a brow.

Izzy grins, "I'm not if you're not.

Good, didn't think you were. Let's go see what we can find out about Eulie."

Eighteen

EULIE – HEART OF STONE

Only the gulls cry for us
~ Eulie ~

The schooner, Eastern Wind, had been caught in the airless heat of the doldrums for days upon days. Eulie pressed a vinegar-soaked cloth to her nose and mouth as she made her way from the cramped cabin below the quarter deck she shared with Joshua. The stench of human offal rising from the hold below the main deck was always noxious; now it was intolerable. The smell of it was in her clothing, her hair and on her skin. She despaired of ever being free of it. The cries and moans from those confined in the coffin-like spaces below crushed Eulie's soul.

With her free hand, she toted a bucket of water laced with the juice of limes. The slaves were allotted a quarter cup twice a week to prevent scurvy. It was the only decent water they would receive the entire trip. Eulie gagged when she smelled the putrid

133

water in the barrels from which the slaves were forced to drink. Women and children were allowed on the main deck during the day light hours. She wended her way through the clutch of officers and sailors on her way to them. The men's bold eyes raked her person, though none dared make advances. Even Hector, his devil-blue eyes filled with wanton malice, kept his distance, though only from her. He made free with any female slave, woman or girl of his choosing. Their cries for help went unanswered. Silas Stone did not partake in this debauchery as did many of the sailors and officers, yet he did nothing to stop it. On the island, with Joshua as her protector, she'd been spared. Here aboard ship, Massa Stone declared her untouchable.

A mere handful of the slaves were from her island. Most came from places in the before land; their names were as foreign to her as their mixture of languages. Eulie paid close attention to Zina, Ozee's sister. Both had been taken. Ozee had fought, even with manacles on his wrists and shackles at his ankles. He had begged Massa Stone for Zina and her children, a child and a babe, to be left on the island. His pleas fell on indifferent ears.

Eulie approached Zina first. The girl kept her shaved head bowed, as much from the shame of her nakedness as her reluctance to set her sight on Eulie's eyes. Every conscript slave aboard ship save for Eulie, Joshua and the personal slaves of those who'd booked passage, were without a stitch of clothing. This being standard practice of the slave trade. It was feared many would hang themselves with lengths of cloth rather than be in bondage. Adding to this humiliation, they'd had their hair shaved off to prevent the spread of lice.

Zina was much older than Eulie, a woman grown and still fair of face, though the weeks on board the schooner had taken its toll. Once, she had been the most beautiful of girls on the plantation. Her babe, a boy, clung to Zina's breast like a sea urchin. Five-year-old Jamila lolled against her mother's knee. Her eyes dull, her movements as listless as her mother's.

"Zina, I have clean water for you and Jamila," Eulie knelt beside her. Zina turned away, her arm warding off Eulie's presence. "Zina, you must have this medicine, or you will become sick. Please, Zina, for your children."

"It is better we die," Zina turned her back on Eulie.

"If you die, Zina, Ozee will chose death also. Do you want to be the cause of his death?"

Eulie waited. In her heart, she knew Zina would not want to be the cause of her beloved brother's death. Her patience was rewarded. Zina held out her hand for the cup. She gave Jamila the cup. The child gulped it down. Eulie ladle out more than a quarter cup for Zina. Her desire for Zina's survival equaled her desire for Ozee's survival. The siblings were as much a part of her as was the island. They would live. She would make it so.

The women were gathered around a large copper kettle. A young sailor, designated as a cook, stirred tepid mush inside the kettle, a mixture of corn meal and horse beans. As each woman or child approached, the sailor ladled a portion into their outstretched hands.

To see the women licking the mush from their fingers added yet another layer of disgust she felt toward the slavers. If they'd at least given the women wooden spoons so they might have the dignity of dipping into the kettle themselves, Eulie's disgust might have been tempered. Some women had refused to eat altogether. Starving to death being preferred over indignity. Yet, even this was denied to them. They were held down and forced fed with a scissor-like instrument, a *speculum oris*.

Joshua, fearing Eulie would interfere, threatened to keep her locked in their cabin.

"Many will die regardless," he'd told her. "The strong survive. You, my dear, must survive."

She had argued with him. "Why should I, for what purpose? I am no different than those naked, suffering women. I should be with them, not here in our comfort."

"Because you have a purpose, Eulie. I have known it from the first moment I set eyes on you, and you no more than a babe in Serafina's arms.

"You knew my mother?"

"Indeed, I did. She was beautiful, but she did not have iron in her spine, as you have. I watched you from afar, knowing one day you would be old enough to be a house slave. It was I who selected you."

"You, not Massa Stone?"

"I was allowed this for my service to him. He knew I was educated by my former master. It is our secret, such as you and I have. One of my tasks is to read the correspondence of the overseers. I monitor the account books, and, as I am considered ignorant, none are the wiser."

"Because you have educated me, I have a purpose?" Eulie knew an educated slave was a rare thing, though it also put her in danger. Joshua had warned her about slaves caught reading or doing numbers; their masters had them killed or they were sent to the fields to be worked to death.

"No, although educating you was essential. See me, Eulie and know what I tell you is true." He cupped his hands over her hers, his black eyes boring into her violet ones.

"Even though I was taken when I was a small child, Eulie, I

remember our village in the before land. I remember my grandmother, Imani. She had the gift of sight. She said the future was
not an arrow, that the future could be altered, but only by the
strong. She told me I had the gift of sight, and that I too could
see into a person's heart and soul. This gift has served me well.
Everything I have done led me to you. My life has not been
without toil and trouble, nor will yours be, Eulie." He raised
their joined hands. "What do you see, Eulie?"

She blinked, confused by his question. "I see our hands,
Joshua."

"Eulie, see how my black hands cradle your pale hands; it is
the way night cradles the moon. In my village, it was said our
souls are born among the stars. When a star falls to earth, it is a
soul ready to be born."

Eulie, her heart hardened by the callousness of men, raised
her gaze to the night sky, "There are no stars tonight, Joshua."

"Remember these words, Eulie, for one day their meaning
will become clear to you."

She endeavored to keep his words in her mind, if less so in
her heart.

Most days, from her place among the women and children, Eulie scanned the deck beyond the main mast for Ozee. Shackled and
chained, the men and older boys were allowed on deck, although
no more than fifty or so at a time. They were separated from the
women by a ten-foot-tall wooden fence the sailors called the *barricado*. It bisected the deck at the main mast and extended beyond
the railings. Sailors armed with half-pikes and muskets stood guard.
The barricado served as protection for the crew.

Ozee's strong body had not gone unscathed. He was painfully thin; his broad chest and muscular arms sagged with loose

flesh. Despite being manacled, he covered his privates as best he could. His eyes, when she caught a glance, blazed with hatred. She had tried many times to garner his attention. Still, he avoided her eyes. In Eulie's mind, this would not do. Slave revolt and insurrection were common on *Guineaman* slave ships, Joshua had told her. She feared Ozee would be killed. She needed him to know she was taking care of his sister and the children. He needed to know they lived, and in knowing this, he would desire to live for them.

The officers, accustomed to her assistance with the women and children, allowed her to move about the deck. Soon they ignored her, allowing her to get close to the barricado. She cared not that the shackled men eyed her with revulsion, believing her to have willingly traded her body for clothing and food. They spit on her person, on her face, sneering and hurling words in languages foreign to her.

Unfazed, she continued until she reached the portion of the barricado where Ozee stood.

"Ozee, she called to him, her voice just above a whisper. It was forbidden to speak to the male slaves. "See me, Ozee. I have word of your sister and the children. They live. I take care of them. They will survive as you must survive for them."

Ozee cocked an ear in her direction, his gaze resting on her for a moment. He dipped his head, indicating he'd heard her. She responded in kind before turning on her heel. It was best not to attract the guard's attention. While she made her way back to the women, she felt him watching her just as he had on the island. She prayed her words had been enough.

Many weeks passed, and with their passing came a shortage of supplies. Eulie and Joshua felt the shortage in their stomachs as rations grew lighter by the day. The crew suffered along with the passengers. The slaves, valuable as they were, had their mush cut back from twice daily to but one noonday meal. Eulie smuggled hard biscuits to Zina. It was a slight of hand endeavor, because if the other women caught sight, a riot would ensue.

Death was an equal diviner. Though many slaves continued to weaken and die, so did several of the passengers and crew. Eulie wept for the dead when they were flung into the sea.

Yet the true horror was still to come.

Under the hot blue of a southern sky, Eulie doused washrags in vinegar water for the women and children. The scourge of dysentery had taken its toll on the slaves as well as the crew. It was on this day the quartermaster, a Mr. Gibbons, had ordered a culling. Unease stirred within Eulie's breast. What was this culling?

Dozens of male and female slaves were taken from the hole below deck and lined up. The men were chained together. Ozee was not among them; Eulie's heart trilled with relief. The slaves who were too weak to stand sagged against others. The ship's surgeon strolled along the line. He looked into open mouths, prodded flesh and bloated abdomens. With a jerk of his head toward a slave, that slave taken from the line until more than two dozen were separated. Children were ripped from their mother's arms.

"Come with me, Eulie." Joshua placed a firm hand on her arm. I need you in the cabin, now."

"What is this? Why are they being separated," Eulie resisted him.

Joshua cupped her face with gentle hands. "See me, Eulie, and know I speak true. If you witness this, your soul will be forever marred. To know this is one thing, to be present, is quite another. Come now."

Eulie's knees buckled. She crouched amid her flock of women and children, her arms enfolding all who were near. "Zina, Jamila, come to me." Her flock were weak, painfully thin, but free of the dysentery. She had made it so. Still, her mind reeled with fear. She would not let them take one of hers.

Eulie clasped Jamila to her chest.

Resigned, Joshua knelt beside her.

Fear crackled through the ship. Pleas fell on deaf ears as the culled were dragged to portside. Dull eyes widened, white with fear; arms and legs thrashed against their captors. By twos and threes, the crew flung them into the endless deep. Screams rent the fabric of the air; the water below roiled. Sea foam turned crimson as the great scavengers of the sea tore into living flesh.

Eulie did not breathe, and for one moment of eternity, her heart stopped its beating. Joshua startled at the sight of her face, drained of all color. When at last her lungs forced a breath, her heart lunged forward; the beats slamming hard as stones within her chest.

Nineteen

The past is alive, whispering while crouched in dark corners
~ From Leela's Verses ~

Creeping on tiptoe, Leela and Izzy make their way down the hallway to the narrow attic door. Tugging it open, its rusted hinges groaning, Leela eyes the narrow opening. A faint shaft of light reveals layer upon layer of spider webs.

"Oh," Leela steps back, "I...I think we're gonna need a broom and a f-flashlight, Izzy. Wait here. There's a b-broom in the linen closet. I have a flashlight under my bed. Granny gave it to me for when lights go out in a s-storm."

When Leela returns, Izzy is rubbing at the goosebumps chasing along her bare arms.

"I don't know, Leela, so many cobwebs. Doesn't look like anyone's been up here for ages."

Leela responds with an impish grin, "You scared of spiders?"

"Course not," Izzy thrusts out her chin.

141

"Didn't think so. I'll go f-first, Izzy. You stay close. Aim the light ahead of me." Leela brandishes the broom, sweeping away the cobwebs as she goes. She tries the first step. It's solid beneath her weight. She takes another step and another. When she reaches the last step, the attic opens wide and deep as a cavern. Dusky light shows through arched windows.

Izzy scoots in behind her, "Lordy, I've never seen so much stuff piled up in one place."

"Me neither," Leela holds out her hand for the flashlight. She sweeps a wide arc of light. Shadows play against the rectangular shapes of furniture, boxes and trunks. A dressmaker's manikin wobbles as their footfalls send tremors along wide planks of flooring. After numerous sweeps of the light, Leela stops, aiming the flashlight at a row of picture frames. Even covered with dust and cobwebs, the elaborate frames glint with gold and silver edgings.

"Let's check these out, Izzy." Leela moves ahead, not waiting for her answer. "I want to see what my ancestors looked like." Weaving through trunks, boxes and large woven baskets, Leela makes her way to the wall of portraits. They are of varying sizes and types of frames. She stops at one of the largest frames. It's an oil painting of two bearded men with reddish brown hair. One of the men is younger looking than the other. They stand by a coal black horse. The older man holds a whip across his body. The men are posed by the house, her house. It gleams with white paint and vivid blue shutters. Leela wipes away the dust on the engraved name plate with her fingers. It reads, Silas Stone and Seamus Stone 1845.

"The older one, Silas, is the one Eulie named as her owner. He's the one who brought Eulie here, Izzy. And there are my bedroom windows," Leela points to them. "It's where Eulie stayed, I'm sure of it. She p-painted the mural about that time, I think. I'll know more when I finish my tracings."

"A blonde lady is in the next portrait," Izzy bends down to get a better view. "She doesn't look very happy, does she?" It says her name is Caroline Clayton Stone. She must've have been one of the founder's daughters."

The next portrait shows a grouping of three children of varying ages. The two girls have pale blonde hair and the youngest, a boy, has coppery brown hair. "They must be his children. Leela swipes her finger over the name plate. Leela reads their names, "Sarah, Sophie, and Simon Stone 1857."

They move on down the line of portraits as oil paintings turn to sepia photos and modern photographs in modern frames.

"This must be granny Vernell when she married my grandfather, Samuel Stone. She looks almost pretty with her long, dark hair. This one must be his mother, Laura Lee, the one I'm named after. She's beautiful.

"I don't know who my ancestors were. It's just my nana, my mom, her brother and his family," Izzy stands, letting out a long, slow breath.

"I'm sorry, Izzy. I wish things had been different," Leela slips her hand into Izzy's. "Come on, let's see what's in one of those trunks."

"I, I think I hear someone calling out," Izzy freezes in place.

"Rats, it's granny. I'd know that voice anywhere. Come on, we better get back to my bedroom fast before she finds us."

In their haste, they bump against boxes and trunks. Leela trips, stubbing her toe on something hard. She lets out a muffled, "Ouch," and aims the flashlight toward her feet. An elongated metal case, its lid flipped open and tipped to its side, has loosed shives of paper. Leela hands Izzy the flashlight.

"I'm taking these, Izzy," she whispers. Scooping up the papers, she stuffs them back into the case. With it tucked beneath her arm, she follows Izzy to the stairs.

When they are back in Leela's bedroom, breathless, they fall on the bed amid muffled giggles. Leela slides the metal box beneath her bed just as granny Vernell bangs open the door.

"Y'all deaf? I've been calling out to beat the band. We got news on Abraham. The two of you get your shoes on and come to the kitchen. Brick has somethin' to tell y'all."

Twenty

In every frozen heart there is a drop of love,
just enough to feed the birds.
~ Henry Miller ~

Leela and Izzy nearly trip over their feet as they rush downstairs, sure that Brick has found Ham and brought him back. Their excited smiles freeze when they see Brick's solemn face. The pinched look on Sable's face sends Leela's heart plummeting.

"Sit down, both of you," Brick waves them over to the kitchen table. "There's been trouble. Ham is in the hospital."

"W-what? Ham in the h-hospital? How, I, I mean, is he okay?" Leela sputters.

"Oh no," Izzy groans, covering her face with her hands.

"No, I'm afraid he's not. He was beaten-up by a group of boys. Finn tried to intervene, and they roughed him up, though he's okay, just bruised pride. When a patrolling deputy came by, the boys ran off. The deputy told me Ham doesn't know who the boys were. Finn is being questioned by the sheriff. His parents are with him.

"Izzy sobs into her hands. Leela is white faced with outrage.

"Now girls, this is what's going to happen," Brick's blue eyes narrow, though his tone softens as he breaks his news to them, "I don't want either of you working at the grille for the rest of the summer. Izzy, you need to stay close to home in White Oaks. I've no doubt your parents won't want you out and about. Leela, the same goes for you. It's important you understand this is for your safety."

"It's not fair," Leela slams the table. "I hate the people who hurt Ham. He's never hurt anyone. I hate that I can't work at the grille. It's not fair."

"Calm down, Leela," Sable reaches over for her hand. Things will go back to normal in time. We need to be vigilant right now, all of us."

"Back to normal? I don't think I like normal, Mom. I don't like Jim Crow and his so-called laws. I don't like that Izzy and Ham must use a back door to get into the grille. I don't like that we can't go to the same school. It's not fair. It's not right."

"Oh, hush now, Leela, yer makin somethin out of nothin," Vernell flicks her hand at Leela. "The coloreds know where they belong and where they don't. We've been getting along just fine until now. It's those Yank outsiders causing trouble again."

Leela, her violet eyes ablaze, turns her wrath toward Vernell. "Why should the coloreds have to know their place? Why is that? They have as much right as us to go anywhere they want. What's wrong with you? How can you say these things? You're mean, Granny, your heart is mean."

146

"If that don't beat all, my own grandchild talkin down to me. Why I never…"

"'Ma stop. You've said enough. Leela's upset and rightly so."

Vernell pushes away from the table, stomps out of the kitchen while muttering under her breath.

Izzy bolts from the table, her face haggard, tear streaked. "I want to go home now. Please, Mister Brick, will you take me home?"

"Yes, Izzy, we'll go right now." Brick moves from the table.

"Leela takes Izzy's hand, "I want to go along, is that okay, Brick?

"It's up to your mom, Leela."

Sable hesitates, "Is it safe, Brick?"

"I've been deputized, so yes, we're safe. I'll have her back before its full dark."

"Leela honey, we'll talk about *things* when you get back," Sable stands, goes to Izzy. Wrapping her arms around the girl, she wipes away Izzy's tears. "Anytime you want to visit us call and I'll make arrangements to get you here. Leela will miss you. Tell your mom and Abraham's mom we're praying for his full recovery."

"Thank you, Ma'am," Izzy dips her chin.

Leela and Izzy squeeze into Brick's cab. Leela keeps a tight hold on Izzy's hand the entire way. The streets are ghost town quiet and empty, save for patrolling police cars and the occasional army-green jeep of the national guard. Rifles are cradled in the men's arms.

When they get to the outskirts of colored town, Leela sucks in a breath. Izzy stares wide-eyed at the smoke and ash of a burned-out church. An enormous wooden cross planted on the church's front lawn still smolders. When they get into the town of White Oaks, they see more destruction. Businesses have been vandalized. Glass from broken windows litter the sidewalks. More burning crosses have been planted in residential areas.

"Why would anyone do this?" Leela asks, bewildered by it all.

Shaking his head, Brick grits his teeth, "What the hell? Where's the guard? They were supposed to intervene. They were supposed to stop the Klan."

"Klan? What's that?" Leela asks.

"The kind that wears white robes and hoods," Izzy mutters.

Leela is disturbed to see how hard and closed off Izzy's face has become.

"They're a misguided group of men, Leela. White men who've become vigilantes," Brick tells her."

Izzy turns a cold eye to Leela. "They've been working against us coloreds for more than a hundred years, Leela. They hate seeing us coloreds walk free, living free." Izzy pulls her hand from Leela's. "But the thing they like best, is to see us hanging from a tree."

Twenty-One

❧ ALONE AGAIN ☙

I took a deep breath and listened to the brag of my heart,
I am, I am, I am.
~ Sylvia Plath ~

After a week, the curfew lifts. According to Leela's mom, businesses have reopened, including the Catfish Bar and Grille. It makes little difference to Leela. Her life has come full circle, no friends, no job, and no place to go. Finn, she is told, has been sent to visit relatives in Atlanta for who-knows-how-long. Izzy doesn't return her phone calls. Leela had called so many times that Izzy mom, Mirabel, asked her to stop calling.

Her self-pity turns to self-shaming when Brick takes her and her mom to see Ham in the hospital. He'd been beaten so badly his is face swollen to twice its size. She doesn't even recognize him. His jaw is wired shut. His family are polite enough, but Leela sees the blame in their eyes. He'd befriended her. Been seen with her. Her heart breaks open spilling out equal parts of

149

love for the friendship they'd shared and burning hate for those who'd hurt him. She suspects Darla and her friends were involved. Thoughts of revenge stitch together the pieces of her broken heart. She vows the guilty will pay for their crime. Somehow, someway, she will make it so.

Leela had not spoken for years, now she has words in abundance and no one to talk to. She and her grandmother aren't on speaking terms. Her mom is gone most days at the library. Confined as she's been in the rambling old house, she doesn't feel completely alone. She has the painting and Eulie's words. And there are countless words yet to be revealed. Eulie has come alive in Leela's heart. She weeps when Eulie weeps. She feels the fear and the hatred Eulie feels. She finds herself speaking to Eulie, sharing her feelings with the long dead girl as if she were alive and listening.

And she has the contents of the mysterious metal box. Late one evening, when she's sure granny Vernell and her mom have settled in for the night, she retrieves the box from underneath her bed. She sorts through the yellowed shives of paper. In her hands, they crackle with age like dried leaves. The ink is blurred, faded by time. Leela uses her flashlight to illuminate the elaborate scrawl of words and dates. Much of it describes accounts, bill payments and letters, all written in the same hand. A ledger of worn tooled leather opens to reveal a ship's manifest. She follows the writing with her fingers:

Manifest of Slaves transported on board the Brig, Eastern Wind of Charleston, State of Georgia. Whereof Silas Stone is Master of the burden one hundred thirty-six tons and bound from Isle of Martinique for port of Savannah, State of Georgia this 27th day of July 1850.

Leela sucks in a breath. Martinique? That must be Eulie's island. Leela runs her fingers across the top of each page which identifies the names, sex, age and complexion of the slaves. Her fingers tremble with nervous excitement. This had to be the schooner that brought Eulie and the others. And Silas Stone, the captain.

Most of the slaves are merely numbered along with approximate age, gender, the owner's name or consignee's name. The writer remarks about their complexion being black, brown or mulatto and states place of origination. The remarks like lashed, diseased or deceased caused bile to rise to her throat. Eulie had written how dozens of the weak or diseased had been thrown overboard while still living.

Holding her breath, she trails her finger down the lengthy list of those enslaved. Her racing heart slows with relief when she comes upon Joshua's name, then Eulie's. Ozee, Zina and her children are listed soon after. Leela tallies up the list. Of the 376 slaves who began the voyage, only 253 survived to reach the port of Savannah. Silas was the named owner of more than a third of the slaves. Most of his slaves had survived. Survived only to be sold to the highest bidder. What kind of human feels the need to own another person? Leela shakes her head, her stomach twisting with revulsion. What had happened to Ozee, Zina and her children? Had they been sold away from each other?

She replaces the shives of paper and the ledger into the metal box, sliding it back under her bed. Going to the painting, she runs her fingers over the words left to be revealed. Were the answers to her questions here? The act of tracing the words had been slow and delicate work. If she rubs the lead of the pencil too hard over the markings, the paper tears, or the words blur.

Thinking of the words, Leela, has a vision of the burned-out church in White Oaks. Was the church in the piney woods in danger of being burned down? Her chest seizes at the horror of the flower painting being burned to ashes. She felt sure Eulie had painted it. Had Eulie hidden a story there as well?

When she finally settles into bed, her mind racing with ideas, she comes up with a plan. One that would save the painting. Should she find words hidden in that painting, those she would trace. Her plan set, her mind at ease, Leela drifts off to sleep dreaming of answers to her questions.

Twenty-Two

Look for it, for it cannot be seen
~ Lao Tzu ~

It is days later before Leela can put her plan into action. Her granny is off to do a fitting. Her mother is working at the library. They've left her believing she is in her room reading and writing poetry. And up to their leaving, she had been. Until recently, she had never disobeyed her mother, never told an outright lie. In her mind, the greater good of what she plans overrides her deceit. The greater good being the saving of Eulie's words in the painting.

When the time is right, she will tell Ham, Izzy and Finn about the secrets in the mural. And someday, her mother. Not Granny Vernell. No, never her because of her heartless contempt to the plight of the coloreds. Although in this, she has been conflicted. She has always loved her grandmother, the only grandmother she has ever known. How can someone as good as her grandmother

153

be so narrow minded, so hard of heart just because someone's skin is different than hers?

Perplexed as much as conflicted by these thoughts, Leela gathers tracing papers, pencils and her Brownie camera, last year's Christmas gift from her father. She and her mom had celebrated the holiday alone. The gift had come in the mail. She had not wanted it, had put it in the back of her closet. Her mother insisted she take it with them when they left for Georgia. Now, she can use it to photograph the painting of the women and their flowers. She felt sure it was Eulie's hand that had painted it.

With everything she needs in the tote bag, she slings it over her shoulder. She closes her bedroom door and heads down the narrow hallway which leads to the kitchen's backstairs, though it is not those stairs she is intent on using. She'd discovered a forgotten staircase by chance when she was looking for extra towels. She'd thought it was another linen closet. When she tugged at the door, it creaked and groaned as if it hadn't been opened in a century. What she found was a narrow passageway and a series of crooked steps that led down to the back porch. Beyond the porch, old brick threaded with moss and weeds revealed a free-standing chimney. She'd seen the chimney before when helping her mom weed the vegetable garden. Granny said it was part of the old kitchen back when all the cooking was done outside the main house. Leela hadn't given it much thought at the time.

Though now, the thrill of having her own secret passage assuages her lonely heart. She can come and go without her mother or granny knowing. This newfound sense of freedom sends her out of the doldrums. Nervous excitement bubbles up in her chest.

Wearing old jeans, a loose shirt, her worn saddle shoes and a baseball cap pulled low, she slinks down one alleyway after another. The town was built on a grid of these narrow tracks making it easy for her to avoid most of the cross streets, except the four-lane thoroughfare. She's making her way toward it through a vacant lot when a screech of tires sets her heart thrumming. Her first mistake is to look up. Her second is to freeze in place. A red truck is pulled up by the curb, not twenty feet from her. Several boys hang over the edge of the flatbed.

"Hey, it's her, she's that nigger lover." The driver, one she'd seen before with Darla, yells back to the others. "Go get her."

Something snaps inside her, something raw and ancient. She is running before she thinks of running. She does not think. A fear as old as the world itself, propels her. Everything around her blurs. Instinct, as deeply ingrained as those of any animal, brings her to the cemetery's gate. She feels no pain when she grasps the spiked iron railings, scrambling over them and through the heavy foliage. She keeps running, over tombstones and stumps. The voices behind her fade into nothing. She is in the forest now, her pace slowing. Kudzu vines close behind her, a door shutting out one world from the other. She is alone, the rapid thudding of her heart and her ragged breaths the only sounds. The silence is deafening. All at once, as if the forest has accepted her presence, birds chirp and call, squirrels chatter, whishing their tails, and whatever is sliding beneath loam and leaves, resume its travels. She returns the birds' call notes, mimics their songs, feeling the kinship she's always had with birds.

Her head down, her eyes on the twisting path, she moves onward, even as branches tug at her cap and scrape against her arms. At some point, she loses sight of the path. She steps through

155

tumbles of leaves, leaps over fallen branches. There is no music, no clapping, nor the stamping of feet to guide her this time. Yet, she is inexorably drawn as though something is urging her on. The fear in her throat melts away.

After a time, the trees thin and the church's clearing opens before her. First there is the scent of flowers and then the sound of bees, hundreds, maybe thousands of them. When she'd come to the Gathering, she noticed the flowers and their scents, not the bees. She been too overwhelmed with everything else to pay attention. Now, she sees the row of hives beyond the church. The church itself is surrounded by mounds of blooms.

Amid all this beauty, hate burns in her chest. Those boys, she grimaces, those terrible boys. She collapses on the church steps. With hands to her face, hot angry tears spill. When she is spent of tears, she wipes her wet hands on her shirt. She is surprised to see streaks of blood there. There are cuts, deep ones, on her palms. Now they begin to throb. Tearing strips from her long shirt, she wraps her palms. How is she going to explain this to her mom?

Taking deep, calming breaths, she stands. Her legs tremble with the effort from the scare she'd had. She turns the door-knob, it doesn't move. She pulls at it, jiggles it. It's locked. After everything she's done to get here, she can't even get inside. She had imagined this moment so many times, but never given thought to the possibility of the church being locked.

"L-L-Leela," a voice calls out. Heart jumping to her throat, she twists around.

In an awkward lope, Ishmael makes his way to her. "L-Leela," he repeats. One arm is full of blooms and in his hand, a garden trowel.

"Ishmael, why are you here?"

"I g-garden." He taps his chest with the trowel, then gestures to the church.

"Oh, the flowers are wonderful. Did you make the garden at Granme´ Delia's house?"

Ishmael bobs his head, grinning a lopsided grin. "F-flowers f-for c-church."

"I see. It is alright if I go in with you?"

He stares at her. L-Leela, you h-hurt?

"Oh, it's nothing, I-I hurt my hands on the cemetery gate. That's all." She shows him her wrapped hands.

"I-I help. Ba-bandages," he points to the church."

He bobs his head again, thrusting the blooms at her. She gathers them to her chest. He sets the trowel down on the steps and tugs a metal ring from his overall's pocket. A key is dangling from the ring. In what appears to Leela as a much-practiced movement, he manages to insert the key into the deadbolt lock. Opening the door, he steps back, allowing Leela to enter first.

With her arms full of flowers, Leela approaches the nave and the alter. A glass vase on the alter hold wilted flowers. Ishmael follows. He motions for her to put the flowers down.

"Leela w-wait. Ba-bandages," he says, going to a cabinet in the front of the church.

While he's busy getting the bandages, she moves to the painting. She reaches up, gliding her fingers over the rounded bellies of the girls and their flower buds. Leela searches for the marks the way a blind person traces over braille. If Eulie had painted this, then she probably left words here as she had in the mural. On the lower right corner, she finds the first series of marks. "Eulie," Leela breathes her name like a prayer.

Hearing Ishmael return, Leela steps away from the painting, her thoughts churning with a plan. She will need Ishmael's help.

He hands her a fistful of band-aids. "Y-you do. I-h-help."

"Thank you, Ishmael. I can do this."

He bobs his head, watching her unwind her makeshift bandages. Holding out his hands, he takes them from her. The bleeding has stopped. Crusts of blood hide the punctures. When she's finished, she looks up. "I'm fine now."

He gives her a skeptical glance and bobs his head. W-wait."

From the alter, he retrieves the vase with the wilted flowers. "I-I be b-back."

After a few minutes, he returns. The vase is empty of flowers. Fresh-water sloshes inside the vase as he places it on the alter. One by one, Ishmael painstakingly places each stem into the vase. When he's finished, she admires his lovely arrangement.

"Ishmael, that is so beautiful. Do you come every day?"

He shakes his head, holds up one finger.

"Oh, only once a week?"

"Y-yes, L-Leela. You, d-don't ta-talk with ha-hands? Ta-talk good now.

"Yes, I talk all the time now. Granme´ Delia showed me what I needed to believe."

He bobs his head, giving her a knowing look.

"Um, Ishmael, I ah, I need your help. There is something I need to do here. It's sort of a secret, but very, very important that I do this. She goes on to tell him, all the while he's smiling and bobbing his head. She shows him the camera and the tracing papers.

"Y-yes, y-yes. Th-this is g-good thing."

Leela takes photos of the painting and then the rest of the church. The afternoon light threading through the church's high set windows gives her enough light to capture the details on Eulie's painting.

She asks if the next time he comes, will he meet her at the cemetery gate.

"W-why there?" He lifts his hands in a question.

"Is there another way, Ishmael?"

"Easy w-way. I s-show you."

"Okay, but I don't want to be seen coming and going. Are there alleyways?"

"W-why?"

"My mom and granny Vernell wouldn't approve, Ishmael. This has to be our secret."

Ishmael's eyes narrow at her words. A frown replaces his lopsided grin.

Please, Ishmael. I'll be so careful. I promise to tell them when I'm done."

With an of slight shake of his head, he says, "O-kay, I shh-show you."

After he locks up, Ishmael takes her in the opposite direction of the way she'd come. They walk a winding path through the piney woods until they reach a vacant lot concealed by a row of several buildings. They cross over the four-lane highway. He takes her through several alleyways and behind vacant houses. In no time at all, they've reached the alleyway leading to her house.

"This is easier. Thank you. When will you go to the church again?

Ishmael tells her he'll be back in a few days. Her face reflects her disappointment.

"Here, L-Lee-la. He takes out his key ring, "Y-you go, go w-when you l-like."

She shakes her head. "But Ishmael, this is your key."

"Y-you t-take." I ha-have m-more." He gestures for her hand, placing the key gently on her palm.

"Thank you." Leela beams. Her eyes, catching the afternoon light, reflect a kaleidoscope of colors.

Ishmael's eyes widen. L-Lee-la. P-pretty eyes.

"Well, I'm happy you think so." She is even happier for finding him at the church. Now she can trace the words, the story she is sure Eulie has left for her in the painting. Well, maybe not for her specifically, but for someone, someone like her.

He waves bye to her. She watches him go. She's seen how the kids and even some of the adults have made fun of him, yet he remains kind and gentle. And she knows all about ridicule. She'd been ashamed and angry. She'd given up on speech until the gathering, until Granme´ Delia. There had been power in Granme´ Delia 's voice, her words. Leela is pleased with the sound of her own voice, her words. Voices have power. She knows this now. She knows too, that there is power in the written word. She thinks of Eulie's words.

As she makes her way down the alley, she wonders why her own grandmother dislikes Ishmael. It doesn't make any sense. Which brings to her mind other questions. Questions about her mom and Brick. That they'd been more than friends in high school had become obvious to her. Brick has eyes only for her mom. Her mom looks younger, acts younger whenever he visits. If they'd been in love back then, what had happened? Why had she married her father instead of Brick? Her father was not kind or loving, at least not to her mom. And that indifference had transferred itself to her, his only child. Leela had loved her father. Over time, his disregard for her and her mother had whittled that love down to a sliver, barely there. It was easy to hate him now.

She puts aside those questions to think about Eulie, her mural and her painting in the church. Her fingers itch to make those tracings. What do the flowers mean? Why had Eulie painted it? If there are answers to be found, she intends to fine them.

Leela hears the rattle of cook pans in the kitchen as she sneaks up the crooked stairs. The door moans, creaking like ancient bones when she opens it. She stops, holding her breath until she hears the clatter of dishes. She makes a mental note to grease the hinges before using the door again. She pauses to remove her saddle shoes. In her stocking feet, she goes to her bedroom. Closing the door behind her, she blows out a long breath of relief. She's done it, and no one is the wiser. She falls back onto her bed. The thrill of escape and the fear of being caught seeps from her trembling limbs, leaving her weak and spent. As much as she wants to, needs to, she can't allow herself to rest, just yet. There is still one more thing to do. She can't be caught wearing what she has on. She kicks her dirty saddle shoes and socks under the bed. She'll clean them later. Slipping out of her shirt and jeans, she bundles them up before slipping them too beneath her bed.

After washing up and dressing in the shorts and tee shirt she'd worn earlier, she flops down on her bed. Maybe she'll have time for a quick nap before she gets called down to help with dinner. She's not looking forward to it, not with granny Vernell stomping around the kitchen and grumbling under her breath. Her mom's attempts to carry on as if ugly accusations hadn't transpired between her daughter and her mother.

That night, Granny Vernell is the first to leave the table. She huffs, muttering under her breath. After Leela has finished up in the kitchen, her mom takes her aside. "Leela, honey, you're going to have to make amends with your grandmother. You need to understand she's set in her ways."

"Why can't she learn new ways?" Leela juts out her stubborn chin.

"Leela, your grandmother was born and raised in the south. Things, as you are now aware, are different here. It takes time for people to learn new ways of thinking. Change is hard, and I suspect things here will get worse before they get better. In the meantime, you need to respect her right to believe as she does. You are her only grandchild. She loves you with all her heart."

"She doesn't act like she cares," Leela insists.

"Yes, she's gruff. It's just her way. Her life hasn't been an easy one. Someday you'll understand. If not for her, do it for me. We can't go on like this."

Leela stares at her feet. She'll try to make amends, but only because her mom has been through enough already. "Okay. I'll try Mom."

"I've meant to ask, what happened to your hands, Leela. Why do you have band-aides on them?

A lie forms on her tongue. One of many she'll probably have to tell in the coming days.

"Oh, I nicked them when I was slicing the tomatoes."

"Well, be sure to put rubbing alcohol on them tonight."

Later, in her bedroom, Leela takes out her tracing papers and pencils. She'd finished tracing the words about the island and the three masted schooner. Those pages, over two dozen at last count, she'd numbered and pinned together. Sliding her fingers over Eulie's depiction of a wharf and the town square where the coloreds huddle ready to be auctioned, she finds marks, and there are many, so many.

Twenty-Three

I am not shackled, though I'm as much
a slave as those who are.
~ Eulie ~

SAVANNAH, GEORGIA 1850

Under the blistering noon heat, Eulie, her hands fisted against the edge of the wagon seat, watched the enslaved being herded through Wright Square, Savannah's slave trading district. Women and children, tied at the wrists and linked by rope, trudged behind cobbled men and boys. Ozee and about sixty other males, shackled and manacled, shuffled behind the wagon she and Joshua were seated on. She glanced back hoping to catch Ozee's attention. Often, while on the Eastern Wind, she'd found him watching her from behind the barricado, though each time she sought to catch his gaze, he looked away.

The city of Savannah teemed around her, sending her heart racing and her head spinning. To her untrained ears, the city's noise was deafening. Carriages rumbled through the streets.

Hooves clattered on stone and brick as riders dashed here and there. Rows of shops and open markets lined the streets. Countless people mingled hawking their wares. Negresses, balancing woven baskets on their heads, weaved through the crowds. The pungent scents of horse and dung mingled with the tang of unwashed bodies. It all was too much. Closing her eyes, she put her hands over her ears. When the dizziness passed and her racing heart slowed, she lowered her hands and cracked one eye open, then the other. Joshua pressed a flagon to her lips. The liquid burned her throat, numbing her senses.

"Take deep breaths, Eulie. It will pass." Josh tipped the flagon toward her lips again. With a trembling hand, she pushed it away. "I am better now, Joshua."

"Good. You will soon become accustomed to all of this, Eulie." He made a circling motion with his hand.

Taking another deep breath, she keened her eyes to the line of the enslaved moving beside the wagons. Eulie's heart constricted painfully as she searched for Zina and her children. She had begged Joshua to intervene on Zina's behalf, but to no avail. The Massa intended to sell all but those who were fit enough to work on his rice plantation. Many of those men had come from the rice growing regions of Africa. These men were particularly valuable, Joshua told her, as they were skilled in its cultivation.

Prior to disembarking the Eastern Wind, Silas Stone had directed the hated overseer, Hector, to have the crew prepare the enslaved for auction. Naked as they had been throughout the long voyage, they were now washed, clothed, and oiled to look healthy, though they were anything but. The women, their wooly hair growing out in sprouts, wore ankle length coarse muslin shifts. The children wore knee length shirts of the same material. The males wore loose muslin shirts and dun colored breeches looped at the waist. All were barefoot, their heads bowed, eyes shuttered against the hustle and bustle of the busy thoroughfare. To Eulie they were like ghosts walking, as if they were no longer of this world.

"Zina," Eulie called out. Zina raised her head for a moment, her eyes blank, unseeing. The babe was hitched to her hip with a length of muslin, his tiny head lolling and jerking with each of her steps.

"Zina, I'm here. I'll help you. Please don't give up, please," Eulie entreated. She made to jump from the wagon. Joshua's strong arms encircled her waist.

"No Eulie," he gave her a hard look. "Do not give Hector a reason to beat her with the paddle. You have a different path. Do not waste it with useless hysterics."

Eulie's breath caught in her throat. She sunk back into her seat, knowing he was right. She wanted to walk next to Zina, to be sold with her, though there had never been any hope of that. Silas Stone, she refused to title him with Massa in her thoughts—had told Joshua she was to be a maid for his wife and children. She would be installed in his house at a place called Bateaux Bay. Joshua reminded her daily of her good fortune. He said it was a large structure situated on a bluff overlooking a bay. Said it was a grand place with tall glazed windows and numerous fireplaces.

I don't care, she'd replied when they'd spoken about it. I don't want to be his wife's maid. So," he'd said to her, "you would rather be a fancy and sold to a brothel? For that is where young and pretty quadroons like you are destined. At his words, she'd bitten back another retort. No, she did not want that. Still, her stomach roiled when Joshua told her Massa Stone's slaves were to be held at the slave yards in Johnson Square where they would await inspection by prospective buyers. Eulie was unable to conjure in what manner the slaves would be held, or what the inspection entailed. When she asked Joshua about it, he'd declined to answer.

The driver, an elderly negro with a shock of white hair, pulled the mules to a stop by a board and batten two story rowhouse on the outskirts of town. Joshua hopped down. He held his hand out to her. "Our lodgings are here."

Eulie slid off her seat, her bare feet landing on hard baked red dirt. She was attired little better than Stone's other slaves. Over her muslin shift, she wore a quarter sleeve smock gathered at her narrow waist with a length of muslin. The lengths of her coppery hair were pulled into a bun at her nape. The tigon, with its bright splash of colors, was the same one she'd worn on the island. Scanning the line of shackled men, she sought a final glimpse of Ozee. The corners of her lips curving into a sad smile, she called out his name. He turned his head sharply at the sound of her voice; his dark eyes met and held her gaze. Eulie sucked in a breath, her eyes widening in surprise. He called out his sister's name to her. She pressed a hand to her heart in a silent promise. He returned her gesture by bringing his manacled hands to his lips, sending her a kiss.

The moment was lost when Joshua came between their sightline to gather his valise from the wagon. When the wagon moved forward, the men shuffled behind it, their bare feet kicking up red dust. Ozee met her gaze again, holding it, and craning his neck until she was lost from his sight. She watched as the procession disappeared around a bend. He was gone, and with his leaving, went her heart's longing and a promise she meant to keep.

She stood solemn and resolute behind Joshua with her hands

clasped at her waist. Joshua rapped on the weathered door. It was opened by a young mulatto girl.

"Mister Cartah, we been waitin fer ya all dis mornin long."

Eulie blinked back her surprise. Carter? Joshua had a surname. She'd never conceived of him having one. Only the bekes, the whites on her island had surnames.

"We're more than ready for our accommodations, if you please, Tansy."

Eulie's eyes widened, taking in the girl's appearance. She wore a full skirted gown, green as island ferns. The sleeves were puffed from shoulder to elbow. A white collar and cuffs were scalloped at the edges. Her ebony hair was smoothed back, parted in the middle and curled into ringlets over each ear. She had caramel colored skin and dark eyes. Most surprising to Eulie were the girl's shoes. They were black patents, shined to a high gleam. Eulie had only ever seen whites wear patents.

But it was the girl in her fine dress who sucked in a breath upon her appraisal of Eulie.

"Tansy," Joshua cleared his throat. "This is Eulie. I assume you have the item sent over by the purser for us?"

The girl nodded. She stepped back into the narrow hall, casting her gaze from Joshua back to Eulie. "Yessa, a parcel come early dis mornin."

The girl kept staring. Eulie's flush darkened. It was her eyes, wasn't it? Even here in the Americas they feared the eyes of the deadly serpent Basilisk. Eulie gritted her teeth. She wasn't having it. Not here, not anymore. Eulie arched her neck, giving the girl stare for stare.

Tansy, startled, shifted her gaze and took the valise from Joshua's hand, "Dis way, Mister Cartah, ya both be lodged upstairs." The girl led the way, a flash of white petticoat showed when she lifted her skirts away from the risings. As Eulie went up the stairs behind Joshua, she took in her surroundings. Across from the stairs, she saw a room fitted with a settee and several upholstered chairs. Voices emanated from somewhere else in the house. Dishes clattered and the faint scent of food made her mouth water. She and Joshua had broken their fast at dawn with a bit of cheese, dry biscuits and dank water. She swallowed hard.

Eulie's eyes were drawn to what looked like a painted garden on the stairway walls. When she got closer, she saw the walls were flocked with a pattern of flowers and sprigs of green, not painted, instead it felt of coarse paper like the broadsheets. So, this is what Joshua had spoken of, wallpaper. Lightly, she ran her fingers over it. It was smooth, unlike the painting on the dining room wall at Stone's house on the island. That had had ridges and swirls of thick bright paint. The colors here were muted and flat.

The girl opened a door at the end of the hall. She stood back to let Joshua go first. Eulie hesitated, waiting for the girl to enter. The girl stood aside, gesturing for Eulie to go ahead. The girl followed. The room was a good size with two single beds. A thick, cloth wrapped parcel was on one of the beds. There was a mirrored, low dresser situated against one wall. It held a basin, a layer of towels and a stone pitcher. Flowered curtains fluttered by a narrow, open window. The walls were papered the same as the hallway.

"Supper be at four on the clock. Chamber pots get emptied ever mornin. Nice ta see ya again, Mister Cartah." The girl bobbed a curtsy, closing the door behind her.

As soon as the door shut behind the girl, Eulie turned to Joshua.

"Are the Negras in America afraid of the Basilisk."

"No, why do you ask?"

"Why then did this girl stare at me so?"

"Eulie," Joshua took her hand, leading her to the oval glass mounted on the dresser; it reflected aspects of the room. She'd seen a mirror but once when she'd been tasked to polish the furniture in Silas' bedchamber. Then, she been afraid to see her reflection. Some of the slaves on her island believed it would catch and keep a body's soul.

Eulie averted her gaze, ducking her head.

"Eulie, "Joshua sighed, "A mirror does nothing more than reflect. "Trust me."

And she did trust Joshua. Slowly, she raised her head. For the first time in her life, Eulie took stock of herself. She saw skin the color of pale cream. Hair the color of a burnished copper kettle. Her nose was straight, her nostrils softly flared. Her lips were pleasingly shaped and full. And her eyes, the eyes that had terrified those of her kind, were as violet as the frangipani flowers that grew in abundance on her island. Her mother had never spoken about the man who'd fathered her, and Eulie had not been old enough to question it at the time. Now, she was desperate to know.

"Joshua, do you know who fathered me?"

"You were born before I came to the island." He dipped his head, avoiding the questions held in her violet eyes.

"Come, the parcel is for you."

"For me?"

"Yes, my dear. You must be clothed befitting a house maid." He held out the parcel. She took it in her hand, feeling the weight of it. She sat on the bed with it in her lap.

"Dress now, Eulie. I will return shortly."

The parcel was wrapped in a strip of coarse muslin. Unwrapping it, she found a soft cotton shift, a linen smock and an apron made of white linen. Beneath these was a swath of deep brown material. When she shook out the folds, it became a quarter sleeved gown with a high neckline and a full skirt. A white triangle of material, she supposed, was meant to be a head scarf.

She stripped off her dingy shift and smock. Filling the basin with cool water from the pitcher, Eulie washed and dressed. The slip and gown were overlarge for her. She double wrapped the apron straps, cinching in her waist.

Sometime later, Joshua rapped on their door. She opened it to find him carrying yet another parcel and a straw bonnet.

"I believe these will fit." Unwrapping the parcel, he held out a pair of brown leather shoes he said were called brogans and a pair of muslin stockings. Eulie's jaw dropped. Shoes, she was to have shoes. Joshua turned his back while she pulled up the stockings, fastening them at her thighs with the attached cloth ribbons. The shoes held a strong scent of tanning dye but fit well enough. They laced up to her ankles. She paced the room, getting the feel of the brogans. She'd never worn so many items of clothing in her life. When she looked in the mirror, she blinked twice. The girl from the island was no more. In her place stood someone she was still to know.

"When is the auction to be held, Joshua?"

"Tomorrow. Why do you ask?"

"I must see to Zina and the children."

"No Eulie. It is not a place for you. Few women attend, and those who do remain in their carriages. They are accompanied by a manservant or relative. As it is, I will be engaged with Hector and Massa Stone during the auction.

Eulie bowed her head so Joshua would not see the defiance flashing in her eyes. She twisted the folds of her gown. No, no, her mind reeled. She must see Zina. She must be there for her. She would find a way.

Twenty-Four

We are as chattel, beasts to be exploited.
~ Eulie ~

"Can we not venture out to see the city?" Eulie studied her hands. He knew her well enough to perceive the deception in her eyes. Her true goal was to find the location of the auction.

"That would be unwise. Our master made his intention clear, and I do not wish to disregard the master's intent. He is aware, as am I, of the number of unsavory men drawn here by the auction. Think no more on this, Eulie."

As the morning wore on, Eulie paced the room while Joshua sorted through his valise. He pulled out several books offering her one he knew she wanted to read, Ivanhoe, volume one by Walter Scott. She took it, putting it aside on the bedside table. Joshua arched his brow. Seeing her worried and listless, he tugged out a sheaf of foolscap.

"I've seen you draw on the muslin tigons you've made. Here you have a fine view from the window." He handed her the foolscap and a stick of graphite. "Draw what you see, Eulie. It will pass the time."

Her eyes lit up to see the foolscap. She'd never had true paper to draw upon. She would indeed draw, but not from the view. She would draw from her memory those she loved, Ozee, Zina and the children. And Joshua. "Thank you, Joshua."

The day sped by. Eulie kept herself busy with her sketches. Joshua spent time reading and in between, he dozed. They took their supper in the room. Both read until the light became too dim for reading. Joshua left late in the evening to meet with Silas. Eulie nodded off and was asleep before he returned. The comfort of the first true bed she'd ever slept in did not prevent troubled thoughts that kept her tossing and turning during the night.

Joshua was up and dressed before she opened her sleepy eyes. He left the room so she could dress in private, saying he would meet her in the common room for breakfast. She bound her braided hair in a tigon and slipped on the dark gown and smock he'd brought her yesterday. Her new shoes clicked against the risers as she went downstairs. Following the sounds of muffled voices, she found her way to the common room. She paused at the doorway, her eyes widening at the sight of such a place. Tapers in silver sconces lit the long room. White tablecloths covered the numerous tables. A highly polished sideboard was laden with silver platters. If not for it being peopled with Negras, Eulie would have thought she had entered a white establishment. Joshua waved her over to his table. He stood, pulling out a chair for her; it was as beautiful as any chair she'd seen in the house on her island. The table was set with rose patterned china. Her gaze traveled the room. The negroes here were dressed nearly as fine as the whites she'd seen.

Her wide-eyed stare was returned by others who chanced to see her enter. She took her seat, blushing.

"Eulie, you may serve yourself from the sideboard. Tansy will offer you a choice of coffee or tea." As soon as those words left his lips, Tansy appeared by the table bearing two silver decanters. "C-coffee, p-please," Eulie sputtered, though she'd never tasted coffee. It was black and bitter. Eulie spit it back into the cup. Joshua, seeing this, pointed to the milk and honey in decanters. By the time she was finished mixing those in, the coffee was a pale as cream and as sweet as the honey she poured. When Tansy left their table, Eulie asked the question that had been burning on tongue. "Joshua, are these Negras not slaves?"

"No, they are not," he shook his head. "Those you see here are freemen. They have bought their freedom or have been emancipated by their owners."

"One may buy one's freedom?" This was a concept unknown to her. On her island, many had run to the mountains for freedom; they were maroons, though they were not free. They were hunted like animals.

"How do they earn money to buy freedom?"

"Some slaves have special skills. Their masters allow them to keep the money they earn during their free time."

One could buy one's freedom, but only if one has special skills. Eulie wondered if painting the tigons counted as a special skill.

While Eulie picked at her food, she listened to the conversations of those near her table. All spoke English, though their accents were varied. One couple near her table drew her ear.

Their language had a musical tone to it, though it was English as she'd never heard. "What language is this, Joshua?"

"They are Gullahs, Eulie. The language they speak is a combination of English and their native tongue, it is called Geechee."

Eulie watched the couple until she found herself under their perusal. She ducked her head, blushing.

Later, back in their room, Joshua warned her again. "Do not leave this room, Eulie. It is dangerous for one such as you to be on the streets. Lock the door behind me. I have arranged for Tansy to bring you supper."

After he'd gone, she paced the floor. She'd seen the broadsheets advertising the auction. It was to be held, she'd read, at a place called The Racecourse, three miles outside of Savannah. The number of slaves to be auctioned was staggering. It was in the hundreds. Joshua had told her there would be large crowds of men. As a lone female, she'd be suspect. But as a boy? Her eyes flit to Joshua's valise.

A short time later, Eulie was dressed in a pair of Joshua's breeches and one of his linen shirts. Her bright hair needed covering. The bonnet would not do, nor would the tigon. At the bottom of the valise she found a floppy hat, a rain slicker made of tanned leather. She'd seen Joshua wear it many times on the island. It was too large for her head, but that served her purpose. Pulling it down over her ears, it concealed much of her face. She studied her appearance in the mirror. A young boy with violet eyes stared back at her.

From the broadsheet, she knew the address of the auction. Yet, how was she to find her way there? Did she dare ask for directions from a stranger? Surely there was little danger in a simple question.

Barefoot, her shoes held in one hand, she was down the stairs and out the entrance door. She took off down the hardpacked earth, not stopping until she was a good distance from their lodgings. Under the shelter of a leafy oak, she brushed off her feet and slipped on her shoes. Taking deep breaths to calm her racing heart, Eulie's eyes widened to see the crush of travelers on the road. All sorts of wagons, carriages and men on horseback were passing by. Other men, those who had the look of country folk by their clothing, walked beside their carts and mules. There could be little doubt as to where all were headed. Relief washed over her. She need only to follow them.

Billows of clouds rolled overhead, their dark underbellies auguring rain. Eulie, her heart thumping hard, gathered her courage. Stepping out from behind the tree, she merged with the travelers. Keeping her head down, her violet eyes shuttered, she sought a place behind a cart pulled by a plodding mule. No one paid her any mind. She was just another boy among other boys.

It seemed to her as if miles had passed beneath her feet when the cart and wagon veered off onto a side road. The travelers spread out among a melee of men, horses and carriages. A din of loud voices rang in her ears. Cigar smoke wafted on the air. She was pushed and shoved as the crowd surged ahead. Her breath came fast and hard. Wedged between a wagon and the brown withers of a horse and rider, she pushed back, wending her way through the crowd.

Ahead of her was an enormous building open on two sides. Inside the building there was a raised platform with risers on both sides. All manner of men crowded around it. Some were dressed in fine swallow-tailed coats and stove-pipe hats. Others looked to be straight off farms and plantations with their grimy clothing and unlacquered boots.

As Eulie drew closer, she saw a high fence of latched railings cordoning off hundreds of slaves. She went numb. Her heart banged within her chest, beating so hard she thought to die where she stood. How was she to find Zina and the children among so many?

Mary, Mother of Jesus, show me the way. Lead me to my loved ones, Eulie prayed as she had never prayed before. She moved forward and kept moving until her outstretched hands clutched at a railing. No one stopped her. Had Mary, in her divine mercy, rendered her invisible? Calling out Zina's name, she moved down the railings. Those soon to be sold glanced at her with disinterest. Many had their heads bowed. Other stared straight ahead with blank, unseeing eyes. Children whimpered. Families of three and four clung together, anguish drawn on their faces.

Toward the end of the building, Eulie came to rows of horse stalls. Between the stalls was a bricked walkway. Slaves inside the stalls reached out to her between narrow bars.

"Zina," Eulie called out, peering into each stall. She was stepping over to the next row of stalls when a ruckus of men entered. Terrified, Eulie hid inside an empty stall. Through the bars she saw two white men dragging a young negro male by his elbows. His arms were shackled behind his back. His feet bound. He'd been stripped naked. Thrusting him onto the brick floor, belly down, the men looped a rope through this wrists and feet. They pulled the rope taut until the boy stopped arching his back. One of the men held a paddle. Eulie cringed at the sight of it. She'd seen this kind of punishment on the schooner. This instrument of evil was a narrow board, two inches-thick and about two feet long with holes drilled throughout. When the paddle met flesh, it left deep, bloody blisters along the buttocks. This, Joshua had told her, was inflicted instead of the whip as the whip left scars along the back. Perspective buyers drew away from slaves with whip scars as it indicated a rebellious slave.

Eulie covered her ears, whimpering with each whack of the board on the boy's bare buttocks. The boy's screams pierced the air. Eulie bit down on her lip until it bled. When his screams abated, they dragged him away. She sunk to the straw covered floor, drawing ragged breaths. Wiping a smear of blood from her lip, she rose, weak-kneed, yet determined to continue her search when several more men entered. Peering through the bars, she saw they wore fine cuts of cloth. Their boots were highly lacquered. In their hands they held sheets of paper and sticks of graphite.

One man strode toward a stall opposite where Eulie hid.

"This female is a fine mulatto and a breeder as you shall see." He tugged back the sliding lock and opened the stall door. "She is chattel number thirty-eight in your catalogue. Meena, come," he barked, snapping his fingers. With great hesitation, a tall, willowy young woman stepped past the stall door. The man kicked it closed behind her. Clinging to her side was a child of about seven. Both mother and daughter had honey toned skin and black hair thick with tight curls.

"Ah," said the men, moving in close to the young woman. They bade her show her teeth, pinching her cheeks until she did so. Their hands pawed at her breasts, her buttocks. One of them pulled at her thin shift, ripping it until a breast was exposed. He stood back, laughing at what he'd done. "Yes, she will do. I do not need the child."

"Come now," the owner said, pointing to the little girl. "Two for the price of one. She will grow."

"No, my good man. I purchase this for another. His request is for one only."

The young woman, Meena, dropped to her knees prostrating herself before his shiny black boots. "Mas'r, please, please, Mas'r." She continued to beg him, her arms around his boots. "Get off me, woman." The man kicked at her with the tip of his black boot. "I'll settle with you now, sir, and take her with me."

They shook on it. The owner jerked the child from the mother's arms. The little girl screamed and fought. The man smacked her on her head before shoving her back into the stall. The young mother, bent over with gut wrenching sobs, was shackled and dragged away. Her cries echoed through the stalls. Voices of the enslaved took up her lament.

Sobs worked their way up Eulie's throat. To stop their flow, she brought her fist to her mouth and bit down hard. If she fell to wracking sobs now, she'd be lost to grief for the mother and child. Her lips moved against her fist, a vow forming there. "No child of my blood will be in bondage. No matter what I am brought to do, no child of my blood will be in bondage. She repeated her vow until it became one with her soul.

Her breath still burning in her chest, she checked the other stalls, calling out Zina's name again and again, to no avail. She had little choice but to return to the enclosure and find a way to get inside.

She followed the shrill, rapid voice of the auctioneer as he called out the numbered chattel. Bids for the well-muscled negro man on the platform rang out. Behind him stood a woman in a field hand's garb. The man stood pliant, searching the crowd until he focused on one bidder. "Suh, I be ah fine hand in de rice fields. Suzie," he gestured to the woman, "she be one of de best, Suh. We together, Suh."

The bidder paused, then nodded his head, to the obvious joy of the negro man. "Thankee, Suh, thankee."

Eulie eyed the bidder. He was middle-aged and finely attired. His eyes were a soft blue. He had a pleasant expression on his face. The negro man had discerned who he hoped would be a kind master.

Eulie kept an eye out for Joshua and Stone as she moved through the crowd of men. Stone would not take notice of her, but Joshua had a second sense about him. If he was anywhere near her, he would see clear through her disguise. She ducked her head and wended her way behind the platform. An elderly negro stood sentinel by a gate attached to the fence enclosure. Looking up, she saw there were other gates and other sentinels. Owners directed the men, pointing to the slaves to be brought forward through the gates.

No one took notice of her as she trailed along the fence. Behind a fence near Eulie, a young woman had sunk to the ground. At her shoulder, a babe slept. A little girl stood by sucking her fingers. Her shift was dirty and torn. Pieces of hay stuck to her wooly hair. Eulie blinked. Jamila? Eulie's breath caught in her throat. She fell to her knees, clutching the fence.

"Zina, Zina, it's me, Eulie. Look at me, Zina." Jamila burst into tears. She clawed at the fence to get to Eulie. "Eulie, Eulie, she cried. Only then did Zina turn. She looked passed Eulie with a blank expression. "Zina, I'm here. I'm going to help. I'm going to get you out." Though what she would do with Zina and the children once they were freed, she'd no idea.

Eulie had taken to shaking the fence to get Zina to look at her when two large, firm hands settled on her shoulders.

"Eulie, come with me before Stone sees you or you may well end up on that platform with men pawing you."

"Joshua, I, I can't leave her. I can't leave them."

"I have obtained a good, God fearing man who will purchase all three. They will be fine. It is you who are the problem at present. Come now before Stone is tempted to turn a handsome profit at your expense."

With her burden lifted, Eulie spoke once more to Zina. "You are going to be fine, Zina. You and the babe and Jamila. Joshua has seen to it. I will see you again one day, I promise."

Jamila wailed and wailed. Zina was numb to the world around her. Eulie got to her feet. Keeping her head down, she followed behind Joshua.

Twenty-Five

Everything we see hides another thing
~ Rene Magritte ~

L eela stirs from a deep sleep. She glances at her bedside alarm clock. Yawning and rubbing her eyes, she sees its near midnight. Muffled voices, discordant, reach her ears. Tracing papers are scattered over her bed. She gathers them, sets them aside with all the others. The voices grow louder. Granny and her mom, arguing? Have they found out about her visit to the church? Stumbling to her bedroom door, Leela goes to the landing, squats down. Their voices are clear now and growing angrier.

"I won't give him up, not this time."

"What're you talkin' about?"

"Ma, you know exactly what I'm talking about."

"I know Luanne's been spreadin' rumors about you and Brick and you a married woman, Sable."

183

"Did you know Luanne called Dale, told him about me spending time with Brick. I guess she thought Dale would be coming back for me. Well, her ploy backfired. Dale wants a divorce and I said yes. It was going to happen anyway. Dale's been living with some woman, wants to marry her."

"You'd shame our family with a divorce, Sable? Your poor father is rolling over in his grave."

"Me, shame our family? Oh, that deed was done long ago, Ma. The whole town knows who Ishmael's father is."

"Don't you bring that ill-gotten retard up to me, you hear. I won't listen. It's lies, all lies."

"Not lies and you know it. Ishmael's my half-brother and it's not right the way you treat him. Pa fooled around with Monique Dubois. It's common knowledge."

"Stop it, I won't listen to these lies. Samuel did no such thing."

"Sebastian has a copy of Pa's will. And you know what? Ishmael is in it. Stop lying to yourself, Ma. Pa did what he wanted. Look what he did to me. Where do you think Pa got the money to keep his fish packing company going? Pa made a deal with Dale, Ma. I know you knew, because Pa told me. I was just seventeen, Ma, a high school beauty queen sold to the highest bidder. You went along, helped it along. Well, I won't give Brick up this time."

Vernell harrumphs. "It was a dowry, is what is was."

"Not to me it wasn't. Brick and me, we've always loved each other, since we were kids. I never loved Dale. I tried to make it work for Leela. She's the only thing good that came out of my marriage. Dale might try to take her, but I won't let that happen. Sebastian's on my side, Ma. He's a divorce lawyer, one of the best in Atlanta.

Well, it's a damn good thing he's comin' because Luanne and her pa have set the back taxes on us. They're trying to take the house right out from under us. Bet you didn't know that."

"What?" Sable gapes, dumbfounded.

"Edwina down at the courthouse told Loretta. Said our place is gonna be put up for auction unless the taxes get paid by the end of August. While you've been foolin around with Brick, Luanne and her pa have been trying to buy us out. Been trying fer years. Well, now they got the back taxes brought up. We owe a ton of money. I ain't got it. Do you?" Vernell shuffles to a kitchen chair, sinks wearily into it."

Sable takes a seat next to her. "We won't let that happen, Ma. Sebastian and I are co-owners of this house, and he has financial resources. Pa provided for you. Written in his will is a codicil, meaning you have Survivorship until you pass. I had no idea pa hadn't laid aside tax money."

"Well, he didn't. So, whatever it is yer gonna do, you'd best get doin' it 'cause the clock's tickin'."

"How about some tea Ma? We both need to calm down and talk this through."

Leela, her mind spinning with questions, gets back to her room and flops face down on her bed. A divorce? In her heart, she was glad. Her mom deserved someone who loved her, someone like Brick. Thinking back to her days with her father, it was clear to her now, her dad had never loved her mom.

The question was, why did her father threaten to take her away from her mom? He hadn't acted as if he wanted her when he'd had her. All these weeks and not a word from him. She knew he could be mean. Would he try to take her just to hurt her mom? Leela clenches her hands, hot anger towards her dad burning in her chest. She will never go back to him, never. She'll run away first.

Leela rolls over, covers her face with her hands. The shadow of her recurring nightmare tugs at her. An unnamed terror crawls up her spine. She's had this same nightmare since she was little. The nightmare itself always becomes a blur when she wakes up, her heart pounding in her chest. Leela rolls off the bed, planting her feet on the floor. She can't go back to sleep, not with the shadow of her nightmare still lingering in her mind. She goes to the mural, slides her fingers over its contours. The mural and the feel of Eulie's words beneath her fingers eases her mind.

Leela's thoughts turn to Ishmael. His mother, Monique, is Granme´ Delia 's daughter. If grandpa Sam *is* Ishmael's father, that makes Ishmael her uncle. Her heart warms. Ishmael, her uncle. She can't wait to tell him they're related. Of course, he might already know. If the town knows, as her mom had said, then everyone knows, even Finn? If he doesn't, she'll tell him. That is if he ever comes back to Bateaux Bay. Who is this Sebastian? Leela remembers her mom saying she has a cousin who is a lawyer. Grandpa Sam had a brother named Seymore. So, it makes sense that Sebastian is her mom's cousin and her uncle.

With all that settled in her mind, her thoughts turn to Darla and her mother, Luanne. Leela clenches her teeth. If they win, if they take the house, they will tear it down and build a new house. She'd heard as much from granny Vernell. Eulie's beautiful mural will be lost forever. There must be a way to stop them. She'd made a promise to Eulie she would protect her words, her mural. Leela gathers up the latest tracing papers. She clips them together. Before long, she will finish tracing all the words, what then? What should she do with Eulie's words, her story? While she's cradling the papers an idea forms, taking on a life of its own. She will need lined writing paper, lots of it and a binder. Leela slides her fingers over the house in the painting. Someday, Leela promises herself, she will make this falling down house grand again. Eulie's words come to her. She will find a way. She will make it so.

Twenty-Six

What is this path I am to walk?
~ Eulie ~

BATEAUX BAY, GEORGIA 1850

E ulie was well and truly hated by Silas Stone's wife, Caroline. "I will not have this creature roaming about my home," Caroline screeched upon her first sight of Eulie. "Her eyes have a wildness about them, and that hair, the vulgar color of it."

Silas Stone shook his head. The ponderance of his sigh one of long practice. "The girl has a fine hand. Send her to the sewing room then, if you are so bent against her person. I had no wish to vex you so, wife. She was meant a gift, a helper for the nursery. I'd been told she had a way with children."

Caroline, visibly agitated, plucked at her full skirts, the citrine colored taffeta whishing as she paced the wide entrance hall. Eulie stood next to Joshua, her head bent, her hands folded at her waist, a sign of submission she had oft practiced at Joshua's insistence. Eulie took in her surroundings in a single glance. She

189

was stuck by the abundance of gleaming wood and patterned walls. Her nose twitched at the over-zealous application of lemon oil. She viewed her new mistress beneath her lashes. The woman had a long, narrow face and a pointed chin. She looked to Eulie bloodless with her pale eyes and translucent skin. A blue vein pulsed at her throat. Her hair, pulled into a severe bun at her nape, was the color of bleached bones.

"Well, this creature will not have her way with mine. All that is within me warns against it, husband. A fine hand, you say. She will keep to the room on the third floor, then. It has a good light for a seamstress, if indeed she is what you claim. The kitchen servants will tend her needs." Caroline snapped her fingers at a servant, a girl about Eulie's age. "Dory," Caroline spat. The girl jerked to attention. "Put the new seamstress in the room by the attic. See to it she takes her meals there." Caroline leveled her icy stare on Eulie. "Disobedience is severely dealt with girl. I am never to see you below stairs."

Stunned by the woman's vehemence, Eulie darted a glance at Joshua. His gaze was directed away from her. Stone ignored her as well. Eulie's chest constricted; her heart thudded in her ears. Dazed, she trailed behind the girl, Dory, caring not for the finely appointed rooms she passed. The girl led Eulie up a series of backstairs to a dark hallway. Dory opened a door at the end of a long hall. She stood back, allowing Eulie to enter.

"My name is Eulie. May I call you, Dory?" she asked, hoping to find a friend in this friendless place. The girl darted a look behind her, and with a shake of her head, shut the door on Eulie's words. The clicking of a door lock resounded in Eulie's ears. She twisted the doorknob, shocked into disbelief to find herself locked inside. Trapped, she was trapped. She brought a fist to her mouth to hold back the scream burning in her throat. Clutching the small bundle of muslin wrapped clothing to her chest, she sunk to the floor. She rocked back and forth. Tears streamed unchecked down her face. Heart-wrecked and spent, and with the hard floor beneath her, Eulie curled into a ball and slept the sleep of the truly hopeless.

Deep in the afternoon, a shaft of hot sunlight flickered over face, stirring her to wakefulness. She'd been dreaming of her island, of the hot sun, the warm water and azure blue sky. The children she'd tended, free of their chores, dashed into the waves. She heard the swish and crack of billhooks on cane stalks, smelled the sweet-bitter scent of the boiling house and heard the whisper of couples as they dashed into the shadowed forest. Oh, to be back there now, she'd kiss the sand and not mind the hot kitchen. Uncurling from her sleep, she stretched her legs. She was stiff all over. Her mouth and throat were dry and sore from her sobs. Getting to her feet, she took stock of her prison. One entire wall was a brace of windows. She went directly to them. Throwing the casements wide, she breathed in the sun-heated, salt laden air. The view of the bay and sea beyond stretched out before her. Birds twittered in the trees, their songs salving her broken spirit.

Below her was the town with its grid of streets, houses and businesses. With a long, slow breath, she turned her gaze to the room. The walls were milk-washed white and barren. A single bed with a wrought iron headboard was pushed up against one wall. By the bed was a chamber pot. A small chest with worn leather straps was at the foot of the bed. On the opposite wall, a wood chair was set next to a long, narrow table. On it was a basin and pitcher. Hoping against hope to find relief from her parched

191

throat, Eulie lifted the pitcher. It was full. She poured the water into the basin. It smelled dank, but she scooped up several mouthfuls with cupped hands. The room, temperate in the morning, had turned viciously hot in the afternoon. Eulie stripped down to her shift. Her stockings and shoes went next.

After folding her new clothes and the clothes from her small bundle into neat piles, she opened the chest. Inside were several worn, ragged shifts and a smock. Digging deeper, her eyes widened to find a tooled leather journal. It was held closed with a leather strap and buckle. A half-used taper and a set of wooden matches were at the bottom. Her fingers were on the buckle's latch when the lock on her door turned. She shoved the journal back into the trunk. Dory entered bearing a tray. Keeping her gaze adverted from Eulie, she set it on the table. With what might have been a nod in Eulie's direction, Dory left, locking the door behind her. Eulie, her stomach cleaving to her insides, ate every morsel of the beans and fatback, wiping the plate clean with a wedge of corn pone.

After her meal, and with hours before nightfall on her hands, Eulie looked to the trunk and the mysterious journal within. Opening it, her face fell to see that numerous pages had been ripped from the spine. The rest of the pages were blank. The graphite sticks Joshua had given her were hidden among her clothes. She knew better than to write on the pages. Others like her had been killed for being able to read and write. There was no law against the making of drawings. She took the foolscap Joshua had given her and folded it into quarters. The sketches she'd made of Ozee, Zina and the children she tucked in their as well.

With nothing but time on her hands, she made room for her clothes in the chest. That done, she opened the journal again.

The empty pages stared back at her. She pictured her island. She would draw all that she remembered. When the room grew dark, she put the journal away. The half-used taper was precious. She would save it for another time. She stood by the windows. Distant lights flickered like fireflies.

After a fitful night's sleep, Eulie woke at sunrise to find Dory placing a large basket by the table.

"Dis de cloze. Missus say do dis ta day. Uh git dem demarra maanin."

"Oh, yes, the clothes that need mending. Thank you, Dory." Eulie replied, her lips curving into a smile. The girl spoke the Geechee tongue. She and Joshua had met several Gullah natives during their stay at their lodgings.

Dory dipped her chin in Eulie's direction before shutting the door. The lock clicked into place. Eulie slipped from the bed drawn to the delicious scents coming from the plate Dory had left. The buttered, crispy hoecake was still warm and topped with figs and honey. The cook, whoever she was, knew her business.

After her breakfast, Eulie examined the basket of mending. It was full to the brim with all manner of children's clothing, adult smocks, shirts and the like. A spool of thread, two needles and a pair of darning scissors were in the basket. Eulie bit her lip. Was she expected to do all of this in one day, as Dory had said? Eulie clenched her hands. Caroline had the devil in her. Eulie was sorely tempted to ignore the mending and return to her drawings. Still, how poorly or well she performed here would surely fall back on Joshua. She would do the mending for Joshua. Her mistress be damned.

Eulie set to work. By early evening, nearing what she believed to be her supper time, Eulie folded the last smock and tucked it into the basket. Later, when Dory opened the door, Eulie held out the basket.

"Tell your mistress the work is done. All of it."

Dory's jaw dropped. The girl had no guile whatsoever. A quirk of a smile revealed a dimple in the girl's cheek. Giving Eulie a shy look, Dory handed her the supper plate and took the basket. The girl dipped into slight curtsey before shutting the door. Eulie waited for the click of the lock. It did not come. Eulie felt her shoulders relax. She could breathe again.

A week, then two went by. There was the mending, though days passed with nothing for her to do but work on her drawings. Late one night when sleep would not come, Eulie stood by the windows while the gibbous moon rose among the stars. A light tapping on her door, gave Eulie a start.

Dory cracked open the door. She beckoned Eulie.

"Ya kum wid me. Tek ya out ter waak." Dory put a finger to her mouth, "Shhh." The girl handed Eulie a shawl.

Eulie draped the shawl over her head and around her shoulders.

Dory nodded. "Dat gooly nuff." She took Eulie by the hand and led her down the darkened hallway through a narrow door and down a series of steps. She opened yet another door. The night air, cool and fresh, washed over Eulie.

"Eulie, ya stay wile wid fren. Eh hab wud wid ya."

"Friend?" Eulie did not know what to make of this.

"It's me, Eulie" Joshua stepped out of the dark.

"Joshua, oh, Joshua." Eulie, unable to restrain herself, wrapped her arms around him. He was not a demonstrative kind of man. Yet this time, he returned her embrace. He had word of Zina and her children, he told her. All were adjusting. They lived on a rice plantation some fifty miles away. When Joshua told her

Zina had a position as a house servant, Eulie wanted to weep with relief.

"Come," he said, "let's walk from the house. The kitchen garden is this way."

"What of Ozee and the others from our island. How do they fare?"

"Well enough, Eulie. The plantation work is hard, the hours long. Take a measure of comfort in that they are fed regularly." Before she could ask him for news of Ozee in particular, he pressed two books to her chest.

"Take care you keep these secreted away," he told her, his way of shutting down further discussion of Ozee and the others. "What of you, Eulie, how do you fare?"

"Well enough. I eat regularly." She fed his words back to him. "I do the mending and I draw some." She would not reveal she was sequestered both day and night. It would bring him pain.

"What are your needs?"

Eulie thought on that before answering. She had nothing to lose by asking. "I would like you to ask Stone if I may enhance the bare walls of my room."

"I see. You spend much of your time there, do you?"

"Yes, quite enough."

On his second visit, two weeks later, he brought her an answer from Stone.

"Aye, the Massa sees no issue with you enhancing your room. He has seen your hand with the tigons. I am to monitor your progress. Indeed, I have purchased brushes, linseed oil and bowls for you. Oil paint, unfortunately, is quite impossible."

Eulie looked to the garden. She'd been down several times on her own in the dead of night with only the moon to light her way. "I know my way around a garden, Joshua. I have all the colors I need right here, just as I did on our island."

"You are clever and industrious as ever, Eulie."

Before Joshua took leave of her, he placed his hands over hers. "You walk the path as foreseen by my grandmother, Eulie. She told me, and I no more than a boy, that one would be born to mark the words."

"Joshua, what does it mean, to mark the words?"

He shook his head. "She did not say, Eulie."

Twenty-Seven

∾ FINN RETURNS ∾

Eulie's path is mine now. I know what I must do.
~ Leela ~

Leela is washing the breakfast dishes when granny Vernell steps heavily into the kitchen.

"I'll be gone till late afternoon. I gotta do a fittin over at Miss Hodges place. There's last night's gumbo in the icebox fer lunch. Take a slice of that lemon pie, if you want. Best you keep the door locked while I'm gone."

Leela, whose head is as stubborn as her heart, offers up a shrug to her grandmother. Her granny might be past those hurtful words she said to Izzy and Ham, but Leela is still filled with the injustice of it. She burns with anger thinking about the damage done to Ham by those white boys.

Granny Vernell harrumphs. "We got to make amends, Leela. It's been long enough. We got enough to worry us without you bein on yer high horse, girl."

197

Leela figured that was as close to an apology as she would ever get from granny. It wasn't enough, not nearly. Still, her mom did have a lot to worry her, what with the divorce and that scheming Luanne Devlin and her father trying to take the house. Leela didn't want to add to it. Swallowing her pride, she answers without turning around. "Yes, Granny. I'll keep the door locked. Should I take the chicken out of the freezer for supper?

"That'd be fine. It'll thaw by suppertime. I'm headin out now."

"Bye, Granny." Leela tosses the words over her shoulder. It was the best she could muster. To her mind, considering her granny's offense, it was more than enough.

She finishes up in the kitchen, takes the chicken out of the freezer, covers it with a kitchen towel and heads up stairs. "Rats, the front door. I'd better lock it," she says to the air. Her granny will have a hissy-fit if she finds it unlocked.

Leela's setting the lock when a sharp rap on the door makes her jump.

Two more knocks come in succession. "Hello, anybody home?"

"Finn, is that you?"

"Yes. Is Leela home?"

She swings the door open. "Finn you're back! Without a second's hesitation, she throws her arms around his neck. He hugs her back. He is sticky-hot, smelling of Tide and boy. His arms are strong, his chest wider than she remembers. Her heart flutters and a sudden warmth in her stomach makes her breath hitch. She pulls away, stepping back from him. Heat has crawled up to her cheeks.

"W-when did you get back." She asks, hoping her face isn't a red as it feels.

"When did *you* start talking?" He stares at her, his mouth slightly agape.

"Awhile now, since the night of the riots. Um, please come in. You must be hot from walking all the way here. How about some cold lemonade?" She moves from the door.

He hesitates. "Is your mom or granny here?"

"No." She lifts her chin, arching a brow at him. "Are you coming or not?"

"I'm coming," he grins, taking a tentative step into the foyer.

Leela grins back. She heads to the kitchen. He's right behind her. She senses he's still grinning. She opens the icebox, gets out the pitcher. Placing it on the table, she sees him staring at her, a crooked smile has replaced his grin.

"What?"

"Um, Leela, I believe you've still got your jammies on."

Leela gasps, looks down at herself. Oh no, she's in her shorty nightgown, the one with the pink ruffles' granny made her. She straightens her spine, shrugs one shoulder.

"I'll be right back." With her face aflame, she makes herself walk slowly, regally, she thinks, out of the kitchen. Then races up the front stairs.

"I'll help myself to lemonade, if that's okay." Finn calls out. She hears him walk to the kitchen cabinets.

"Um, sure." She calls back. In her bedroom, she sheds her jammies, pulls on a pair of madras shorts and a yellow sleeveless blouse. In the bathroom, she splashes her face, rinses her mouth and pulls her hair back into a ponytail. At the last second, she swipes pink lip gloss over her lips. No need to pinch her cheeks. They have a high flush. Her eyes are shining, the violet in her irises, luminous.

199

She takes the back stairs to the kitchen. Finn has a glass full of lemonade and one for her on the table.

He stands up when she enters. "Wow, you look, um, nice, really nice. Hey, I didn't mean for you to run off and change. I just thought you'd want to know."

"Oh, I'd meant to change earlier. I just got busy after breakfast."

"How did it happen? I mean about you talking like now?" Finn stares at her lips, as if seeking the answer in their pink fullness. "The last time we were together you, ah, you weren't talking at all."

"It's a long story."

"I'm listening, Leela. I'd really like to know, if you don't mind telling me. I did spend two weeks learning sign language, after all."

"You didn't."

"Did!" Finn signs, *Please, tell me how you learned to talk.*"

"Finn, that's so good. I mean, really good."

He dips his head at her compliment. "All I did was get a book about sign language from the library. Taught myself."

"Thank you. That's the sweetest thing anyone has ever done for me." She leans over, presses a kiss on his cheek.

"Worth it," he grins.

She angles toward him, whispering, "Can you keep a secret?"

"If it's your secret, it's mine too. I promise." Finn crosses his heart.

Nervous, though excited to finally be sharing her adventure, Leela scoots her chair closer to his.

"I went to a gathering on the Fourth, right after you left me that afternoon. I'm sorry for not telling you. I was keeping a secret, so I couldn't."

"*The* Gathering, as in the piney woods with Granme´ Delia?"

"You know about it?"

"Sure, because my mom and dad know. They've been friends with Granme´ Delia and Ishmael forever. So, how did you know about it?"

"Well, it was Granme´ Delia who invited me through Ham and Izzy. She's a storyteller. She uses her hands, like I used to. There was this wonderful music and dancing and clapping and there was a church, an old, old church, Finn."

"Okay, sounds like a fun time, but what has that got to do with you suddenly speaking like, like you are right now?"

"It has to do with Granme´ Delia. She told us this beautiful story about a bird and when she was finished, she called me into her circle. She laid her hand on my chest, telling me it was past time or something like that. She said my voice was in my heart. And then she asked me to sing with them. I knew I couldn't, but to please her I opened my mouth and the words just came out and then I was singing," Leela's eyes shine at the memory. "Later, when I was signing to Izzy and Ham, they started laughing and held my hands. That's when I heard myself talking and talking. I started crying and they cried with me and then we were laughing."

"And you've been talking ever since?"

"Yep. I just talk and talk. Tired of it yet?"

"Nope, but if I do," Finn leans over, presses his lips against hers. They are as soft and warm as she remembered. A tingling feeling, warm, rises in her body.

"Oh," Leela pulls back, her fingers coming to her lips. "T-that was, I m-mean," Leela sputters.

"Sorry, I couldn't help myself."

"No, no, that was, um, nice. Really."

Finn takes her hands in his. "I have a secret for you too, Leela Hawkins. Can you keep it?"

"Cross my heart," Leela says softly.

"Granme´ Delia is a seer, you know. My mom and I have been to The Gathering several times."

Leela's eyes grow wide at this.

"Granme´ Delia told me that one day I would meet a girl who talked with her hands."

"What?"

"I know, kind of freaky, huh?"

"Maybe not so freaky." Leela's face takes on a glow. She thinks about Joshua, Eulie's friend and mentor. About how he and his grandmother had the *sight*.

"Why not so freaky?"

Taking a deep breath, Leela decides to confide in Finn, "I have another secret."

"Hmm, another secret, huh?"

"Yes, but it's a long story."

"I'm listening."

"I think I'd better I show you."

Twenty-Eight

❧ LEELA'S ROOM ❧

A secret shared is a sacred gift
~ Leela ~

"This secret of yours is upstairs in your room?" Finn waits at the bottom of the stairs. "What if your mom or granny Vernell comes home?"

"Oh, they won't be home for hours. And even if they should come home, unexpectedly, there's a secret way out to the back yard. Besides, you won't understand what I've been doing unless you see what I'm going to show you." Leela knows it's a huge transgression, scandalous to have a boy in her room. Even if it is Finn Connell.

"A secret way out, huh?" Finn looks behind him, shakes his head and follow's Leela up the curved stairway to a landing and more stairs, past a hallway and yet another set of stairs.

"Hey, is your room in the attic or something," he laughs, as he follows her down a narrow hallway.

"Ha, very funny. No, it's a room with lots of windows. Granny said it use to be a sewing room and then a school room like a hundred years ago. I picked it because of the view, but mostly because of the mural. You'll see," Leela says, opening her door. She's filled with a dawning sense of thrill and excitement. Finn will be the only one, besides Izzy and Ham, with whom she's been willing to share her secret. He'll understand what she wants to do. He will want to help. She's sure of it.

"Wow," Finn exclaims, heading straight for the bank of windows. That is some view. You can see the entire bay and glimpse the ocean from here. And the town, the pier and the wharfs. You can see nearly everything from here. It looks like a miniature town. "

"I know. I love the view. It's wonderful, but the mural is even better."

Shifting from the window, Finn follows her gaze. "No kidding, that's a big painting, like almost the entire wall."

"Isn't it just wonderful, so full of life."

"Yeah, the schooner is really done in detail. Who painted it?"

"That's the secret part. No one has ever known, until now. Leela goes to her box of tracing papers. She's hands him a sheet and a pencil. "And now, you'll know."

Finn looks down at what she's handed him. "Okay, so what's this?"

She takes the paper and pencil from him, putting them on the floor by the corner of the mural. Taking his hand, she places it on the spot where she'd found Eulie's name. "What do you feel beneath the paint?"

"Nothin, really, just maybe, I don't know, ridges?"

"Yes, that's right. Now, take the paper and the pencil. Remember when you were a kid in school, and you did tracings?"

"Yeah, once," he laughs, "I remember the girls loved doing it. Not so much the guys."

"Right," she laughs with him. "Rub the pencil gently on the paper over this spot. See what comes up."

He does as she directs and when the words show, he sits back on his heels.

"It says, I am Eulie. Okay, so who's that?"

"Look at what you've traced over."

"A girl in a field of tall grass?"

"That's Eulie in a field of sugar cane. It's the island of Martinique in about eighteen-forty something. She was a slave. My ancestor, Silas Stone, brought her here. He was a slaver. He built this house."

"No kidding, a slaver. Lots of people here had slaves back then. My mom said that back in the day the Stones were some of the richest people in Bateaux Bay. She said many of the prominent people here are related to the original Stones. The Claytons and the Hodges, the Delvin's, lots of 'em."

Leela' eyes grow wide. "I didn't know that. Does that mean I'm related to Darla?"

"Distant, very, very distant cousins, most likely. But yeah."

"Maybe I'll freak her out and tell her we're related. Oh, wait. Are *we* related?" Eulie's stomach twists uncomfortably at the possibility.

"Nope, I'm full Irish, O'Connell. When my grandparents came over from Ireland, they dropped the O."

"Good, that's good. I mean, good that we're not related."

"Okay, then. Eulie was a slave and is the artist. So, mystery solved, right?"

"Yes, but that's not all of it." Leela gets the binder filled with realms of lined paper and her stapled tracings. "I've traced over three hundred words, sentences really. Eulie has told her story inside the mural." Leela points to the sequences of Eulie's painting, explaining how each part of the mural relates to her story. "I have more to trace here. And still more at the church."

"You mean the church in the pines?"

"Uh huh. Do you remember the painting in the church? The one with the women and the flowers?"

'Yeah, I guess. I didn't pay much attention, though." Finn shrugs.

"There are words in that painting too. I've been sneaking out to trace those words. I've just started. If you'd want to, I'd be happy for your help."

You've been sneaking out? By yourself? In the woods, alone?"

"Mostly, but sometimes Ishmael is there. By the way, he's related to me. Did you know that?"

"But he's, I mean, he's colored."

"It's true, Finn. My grandpa, Sam Stone, had an affair with Monique, Granme Delia's daughter. Ishmael is her son. Granny Vernell hates Ishmael because of that."

"I, um, that is—are you sure?" Finn shakes his head in disbelief.

"Yes, my mom said so. I love Ishmael, Finn. He has the best heart. He's so brave. I admire him, the way he lives his life the best way he can." Leela's eyes go deep violet, sparking with streaks of gold.

"Hey, I didn't mean to question it. It's just a lot to take in, you know."

"That's okay. It is sort of shocker, I guess.

"Yeah, sort of." Finn takes Leela's hand. "Things happen, Leela. I'm glad you feel good about it."

206

Leela squeezes his hand before letting go. She holds up the binder of Eulie's words. "Finn, I think the reason Eulie painted the mural and put her story inside it was because she hoped someday someone would find her words. I think she wanted someone to write her story down, to tell people. That someone is me, Finn. I'm going to write her story and then I'm going to send it out into the world."

"What do you mean, *out into the world?*"

"Published, like in newspaper or magazine or even a book. People should know what it was like to be a slave. To be owned. To not have a choice about anything. To be whipped for the slightest offense. To be killed, to be thrown over the side of a ship, *alive*, Finn, alive. To have your child taken from your arms and sold away. People need to know these things, Finn."

"Leela," Finn shakes his head. "If you do this, if it does *go out into the world,* you won't be safe here. Bad things are happening, riots. Things like what happened to Ham."

"Finn, I meant to thank you for being there for Ham, for saving him. If you hadn't stopped those terrible boys..." Leela takes Finn's hand in hers. Were you hurt too?"

'Nah. Well, a few bruises," he shrugs. "The deputy sheriff drove up at the right time. Leela, listen to me. Those boys were ready to beat me the way they beat Ham. Just because you're a white girl, won't stop 'em. It's the Klan.

"I saw what happened in White Oaks. It was terrifying. I think I know the risks, Finn. Besides, I wouldn't put granny and my mom in danger. So, I've decided to use a pen name, a pseudonym. "

"Leela, it's the Klan you'd be messin' with. They'll find out. It doesn't matter what name you use."

"And maybe they won't. I've got to do this, Finn. I promised Eulie."

"What, a dead girl? You promised a dead girl, one whose been dead for over a hundred years. Seriously?"

"She's not dead to me, Finn. Look at the painting. Look at her, Finn. She was just my age, and yours."

"I am looking, okay. She's a mulatto. She's pretty with nice eyes, kind of like yours."

"I know, weird, huh. Maybe that's why I feel so close to her."

"Yeah, but that's no reason to go and get yourself mixed-up with the Klan."

"Finn, if you're so worried about the Klan, you don't need to help." Leela's voice has turned steely. Her violet eyes blaze. "I've done it by myself so far. And I'm going to write her story. I've shared my secret with you, and I'd appreciate it if you kept it to yourself. A secret is a sacred thing, Finn."

"I won't tell anyone, I promise. Listen to me, Leela. People, the wrong people will find out. Darla has it in for you. Her mom hates your mom. It's a small town, Leela. Word gets around fast. I want to help, I do, but I can't put *my* family in danger. My parents care about Granme´ Delia and the church. Going to a gathering now and then raises eyebrows, but that's all. It's different for you."

"Why is it different for me?" Leela's cheeks have grown hot.

Finn pauses, clears his throat. "Well, um, it's like this, Leela, your mom, she was born here. Your people are from here, but you're from up North. Folks think of you as a Yankee, and believe me, they don't cotton to Yanks. They don't like you mixing with the coloreds."

"So, going to the church, being a Yank and friendly with Ham and Izzy have put me on some sort of watchlist?"

"Well, you *have* drawn attention to yourself."

"Oh, well in that case, I don't want to put you or your family in danger. So, consider yourself off the hook. For your sake, you shouldn't be seen in my company." Leela's words are frigid, though her chest burns hot.

"Leela, now hold on a minute. I-I didn't mean…"

"Shhh…listen, did you hear that? Uh oh, granny must be back. Come on, you better follow me." Leela slips off her sneakers and gets to her feet. She motions for him to do the same. With shoes in hand, they sneak down the hall. When she opens the door that looks like a closet door, Finn whispers, "A secret door?"

She nods, putting her fingers to his lips, "Shh."

Finn follows her down the crooked steps to the backyard.

"Leela, listen…"

"No, Finn. Just go." She points to the alleyway, turns on her heel, goes to the door and slips inside.

Back in her room, hot tears spill down her cheeks. She presses her forehead to the mural. I will write your story, Eulie, I promise."

Twenty-Nine

I am fouled by a beast
~ Eulie ~

Eulie was etching a word on the wall when Dory rapped lightly on the door. Eulie slipped the pen knife, one of several Joshua had given her, into the hidden pocket of her smock. Over the past months, the two girls had become fast friends. Dory was fascinated with the sketching and the painting, although she was unaware of the words Eulie marked. It was better, Eulie decided, for her not to know. In any case, Dory could not read. Few Negras did. To be found literate was often a death sentence. The markings were nearly invisible against the white-washed walls Eulie would soon paint over. Even so, Eulie stepped away, going to greet the girl who held two jars in her hands.

"Good morning, Dory. Oh, you've brought me linseed oil and vinegar. Thank you. I was almost out of both.

211

Dory pointed to the mural, "Eulie, dis pooty"

"I'm pleased you think it's pretty."

Eulie took the linseed oil and vinegar to the table. Dory had supplied Eulie with a castoff pestle and stone bowl for crushing the flowers, leaves and berries Eulie used to make the paints. Once crushed and dried, Eulie mixed the powders with vinegar first then with linseed or poppy seed oils. The final step was to mix the paints with egg whites to bind the paint to the surface. On the island, she'd sketched her drawings with charred sticks. Now, with graphite sticks from Joshua, she was able to draw precisely onto the walls. On the island, she'd used urine to fix the dye colors to the cloth. In this new land as well, nature provided most of the materials she required.

Near the same age, Eulie and Dory became more than friends. Dory shared the latest kitchen gossip, whispering things Eulie would not otherwise know. Dory called her, *titter,* which meant, sister. Because of Dory, Eulie went to church with the others on Sunday mornings. She'd told Joshua and he in turn made a request to Silas. He'd agreed, so long as Eulie used the servant stairs so as not to be seen by Caroline. The church was deep in the woods; it was little more than a wooden structure with rough-hewn benches. After the sermon by a young, handsome preacher, dancing and singing commenced. Many of the church goers Eulie came to know well. While others passed through, quietly and nameless. There was an unspoken agreement among the parishioners to never speak of them, except as ghosts. These *ghosts* were runaway slaves on their way North.

At the end of each service, the parishioners gathered. Holding hands, they chanted the names of children. Naila, Mina, Omari, Boni, Farai, Asha, Zain, Uma. The names went on and on, so many

212

Eulie lost count. These were the lost children, those sold away from their mothers. Eulie had witnessed this before on her island and in Savannah. Each time, Eulie felt chills along her spine as their names filled the air. Their loss was a dark shroud upon her soul. She would mark their names, praying their souls would meet their mothers' in heaven.

Between Eulie's work on the mural, Dory's friendship and Sunday church was how Eulie endured her isolation. Thoughts of becoming a *ghost* herself entered Eulie's mind, though she wasn't prepared to leave, not yet. Joshua's infrequent visits kept her abreast of Zina, the children and Ozee.

Dory, who owned a large part of Eulie's heart now, was a magpie of whispered secrets. She knew the comings and goings of the household, especially that of her mistress, Caroline. Caroline garnered no respect from those who served her. *Dat ooman*, as Dory called her, was *biggity*. Caroline preened for the gentlemen callers. One morning, Dory came bearing worrisome news. Massa Stone's brother, Seamus Stone, was now in residence.

"Lawd, Massa's bredder, eh ebil dis buckra man." Dory shook her head, crossing herself.

That Dory believed Stone's brother to be an evil white man, Eulie had little doubt. She'd seen what evil white men, bekes, had perpetrated on her kind. Eulie had no worry for herself, isolated as she was. She worried though for Dory, who was comely with her big brown eyes and sweet expression.

"Uh bed wid dem chirren enn nusry," Dory told Eulie. "Eh ain git ter me."

Eulie breathed a sigh of relief, knowing Dory would be safe.

With little need to worry about her own safety, Eulie resumed her nightly forays into the gardens. Deep in the night, when the

house quieted, when the last taper was snuffed, and all had retired to their beds, Eulie would go down the hidden stairs to the
gardens. The moon and the stars lit the dark. Here, she was free
to twirl, arms wide, skirts billowing around her legs. She'd slip
the shawl from her head, lift her face to the moon, glorifying in
its bright wonder. This elusive taste of freedom was heady. She
wanted more, much more. She thought of Ozee. At fifteen she
was a woman, having bled before she'd left the island. He had
held her gaze, had come to see her every evening on the island.
They had never even touched, but she saw passion in his eyes.
He wanted her, and she him. She palmed the bird he'd carved
for her. She kept it on a leather cord she wore around her neck
and tucked beneath her shift. She dreamt of them running away
together. Others had done so, running for freedom. With this
dream in her mind, she feared nothing and hoped for everything.
Until that night.

That night, the clouds shifted, swathing the moon from time
to time. Stars dipped here and there, blinking on and off. She
stopped to pull at the broad-leafed beets and the tall shoots of
carrots. Bushes of new huckleberries and elderberries drew her
with their sweet-sour scents. Sunflowers bordered much of the
garden; she clipped a few heads, needing their bright yellows and
dark seeds for her paints. What she would not use immediately
she would dry for later use.

That night, the gardenias were in full bloom, their petals
showing bright white against the dark. Their heady fragrance
perfumed the garden. The snap of a twig caused Eulie to pause,
her ears pricked. She was used to the small rodents, rabbits and
such that dug under the fence for a nibble of the greens growing
in abundance. She'd seen a few dark shadows from time to time,

knowing it was one or two of the field hands digging for turnips to add to their larders. Even so, *that night* her neck prickled. She had an unaccountable urge to get back to the safety of her room. Her woven basket was nearly filled. She took a moment to gather a handful of gardenias to sweeten her room. She was reaching over to pick a handful of the white petals when a beefy hand slammed against her face, covering her mouth. The overwhelming stench of alcohol and unwashed body brought bile to her throat. Briefly stunned, she kicked blindly at the man who held her in an iron grip. Suddenly, breath was knocked out of her by a blow to her chest. She crumpled to the damp earth. Dazed, she felt her skirts shoved over her thighs. Wild in her terror, Eulie bit his hand savagely. A blow to her head knocked her senseless.

When she woke, dawn was breaking, the sky threaded with slivers of pink and gold. She was curled on her side, her skirts bunched around her hips. A wetness tinged with blood seeped along her inner thighs. Her entire body ached. Fear of being discovered brought her to her knees. A white man lay snoring beside her. She fisted her mouth to keep from screaming. At first glance, she thought it was Stone, but this man was young, much younger than Silas. Both men had reddish-brown hair. This was his brother, Seamus.

Her first instinct was to run and keep running. She would go to the church, hide there. She would become a ghost and go North. She tripped over her basket, spreading the fruit of her labor over the damp ground. Joshua came to her mind, then Dory. There was the mural, unfinished. Her inscribed words, the marks Joshua's grandmother had foreseen years ago, incomplete. She was not prepared. It was not yet time to leave.

Eulie, her body shaking uncontrollably, limped over to her basket. She scooped the plants into her basket. She was dazed and wobbly from the blow to her head. She straightened and took a deep breath. The shock of pain in her chest nearly brought her to fainting. With unsteady feet, she made her way to the back porch and the door to the backstairs. Each step up the stairways brought more pain and nausea.

Closing her bedroom door, she set the basket down. She stayed conscious long enough to reach her bed.

Eulie woke to a cool cloth being applied to her face. Dory was bent over her. She was singing softly, the way one soothes a baby. A sheet was pulled up to Eulie's chin. She was naked beneath it. She was cool and clean.

"Dat ebil bredder, eh git ter hoona, Eulie. Lawd, uh skade offer eh." Dory's eyes were red and weepy.

"Yes, he got to me, Dory. You must not tell Joshua or anyone. I shouldn't have been out to the garden knowing he was here. I won't go there again until you tell me he's gone. I promise."

During the ensuing weeks, Eulie's physical wounds healed. Yet her body stiffened at the slightest noise. It wasn't until Dory told her Stone's brother was gone that Eulie slept the night through. During the days, Eulie worked feverishly on the painting. Her words, the inscriptions, she did only late at night by moonlight. No one, except Joshua, knew Eulie was educated, that she was able to read and write. Dory did not know, nor would Eulie tell her. It was dangerous for a slave to even be aware of such a thing.

Several weeks after the assault, Eulie woke in the mornings with nausea. She ate ravenously, though much of the food she ate wouldn't stay down. Dory began to eye her speculatively.

216

One day, three months later, a flutter in her abdomen brought her upright. Eulie could no longer deny what she had come to suspect. She was with child. Dread seeped through every part of her body. At the very least, she would be whipped. This she would endure without hesitation, should she'd be allowed to keep her babe. More likely, she would be sent away after giving birth. And the child? This child brought into the world by a man's horrific deed would be taken from her, sold as if the babe's value equated the animals in the fields. Eulie would never be privy to the whereabouts of her child, or even if the child had survived the world it had been forced to enter.

Her isolation was now her salvation, at least until the child was born. For the moment, time was on her side. She had months to devise a plan. She would become a *ghost* like the others. Head North to the free states with her babe hitched to her side.

One morning, weeks later, Dory set down Eulie's breakfast and made a pronouncement.

"Missus Caroline, dat ooman, eh ketch wid bebee. Massa Stone, eh tek wid isself."

"Caroline is with child?" Eulie's eyes widened. She'd no doubt Stone was well pleased with himself. Joshua had mentioned more than once how desperate Stone was for a son, if indeed, Caroline produced a son. For without a male heir, his holdings would pass to his brother. It was no matter to her. She would be long gone. Her own child would be born in a free State.

While Eulie attacked her breakfast with relish—she was always hungry these days, Dory stood by with her hands on her hips. "Eulie, wuh hoona gwine ter do?"

217

Eulie blinked. Swallowed. Took another bite of her scrambled eggs, "I'm going to eat my breakfast and then I'm going to paint, unless Caroline has more mending." Eulie often wondered if Caroline tore her clothing on purpose. Dat ooman, in Dory's Geechee language, was ebil.

Dory shook her head, "Eulie ketch wid bebee luk Missus Caroline."

Eulie choked down her eggs. There was no sense denying it, not to Dory.

"When did you know?"

"Trute be. Uh hab knod fer wile.

"I will have to leave Dory, before the babe is born."

Thirty

~ THE BIG WHITE CADILLAC ~

Grits are for chicken, not people
~ Sheldon (Skeet) Stone ~

From her bedroom window, Leela watches the big white Cadillac grind to a stop over the sand and oyster shell drive. It must be them she figures because nobody in Bateaux Bay drives a white Cadillac. She's dragged her hair into a ponytail. Loose curls have found their way to her forehead. The late July heat had become so stifling, so humid that even breathing took effort. Leela holds out a handful of red berries to the scarlet-marked blackbird who's perched on a branch of the live oak by the roof line. She'd name him Rogue because of the way he chases off the other birds who come to her window. She mimics his call note, *kong-la-ree-o-ka-lee*. He cocks his head, spreads his wings, showing off his scarlet fielding markings before winging to her window. Leela scatters the berries along the sill. Eyeing her, he flits, perching there. Slowly, he makes his way to the berries. His fear of her lessens by the day.

Her bedroom floor absorbs the jarring ring of the downstairs phone. Leela goes to her door, cracking it open to hear her mom's muffled reply to the caller. She can tell by her mom's placating tone it's Finn on the line. He'd been calling every day since the day he'd been to her room. She'd told her mom she wasn't interested in talking to him. When her mom asked why, Leela had shrugged saying, she didn't want to talk to anyone. Finn's repeated calls softened the hard edges around her heart, though it didn't change her mind. She'd made clear her intention and so had he. She's done her best to put thoughts of him from her mind because thinking of him made her heart hurt.

When Leela goes back to the window, Rogue is gone. She watches as the driver's side door swings open. A man comes out in piecemeal, long legs first, then the torso and finally the head. The coppery-brown hair marks him as a Stone. He stretches to his full length. He's even taller than Brick, but thin and angular. Speaking rapidly, he gestures to someone in the front seat of the car. The man's agitation is obvious. He stomps over to the passenger side. The man bangs on the window until whoever is in there opens the door. He drags out a boy. The kid is a Stone, can't miss that hair even with the buzz cut. Leela puts his age to a couple of years younger than she is. He wears turtle shell glasses, a plaid shirt and long khaki pants. Leela has heard their names. Both her mother and granny Vernell have waited anxiously for their arrival. Her mom's cousin, Sebastian Stone, is here to help with legal stuff about the taxes and the divorce. The man is her uncle, which, Leela figures, makes the boy her cousin. She likes the idea of having a cousin. Up until a week ago, she didn't even know she had one.

"Come on down, Leela. They're here." Granny's voice booms up the stairs.

"I'm comin, Granny." Leela hollers back. The frilly, pink dress her granny had made is tossed on the bed. Leela shakes her head. There's no way she's wearing it. She's made up a story about how it's too small for her. Instead, Leela wears a plain navy-blue skirt and white blouse with a Peter Pan collar. Slipping on her sandals, she heads downstairs.

The newcomers are standing in the receiving hall when Leela gets downstairs. Her mom is hugging the man. The boy, seen up close, is skinny with a mass of freckles on an otherwise pale face. Granny has her arms around his stiff body. The boy grimaces at the unwelcomed contact.

Her mom, taking Leela by the hand, introduces her to the newcomers. "This is my cousin, Sebastian. And this is Sheldon, Sebastian's son."

"I go by Skeet," the boy states, in a flat drawl.

"Yes, of course. I remember now. "So glad to see you, Skeet. It's been so many years. Why, you were just a little guy then. Skeet, this is my daughter, Leela."

Leela moves forward, thrusting out a hand. "Hi, Skeet. Nice to meet you."

Skeet offers up a pale hand that is surprisingly firm. "Uh huh." He darts a look to his dad, who arches a brow at him. "Um, nice to meet you too." He quickly drops her hand.

"Leela," Sebastian thrusts out his hand, "Call me, Bass. Everyone does."

"Y'all come on, I got breakfast waitin in the kitchen, grits, bacon, scrambled eggs and fried cornbread. Granny motions for them to follow her.

"I don't eat grits. That's chicken food." Skeet states, twisting his mouth in distaste."

"Skeeter," Vernell glowers at him. "I haven't seen you since you were in short pants, but you'll eat what I put on the table or go hungry."

"It's Skeet. And I'm not hungry anyways." He lifts one shoulder in a shrug.

"Leela, ah, why don't you show *Skeet* around the house and let him decide which bedroom he'd like," her mom says, giving Leela an encouraging nod.

"I don't wanna to stay here, Dad. Why do you have to go away with Melinda?" Skeet demands.

"Skeet, we've talked about this before. Mellie and I need some time—alone. It's only for the rest of the summer."

"If mom were here..."

"She's not, son." Sebastian's voice lowers. "She'd want you to have a stepmom. Now, you go on with your cousin." He looks over to Leela. "I bet there's lots of things to do around here, isn't that right, Leela?"

Leela, taken aback by the idea of this boy staying here for the rest of summer, offers up an obliging smile. Her mom hadn't said a word about him staying here. "Yep, lots and lots of things to do," she arches a questioning brow toward her mom. Her mom had better have some answers for her.

Leela's right hand, strong and supple from all the tracings, latches onto the boy's arm. "This way, Skeet," she says kindly enough, though she'd really like to set him straight for being a spoiled brat. He looks down at his arm making an 'ow' noise.

"Go on now, son. I'll get your suitcase and travel bag from the trunk."

Leela half tugs, half drags Skeet to the staircase. "Watch your step on the way up. It's a long way down to the floor, Skeet."

She says, sweetly. He flashes a startled look at her which makes her giggle. Spots of high color bloom on his cheeks.

"Let go," he says, giving her a dark look.

She lets go, and slowly he follows. The looming staircase, arched in a fine curve, wobbles as their feet hit the treads. Leela's gotten used to the tremble. A hundred years of use had taken a toll. When they reach the first landing, Skeet's face is back to being pale, or a bit paler.

"There are five bedrooms on this floor," she tells him. "My mom has the last bedroom on the right down this hallway. I have the only bedroom on the third floor, the one by the attic. There's a bathroom that way," she points to it, wondering how her mom will like sharing her bathroom with this kid. She has her own bathroom which was a storeroom back at the turn of the century, when indoor plumbing was put in. Granny had said it was put there for a live-in housekeeper. "Follow me, Skeet, I'll show you."

After they've been into several bedrooms, she glances at him. He hasn't asked a single question or shown the slightest interest. His shoulders droop. His bottom lip trembles. She shouldn't have teased him. The memory of her first day here comes back to her. She'd been sad too. She'd felt misplaced. Her heart goes out to Skeet. It hadn't been said out right, but from what Sebastian inferred, it was obvious Skeet's mom had passed away. And now having to share his dad with a new mom, well, that had to be hard.

"Hey, Skeet, why don't we find your bedroom later. I have a secret. You can't tell anyone, not even your dad. Interested?"

Skeet gives her a sideways glare. "What kind of secret?"

"I can't tell you unless you swear a promise." She glares back at him, her arms crossed.

"Okay. Fine. I'll swear, but it better be a real secret."

"Oh, it is. Cross your heart and hope to die you'll never tell anyone, and I mean anyone about what I'm going to show you."

His eyes widen at the word, die.

"Well, not die, really. Just promise. Here, hold out your pinky. It's just as binding."

He rolls his eyes at this as he holds out a pinky. She curls her pinky around his.

"Repeat after me," she tells him. "I Skeet Stone promise to never tell anyone what I am about to see."

"Never, ever?"

"Well, never unless I give you permission. Okay?"

"Okay." Skeet repeats the promise. She can tell by the way he's looking at her, and the way he repeats the promise that he means every word. There's something so sad, so solemn about this kid. If she lost her mom, she figures she'd be solemn too.

When they get to her room, he ignores the view from the window, going straight to the mural. He stands there, mouth agape, staring at it, a look of reverence reflected in his eyes. His hands move over the painting, not touching, but following the brush strokes with his fingers. "The colors, the paint, it's, it's luminous. I've never—wait," he brings his nose to it, sniffing. It's not oil paint, the kind you buy at an art store. It's been done the old way, the way the old masters did it with natural things. They used semiprecious stones, plants, dirt and other organic material. He jerks his head in her direction, his look one of wonder. "Who, who did this? Who is the artist?"

Leela's eyes widen at his words, his knowledge of painting. She holds up her hands, "The artist is part of the promise, okay?"

"Yes. The promise." Skeet repeats. His face is flushed, his breathing rapid.

"Her name is Eulie. She was a slave here a hundred years ago."

"A slave? How do you know? It isn't signed." He bends to examine the painting again.

"Oh, it's there, Skeet. It's just hidden."

"Hidden?"

"It was against the law back then for a slave to learn to read and write. By the way, how come you know so much about paint, about art?" Leela's jaw had dropped while listening and watching how he responded to the mural. There's more to this boy than she figured.

Skeet looks down at his hands, kneading them. "I sort of study art. And, um, I sort of paint, and draw things, stuff like that. My dad's not too keen on it. He wants me to do sports, be athletic ya know, football." His mouth turns down.

"I think art is great, Skeet. I'm a writer, well, I'm going to be one." And it comes to her right then, that writing will be her life. A journalist for sure, maybe even a novelist. And she's going to start with Eulie's story. She sizes up Skeet. As an artist, he will understand Eulie.

"Here's the real secret, Skeet, and it's part of the promise. You have to double swear never to tell, unless I say you can, okay?"

"I double, double swear." Skeet's eyes spark with excitement.

She brings out the tracing paper and a pencil. "You can discover her name for yourself." Leela demonstrates. Pointing to the spot where Eulie stands, she says, "Start here."

Skeet bends to the task like a scientist. He's careful to not tear the paper. When Eulie's name appears," he stumbles back. "Eulie," he breathes out her name. Did she write anything else?"

"Lots more," Leela grins.

By the time Skeet has traced a dozen words, he's flushed with the intensity of an archaeologist who has just discovered an ancient tomb. "There's never been anything like this, not that I know of and I'm keen on art history."

"Well," she offers up a sly smile, feeling a bit like the enigmatic Mona Lisa. "I'm almost done with this painting, but there's another painting I've just started on. Wanna help?"

Skeet's smile lights up his face. He's a whole different boy than the one she first met.

When they finally make it downstairs, Skeet has picked out a bedroom, one with good light and a large desk. They go into the kitchen, chattering like the best of friends.

"Son," Bass stands, "I've been thinking, maybe this trip with Mellie can wait."

"No, Dad. This place is great. Where's my stuff. I need to get settled in my room. You and Mellie have a nice time. Don't worry about me, okay."

"Skeet, ah, you sure?"

"Yep. I'm sure." Skeet goes to Vernell, offering her a crooked smile. "I'm sorry about the grits thing, Miss Vernell. I just don't like the taste of them.

"You ain't never tasted mine, Skeet. And you best call me Nana."

Thirty-One

~~ BUDS OF THE FLOWERS ~~

What happened to these children?
~ Leela ~

The next day, Sable and Sebastian leave for the courthouse to pay the taxes. Granny Vernell is busy at her sewing machine. Leela and Skeet slip quietly down the hallway to what she has dubbed, *Eulie's Door* because Eulie had described it in the mural.

"You can't tell your daddy about the door, Skeet. It's our secret now. Granny Vernell and my mom have probably forgotten it's even here. I think it was used back in the old days by the servants who were probably slaves at the time. And Eulie told about it in her mural. Anyway, this is the way I leave the house without my mom or granny knowing."

"Um, why do you have to sneak out?" Skeet asks, following her down the rickety stairs.

"Well, a few weeks back there was a riot and a curfew, so my mom didn't want me out alone. She still doesn't."

"I've never snuck out before."

"I never had either. But it's the only way. They'd never let us go if they knew where we were going." Leela shifts the tote bag to her shoulder, inside are her tracing papers and pencils.

When they get outside, Leela takes his hand, "Come on, run." She takes off running, pulling him behind her. When they get to the alleyway, she slows down, dropping his hand.

"Skeet, can you run fast, I mean really fast if you need to? Like if a rabid dog was chasing you?"

"Rabid dog?" Skeet darts a look behind him.

"No, not a dog." Leela shakes her head. "Boys, Skeet, a pack of mean boys. They chased me the other day. So, if I say run, don't look back. Just run as fast as you can."

"I'm not afraid of boys, Leela. I know Karate. My dad made me take lessons." Skeet puffs out his chest.

"That's, um, surprising, but good to know. Still, there are lots of them and only two of us. So, if I say, run, just do it, okay?"

"Okay."

She sets a fast pace, past more alleys and old buildings and the four-lane highway. When they get to the edge of the piney forest, Skeets pulls up.

"Are, are we going in there, the woods, I mean?" Skeet eyes the woods as if he's about to step into the Amazon jungle.

"Uh huh. The church is not far now. It's easy. I've come by myself a several times.

Leela makes to take his hand again. He shakes her off.

"I'm not afraid, if that's what you're thinking."

"Didn't think you were."

"Good, cause I'm not."

The footpath is narrow, bordered by tall pines and thick

underbrush. Skeet follows so close she can hear his nervous breaths. The pines give shade from the sun. It's cool and dark and eerily quiet. Before long, the trees thin and the gathering place comes into view.

"We're here, Skeet," Leela heads straight to the church, bounding up the short rise of steps.

"This is the church? Doesn't look like one. Looks like a big old wooden shack, Leela."

"It is old, Skeet. It's from the slave days," she says, unlocking the door.

"Oh."

When they step inside, the interior is bathed in shadows. Almost. Through a high, narrow window, a shaft of sunlight falls directly onto the painting, setting it aglow. Leela wonders if the window was placed there on purpose to light the painting. Skeet looks just as awestruck as he did when he first saw the mural. He heads down the short, narrow aisle toward the alter. The painting is situated on the wall directly behind and above the alter. It's a rectangle, narrow and long, about two feet by three feet.

"It looks so fresh as if it were painted yesterday." Skeet marvels.

Leela sets her tote down. "I know, kind of weird, isn't it? Eulie had a way with paints."

"I want to figure out how she did it. I've read the old masters used a mixture of different things, like salt and vinegar to set the paint. It's sort of what people used to do to make dye." Skeet reverently touches a corner of the painting. "It's painted on wood, isn't it?"

"We don't have much time, Skeet." She hands him several sheets of tracing paper and a sharpened pencil."

Together, they drag a bench beneath the painting. It wobbles slightly beneath their feet.

"Going slowly, delicately, they work for about an hour. Each going through several sheets of tracing papers.

"Look," Skeet whispers, "this says…"

"Let's look at the words later. We need to leave. Now. My mom and your dad will be looking for us. Hopefully, granny hasn't called us down for lunch."

Leela locks the door behind them. They take off for the trail on swift feet.

By the time they get to the backdoor porch and hidden stairs, they're breathing heavy and drenched with sweat from the heat. They pull off their shoes, treading softly down the hallway. The house is quiet except for the hum of the sewing machine.

"Whew," Leela breathes out a sigh of relief. "We made it."

They part ways. Skeet going to his room to change into what he had on at breakfast. Leela splashes her face, combs her hair before slipping on fresh shorts and a blouse.

He raps on her door, jiggles the doorknob. "It's me," he whispers.

She locks the door after him, saying, "Now, let's see what we have."

Together they lay the papers out, matching up words and sentences.

Leela, familiar with the style of Eulie's writing, reads Eulie's words.

The flowers of our wombs have been ripped from our arms. We weep for the lost. One day those who have stolen our flowers will be known. May God have mercy on their souls. There is truth in the stars. I Eulie mark these words as foretold by Imani, grandmother of Joshua.

"I don't understand, Leela. What does she mean by flowers and um, wombs?"

"She's talking about babies. The flowers are babies. She means that their children were taken and sold away. You need to read all the tracings I've made from the mural. You'll understand what she means. What puzzles me is what she wrote about the truth being in the stars. How do we find the truth in the stars?" Leela blows out a long, tired sigh.

"Well, what about the stars in the ceiling."

"What are you talking about? What stars, what ceiling?"

"Don't you ever bother to look up? Wood cuts shaped like stars are up on the ceiling of the church.

"Skeet," she throws her arms around him. Did anyone ever tell you you're a genius?"

Thirty-Two

❧ A FIRE IN THE SKY ❧

People cling stubbornly to their hate
~ Leela ~

"Let's go, Skeet. Ishmael will be meeting us at the church." Leela, her voice whisper soft, stands by his bedroom door. Skeet is at his desk which is littered with bits of flowers and plants. Several canning jars, murky with his efforts to replicate Eulie's paint, are lined up along his windowsills.

"Okay, okay." Skeet wipes his hands down his shirt leaving a trail of equally murky smudges. Leela puts a finger to her lips, "Hush." She points to her bare feet. Her sneakers dangle from her other hand. Her tote bag is slung over her shoulder. Skeet slips off his sneakers, grabs his Brownie camera, slings the lanyard around his neck and pads to his door, closing it softly behind him. The whir of granny Vernell's sewing machine covers their footfalls.

Silent as thieves, they are through the secret door, down the crooked steps and out the back porch. The morning sky is a bright blue. A few fluffy clouds float lazily above them. They jog down the alleys and side streets and empty lots. When they get to the four-lane highway, they stop. A few cars pass by.

Leela scans the surrounding streets and buildings. "Looks okay, follow me." They race over the highway and into the piney woods. Jogging down the path with Leela in the lead, she slows to a stop. "Hey, did you hear that?"

"Hear what?" Skeet asks, coming to a stop behind her.

"I dunno, thought I heard voices."

Skeet keens his ears. The woods are silent. No bird song, no rustle of critters. "I don't hear anything," he says under his breath.

"That's what bothers me, Skeet. It's too quiet."

"We're the ones making noise, Leela. We've scared the critters."

"Maybe." Leela jogs ahead.

When they reach the clearing and the church, Leela scans the area. "Seems okay." Leela unlocks the church's door. As usual, it's gloomy, except for the lone window that lights the alter and the painting.

"There is enough light coming through the door, I think. I'll take some shots of the stars." Skeet snaps one photo before moving around to get better light."

"You keep taking pictures, Skeet, I'll go get the ladder from the garden shed. Ishmael will be here soon. He wants to meet you. When he gets here, don't stare, okay. He's, um, kind of handicapped like I told you, but he's so smart. He's a wonderful gardener."

"Yep, got it. Don't stare."

When she gets back, lugging the ladder, Skeet is taking pictures of the flower painting. Leela sets the ladder in the middle of the nave. "Let's start here, Skeet. You hold the ladder.

"Yes, boss," he smirks.

"Ishmael says the stars are fastened with hooks. This should be easy." Leela says, going up the ladder which wobbles some. She's forced to stand on tiptoe to reach the stars. She hands down the first star. Skeet slips it into the tote bag slung over his shoulder.

Within a short time, the stars, thirteen in all, are down. Of the purple stars, only one had been painted white. Leela runs her fingers over both sides. Her face lights up when she feels faint markings beneath the paint. *Eulie, what have you written here for me?*

Leela, her arms around the ladder, is ready to return it to the shed when Ishmael calls out to her. "Lee-la. G-g-got s-surprise f-for y-you." Ishmael's excitement shines in his eyes. Behind him stand Izzy and Ham.

"Izzy, Ham," Leela cries out. She drops the ladder to the floor and rushes over to them. She wraps both in a hug.

"Careful," Ham says, lifting a hand to protect the arm that's in a sling.

"Oh, oh, sorry. I'm just so happy to see you. Both of you." Tears well in her eyes.

Izzy returns Leela's hug "I'm sorry I haven't returned your calls, Leela. I wasn't ready to talk, not to anyone. Ishmael's been telling us about what you've been doing. Says you're gonna tell Eulie's story to the world. Can you really get it published?"

"Yes, not sure when, but I will get it published someday." Leela squeezes Izzy's hands.

Ham shifts his gaze to Skeet. "So, who is this young man?"

"I'm Skeet Stone, Leela's cousin. Nice to meet you." Skeet thrusts out his hand. Ham smiles, shakes it. "You too," Skeet thrusts his hand toward Ishmael.

"N-nice to m-m-meet you, S-skeet." Ishmael pumps Skeet's hand.

Suddenly, Finn rushes in. "Y'all got company. It's Darla and her gang. Izzy, Ham, get back where they can't see you."

"Finn what are you doing here?" Leela steps forward, her lips are pressed in a thin line, though her heart skips a beat at the sight of him.

"Miss Ina overheard Darla's group talking at the Grille. Said they were up to something. Besides, there's trouble going on at the courthouse. She called Granme´ Delia to find out if Ishmael was at the church. Miss Ina called my house. So here I am. I followed them. They're lookin' for trouble, Leela."

"We're not afraid, Finn." Ham says through clenched teeth. Izzy balls her hands into fists.

"Didn't think you were. Listen, I'm gonna talk to them, see what's up. The rest of you stay back."

"I'm coming with you, Finn. Skeet, stay with Izzy and Ham." Leela moves to the door.

"Ah, not a good idea." Finn holds up his hands to keep her back. "Darla's beef is with you. Look, they out number us, okay. I'm going to try and get them to leave." Finn stands on the first step. Leela and the others group behind him at the door. They jump back when Darla yells, "We know the niggers are in there, Finn. Send them out and that nigger lover too."

The gang of boys behind Darla yell, "Send the niggers out, send niggers out." Their fists pump the air.

Ishmael grabs Finn, tugging him inside. He swings the door closed and drops down a bar and secures the latch.

"N-no, s-stay inside. T-they g-get tired. G-go h-home. W-we w-wait." He stands sentinel in front of the door.

"They, they have a can of gasoline, Leela," Skeet mutters so softly, she almost didn't hear him.

"What did you say?"

"Gas-gasoline. I saw it next to that blonde girl."

"They wouldn't dare. Not here, not at the church." Leela folds her arms against her chest.

Izzy and Ham share a glance, saying in unison, "Yes, they would."

"No, I'll go out. Darla's mad at me. I'll reason with her." Leela heads toward the door. Finn blocks her path, "No. It won't do any good. Just listen to them."

"Ah, you guys, I-I think I smell smoke." Skeet's eyes are round as saucers behind his glasses.

"What the hell," Finn curses.

"W-we g-go n-now. C-come." Ishmael lumbers to the alter, "H-help me p-push. T-this w-way out."

Leela and Finn share a glance. Ishmael's meaning clear; they rush over to the alter.

"I'd heard about an old tunnel, but I thought it was just talk." Ham says, his voice rising in wonder. My granny told us runaway slaves hid here before going to the underground railway. I didn't think she meant *under* the ground, literally. I thought it was a metaphor."

Slowly and with much grinding of wood, the alter gives way. An opening, wide enough for a person, leads to a series of steps going down.

"Ishmael, where do these steps go, the tunnel?" Finn asks.

"De-Delia said o-out to w-woods."

"Okay," Leela looks to Izzy, "You go first, take Skeet with you,".

"Um, did I mention I don't like small, dark places." Izzy eyes the narrow opening.

"I don't mind dark places Izzy. Just hold on to me," Skeet grabs her hand, pulling her to the steps.

"Ham you're next; take Ishmael. Leela and I will be last."

Smoke funnels beneath the church's door.

"Hurry, get going," Finn helps Ham then Ishmael down the roughhewn steps.

"Here, Finn, take the tote bag," Leela thrusts it toward him." Finn takes her by the shoulders, "I'm sorry I let you down, I won't again. Now, let's get the hell out of here."

"No, not yet. I can't leave Eulie's painting." She jerks out of his grasp. "I need your help, Finn. Please."

Tendrils of smoke curl around her. Leela coughs behind her hand. "I won't leave without it, Finn."

"Leela, there's no time, come on."

She ignores him, begins tugging at the painting. It doesn't budge. "Finn, please. It's Eulie's. I promised."

"You and your promises," Finn pulls her close, presses a soft kiss on her lips. "Okay, let's do this. Here, grab one side. We'll pull together." Smoke rises to their knees, then their chests. Coughing and struggling to breathe, they keep at it, their eyes smarting against the sting of acrid smoke. At last it gives, the nails squealing as the wooden painting gives way. Finn tucks the painting beneath one arm, grabs Leela's hand, pulling her down the steps behind him. Finn's feet land on hard packed dirt. Faint light reveals a crawl space opposite the steps. Braces of wood line its ceiling.

Finn, his free arm around Leela, twists them around until she faces the tunnel.

"Leela, you go first. I'll drag the painting behind me."

"Finn—I, it's so dark. I can't."

"Yes, you can. Go, keep going. I'll be right behind you."

She drops to her knees, hands outstretched, feeling her way in the dark, seeking light where there is none. The ground is damp, spongy and lumpy with roots. She crawls forward, moving slowly. The thrumming of her heart and her rapid breathing echo in her ears. After what seems like forever, she sees a pinprick of light. It propels her forward. The tunnel gets brighter as the ground rises beneath her and then she is crawling up toward the daylight. She brushes away dangling roots. Hands reach down for her. Blinking against sunlight, she sees Izzy smiling in relief at her.

When Leela's on her feet, the others huddle around her.

"Get the painting," Finn says, pushing it upward. Leela grabs it, hauling it up and over the dirt and dangling roots. He hoists himself up and takes the painting, securing it beneath his arm.

"Ishmael, where are we?" Finn asks.

Ishmael points to the woods ahead. "C-cemetery."

"Come on, let's go quiet. We're not safe yet. Follow me." Ham's says.

Single file, they follow Ham. It's slow going through the foliage and trees, but soon they are on a narrow footpath. Smoke tinges the air. They pick up speed.

"I think I know this path," Leela whispers back to Finn. "It's to the old cemetery."

"We're going straight to the Grille afterwards," he whispers back.

At the cemetery, they skirt tombstones and piles of fallen stones. Ham leads them to the iron gate. He tows Ishmael behind him.

The group scan the four-lane highway. Sirens blast the air. Smoke billows up into the sky. In the distance, flames lick at the treetops.

"They did it, the really did it, they've burned our church," Izzy cries out. Tears stream down her cheeks.

Leela grabs her hand. "They'll pay for this, I don't know how or when, but they will."

"Listen," Finn says, getting their attention. "After we cross, everybody run as fast as you can to the Grille. Izzy, you stay with Skeet. Ham will be with Ishmael. Leela and I will cross last. We'll keep a watch for Darla and her gang." Finn opens the gate. Ham pulls Ishmael through. Izzy and Skeet go next.

After they've safely crossed the street, Finn and Leela join them. "Let's go."

Skirting the side streets, they run through alleyways and empty fields until they get to the Grille's back entrance. When they burst through the kitchen's door, Mirabel jumps back, her arms up, her mouth open in shock.

"Miss Mirabel, we, we need to find Brick." Ham, breathless, demands.

"Oh Lawd, y'all shouldn't be out and about, not with trouble brewin. Miss Ina's closed the Grille for the rest of the day." She backs away. Her eyes widen when she spies Ishmael. "Ishmael, where you been? Granmé Delia been lookin' for you."

"Miss Mirabel," Finn steps forward. "The old church in the woods has been set on fire. We ran here as fast as we could. We need to find Brick. It was Darla and her crowd who set fire to it."

Mirabel presses a hand to her heart. She steps heavily past the long worktable. "Y'all stay here. I'll tell Miss Ina. Lawd, oh Lawd, those damn heathens." She plows through the swinging doors. They hear her calling out to Miss Ina.

All six, still panting and breathless, lean their trembling bodies against the long worktable. Leela presses the painting to her chest. She takes off the tote bag's strap from around her neck, hands it to Finn.

"You know they'll deny it. They'll try to blame us, all of us." Ham says, wearily.

"That'll be hard to do," Skeet says, his chin raised. "Photos don't lie."

"What?" Leela shifts her stance to him.

"I took a couple pictures of them. I bet one of them shows the gas can."

The group cluster's around him, slapping his back and hugging him.

While they wait for Brick and news of the fire, Leela wipes the dirt from the painting with a one of the kitchen's washcloths. Setting it on the worktable, she gets the tote bag from Finn. Sorting through all the purple stars, she retrieves the only one painted a white. She digs out a pencil and a sheet of tracing paper.

"This must be a special star." Leela puts the star on the table, covers it with the paper. Slowly and carefully she rubs the pencil's tip back and forth over the markings.

The others crowd around, speaking excitedly. "What does it say, what does it say?"

Leela reads Eulie's words.

"Eulie mother of Simon Amadi Stone 1851. Son of Seamus Stone.'

Thirty-Three

My child will live free. I will make it so.
~ Eulie ~

In the end, it was the promise Eulie had made to Joshua that was her undoing.

The day Caroline gave birth to a boy child was a trying one for the entire household. Caroline's groans led to anguished screams. If Silas had been in residence, Eulie would have assigned this drama as a bid for his attention. As it happened, he was many miles away at his rice plantation. Eulie was no stranger to the wails of women in the throes of giving birth. On her island, women, some no more than girls of a seasoned age, gave birth one day and were back in the cane fields on the next. Never had she heard such goings on.

Eulie was in the process of carving the last of the words into the mural, when sharp, constricting pains rippled through her rounded belly. The time for her to run had come and gone. She

243

had promised Joshua she would fulfil his grandmother's prophecy. She could not bring herself to leave it unfinished. It had become a promise she made to herself as well. Her dedication to the mural had consumed her every moment. Over the ensuing months, the painting and the story she carved into it, stretched from one side of the wall to the other.

Eulie stepped back to view her mural. It was finished, finally. The last words she carved were, I am Eulie. Her fingers, indelibly stained with the paints she made, moved softly over the rounded curves of her belly. Speaking softly, she crooned to the babe in her native French creole tongue. Though nothing soothed the babe as well as the call notes of birdsong. The babe within seemed to favor the call notes of the island dwelling gray trembler. It was the birdsong Eulie had used to calm the little ones in her care.

Eulie eyed the stains on her hands. She had scrubbed them with ash soap. It had made no difference. And she was tired, so tired. No one in the household had slept the night through since the birth of baby Simon. Least of all, Eulie. The nursery was directly beneath her room. Caroline's babe was fitful, he cried and wailed deep into the night. Dory told Eulie about Caroline's inability to fully nurse her son. Her milk, when it came, was thin. It did not nourish him. A wet nurse from town had been employed, but even that had not stopped his pitiful wails.

Eulie sank to her bed. Next to it was the basket of baby swaddling and tiny nightgowns she had made from the scraps she'd saved. Early on, Caroline had tasked Eulie with the making of baby clothes. She'd cut and sewn swaddling blankets and countless nightgowns tied with silk drawstrings. The material was the finest she'd ever handled.

Eulie, with Dory's help, had prepared what she would need for the hardship of running. Those items, along with weekly replacements of hard biscuits and jerky, were even now beneath her bed. She would run after the birth, after her babe was strong enough to travel. She prayed constantly for its well-being.

It was several days after Eulie had finished the mural that Dory came to her room bearing dreadful news. She came with a face filled with anguish. Eulie had to calm her down to make sense of her words.

"I have been sold?" Eulie's heart went ice cold.

Dory told her it was not the Massa's doing. It was Caroline. She would do as she pleased now that she'd given the Massa a son. What pleased her was to sell Eulie. She had wanted Eulie gone from the first.

"When, Dory, when will this happen? I must get word to Joshua."

Dory shook her head, sobbing into her hands. She told Eulie the man who purchased her, a Mister Williamson, would come for her on the marrow."

Eulie pressed Dory to her chest, assuring her all would be fine. Joshua would talk to the Massa as soon as she got word to him.

After Dory left, Eulie bit her fist to keep from screaming out her rage, not just at Caroline, at herself. Why had she made the mural so elaborate? The answer came to her unbidden. It was pride, a consuming amount of pride. Oh, how she remembered the Lord's words now, *pride goeth before destruction, and a haughty spirit before a fall.* She should have left months ago.

Eulie, pale and trembling, paced the room, her agitation stirring her babe into fitful kicks. Pain rippled around her belly, becoming stronger and more sustained. As the hours progressed into night, Eulie was unable to sit or recline. She was wracked with pain. Having witnessed births on the islands, she knew what to expect. When the pain became intolerable, she bit down on the old leather strap she'd cut from the small trunk. Kneeling on the wide plank floor, her shift up around her chest, Eulie prepared to give birth. Within arm's reach, she placed the darning scissors and string with which to cut and bind the birth cord. She panted and pushed as she'd seen the women do on her island. When an arrow of moon light pierced where she knelt, the babe's head came. Then the body, slippery as an eel, slid into her waiting hands. His eyes were open, his lips pursed into a tremble. Blessedly, he did not cry out, though he stared at her with angry reproach.

Curling on her side, she brought him to her chest, crooning to him while she swabbed him with her shift. He nuzzled into her and together they rested. She gazed at him with a mother's eye. His forehead was broad, like Silas's. On his head, a tuff of reddish-brown hair, like Silas's. The seed Seamus Stone had planted had taken root. In every regard, her son was white. Yet her blood made him a slave.

She brought the babe to her full breasts which were seeping and ready for him. He latched onto her nipple like a leech, suckling for all he was worth. While he nursed, a plan formed in her mind. Later, when she would recall what she'd done, she came to understand she had been desperate, nearly out of her mind with fear for her child.

By midnight, with the moon as her guide, she bundled him into the swaddling cloth left over from Caroline's material. Seeing him safely settled on the bed, she went about cleaning up the blood and afterbirth. When she was finished, there were no traces left, no traces whatsoever a child had been born on these floors. She stuffed the bloody rags into an old, torn shift from the trunk. With water from the pitcher, she washed herself before dressing in the gown she had worn the first day, the gown Joshua had purchased for her.

Retrieving the travel bundle from beneath her bed, she slipped it over her shoulder. She would miss Dory, the sister of her heart. Dory would understand there had been no time for a goodbye. The mural was illuminated by the moon's glow. She'd put her sweat, tears and blood into the making of it. Running her fingers over it for the last time, Eulie pressed her lips to it. Against the mural she whispered, "I have fulfilled your prophecy, Imani. I have marked the words."

On the bed, the babe stirred, mewling. She went to him. Gathering him in her arms, she went to the open windows. Eulie kissed his forehead, his lips and the tender skin over his heart. Holding him high, she spoke to the moon. "His heart name is Amadi, a free man. I pray the Lord protect him, body and soul."

He would be a free man. She would make it so. Barefoot, with her babe at her breast, Eulie left the room, closing the door softly behind her.

Thirty-Four

AFTER THE FIRE

As sure as the sun rises, they'll try to blame it on us.
~ Abraham Jones ~

"A baby, Eulie had a baby?" Izzy asks Leela, who finds four pairs of eyes questioning her. They stem their questions when Miss Mirabel returns. She tells them to take a seat at the big, round booth inside the restaurant. "Y'all look hungry. Settle down now. I'm fixing to make y'all some burgers."

Miss Ina comes out from her office. "Brick will be here soon. He's bringing the sheriff to take your statements. Things have quieted down at the courthouse, but there's still trouble about town. While we're waiting, I want all of you to call your parents. "Ham and Izzy, you go first. Come on, phone's in the office. Leela, I called your mom. Told her Brick would be bringing you and Skeet home."

Leela pales at that. How much had Miss Ina told her mom? And then there was the part about sneaking out of the house.

Maybe her mom didn't have to know about that. Finn's hand finds hers under the table. He gives it a squeeze. "We didn't do anything wrong, Leela. It'll be all right, you'll see."

"Geez, do I have to call my dad?" Skeet groans. I don't want to mess up his vacation with Mellie."

"I don't know, Skeet. Probably my mom will call him."

When Izzy and Ham return, Finn scoots out. He gives Leela a wink before going to call his parents.

"Leela, did you know Eulie had a baby? Was it in the mural?" Izzy asks when they are alone again.

"I know Silas' brother, Seamus, attacked her. And that she was with child. But there is no mention of her having the baby while she was there. If she'd written it, I didn't find it. I'm as surprised as you. Izzy, do you remember the portrait of Seamus and Silas we saw in the attic?"

"Yeah, I remember. They looked a lot alike, and they were very mean looking."

"Eulie wrote about Seamus, how he found her in the garden. He beat her." Leela's face flushes with anger. It was horrible to even imagine.

"My mom told me that slave owners abused female slaves." Izzy presses her lips into a thin line.

"The big question is, what happened to her baby? I mean, she was a slave even though she was almost white, a quadroon, right? So, did her baby automatically become a slave too?" Skeet asks the question to no one in particular. It was a question they all had on their minds.

"I, I don't know. But it was probably likely. A single drop of blood was all it took back then, I think," Leela tells them. *A single drop of blood.* Those words stick in her mind.

Miss Mirabel came out with a platter of burgers and fries. None of them thought they'd be able to eat a bite after what they'd just been through, but soon they were salivating at the delicious smells. Miss Ina drops off a tray of soft drinks.

"Skeet, I don't think it's a good idea for you to hand over your camera to the sheriff," Ham gives Skeet a meaningful look.

"Why not? Don't they need my photo as evidence?"

"Well, evidence has a way of disappearing. I mean look, Darla's grandfather is a big deal in town. We need that photo, but only after its been developed. A copy of it would be good insurance, don't you think?" Ham chomps down on his burger.

"Ham's right, Skeet. The Clayton's and Devlin's will try to make this go away or blame us for it." Finn scoots over to Leela.

Leela pats the camera beside Skeet. "Hide the camera, Skeet. Don't mention the photo, not yet, not until we see it and we have our own copy." She eyes the group, "Not a word about the photo, okay?"

"Sounds like a plan," Skeet slips the camera beneath Leela's tote bag.

"I wouldn't get it developed here, not in town, Skeet. Too big a risk. Can you send it to your dad to have the film developed in Atlanta?" Finn asks.

"Sure, my dad will do it. I'll get him to send all of my photos here."

A collective sigh of relief goes around the table.

"We all have the same story," Finn reminds the group. "It's what happened. Just tell it the way you remember it happening."

They're digging into Miss Mirabel's peach pie when Sheriff Humphrey, grim-faced and flinty-eyed, comes into the Grille. Brick is trailing behind. Leela gives Brick a wobbly smile which he doesn't return. Leela brows knit in confusion. That wasn't like Brick.

"Finn, follow me," the sheriff's barks "The rest of you sit tight."

Brick gives them a hard stare, and with a shake of his head, follows Finn.

When the door to Miss Ina's offices closes, Ham slaps the table. "Looks like Darla and her gang got to the sheriff lickety-split. While we've been here chowing down, she's been filling his ears with her story. All we've got is that photo."

"We're witnesses. Our words count, remember that. Skeet listen to me," Leela takes his hand in hers, "Don't be scared. Tell what happened, but no matter what he says, or even threatens, don't tell him about the photo. We'll call your dad tonight. Your dad will set things right, okay?"

Skeet, so pale his freckles stand out like brown-splotches, bobs his head. "It's my property. My dad's big on that."

A few minutes later, Finn comes out. His face is red, his hands clenched. The sheriff points to Leela. She slips from the table, giving Skeet's hand one last squeeze.

While following the sheriff into Miss Ina's, she schools her face the best she can. She is innocent, they all are. Still, when the door shuts behind her, she jumps.

"Take a seat," the sheriff points to the chair by Miss Ina's desk. Brick stands by the door, quiet and solemn.

Leela sits, staring back at the sheriff, her look unwavering. Her mom always told her the truth shines like a beacon on an innocent face. She wills her face to shine. For a moment, the sheriff looks taken aback, then his face settles into that grim expression.

"Why were you and the others out to that church today? It's the colored church. What business did you have to be there?"

Leela told him how Ishmael was her friend. He had invited her and the others. She told him Ham and Izzy were her friends from the Grille.

"Who was it brought the can of gasoline?" He asks, going straight to the point.

"We didn't bring it. I don't know who brought it, but I saw it by Darla Devlin, sir." Leela goes on to him tell what happened and how they'd had to crawl through a tunnel to escape the burning church.

"Tunnel, you say. Never heard of a tunnel being out there."

"It's a slave tunnel from back in those days, sir. Only Ishmael and Granme´ Delia knew about it."

"Where's Ishmael now?"

"Miss Ina took him home on account of Granme´ Delia being worried about him, sir."

"So, this is your account of what happened. Is this all of it, nothing else you're leaving out?"

"Nothing else, sir. This is what happened."

"I heard something about somebody taking pictures. You know anything about that?"

Leela's heart stuttered, though her gaze never wavered. "My cousin, Skeet, took pictures of the church. Is that important?"

The sheriff blinks, ignoring her question. "We're done, for now," he rises. She follows him. When they get to the table, she stays behind the sheriff mouthing, *only about the camera.*

Sheriff Humphrey points to Skeet. "Bring your camera, son." Skeet doesn't look at Leela. Pale-faced, he stumbles from the table.

When the office door snaps shut, Leela puts her hands to her face. "Darla told him about the camera and about Skeet taking pictures. He asked me about it."

"Damn it to hell," Finn swears. "Humphrey will take that camera for sure. The Clayton's are trying to put the blame on us."

"Ham and Izzy share a glance, their faces glum. "I knew that'd happen. Always does." Izzy says, her teeth clenched. Ham stares stony eyed at Leela and Finn.

"How much you wanna bet they don't even brother talking to me and Izzy. Already have their minds made up." Ham declares.

As it happened, Ham was right.

Sheriff Humphrey doesn't even bother coming back to the table. Brick walks him to the Grille's entrance. Skeet's camera is slung over the sheriff's shoulder. Skeet slides into the booth. His face is red, an angry red. "I better get my camera back. My dad will have a fit. He won't stand for this."

"What'll we do now with no evidence to back us up." Leela bemoans the loss of the camera and its photos.

"Get this film developed, is what we're gonna do." Skeet digs out a roll of film from his pocket.

The rest gape at him, eyes wide with disbelief.

"What?" Skeet tosses the film one hand to the other.

"H-how, I mean, w-when…? Finn stutters.

"I'm a lawyer's son. This here's exculpatory evidence."

Thirty-Five

Here's the truth Leela, justice ain't always blind.
~ Skeet Stone ~

Once Sable learned the whole story about Leela and the others being locked inside a burning church and forced to escape through a tunnel, she was ready to leave Bateaux Bay far behind.

"I won't stay here where you are put in danger, Leela. I won't have it, you understand me?" Sable stood by the kitchen table, her face pale, her hands clasped to her chest.

"Mom, we can't just run away. If we run now, we'll be running forever from people like the Claytons. Ishmael kept us safe. He knew all along we could get out. This is our home, Mom, my home." Leela stares her mother down, though inside, she's quivering. What she fears is leaving the only friends she's ever had. And Eulie's mural. She can't leave, not yet. In a few years, she'll go away to college. Until then, she has Eulie's story to

255

write. She has questions needing answers. What happened to Eulie and her baby? And the star babies? What happened to them. There's bound to be clues among all that stuff in the attic; she's sure of it.

In the end, it was Skeet who tipped the scale.

Ten days after Skeet sent the roll of film to his dad, Bass shows up ready to take on the entire town. The photos clearly show the gas can at Darla's feet. According to Brick, who attended the meeting, Sheriff Humphrey was not swayed. He told Bass the only thing the photo proved was that a gas can was present. Until he had proof who the culprit was, there was not much he could do. The case, he said, remained open. He returned Skeet's camera.

Bass knew a stalemate when he met one, though he let the sheriff know he'd be back should there be further developments in the case.

Not only were there no consequences for her dire act, Luanne took Darla on vacation, which added insult to injury. The friendship Brick had had with the Devlin's and Clayton's was now non-existent. Miss Ina decided to serve up her own justice. She let it be known their patronage of the Grille was no longer welcome. The only other restaurants in town were the Skillet, a breakfast joint and the Shrimp Box. Both were little more than down at the heels watering holes for fishermen. Thus, Leela and Skeet considered justice served.

The next morning, Bass is packed, ready to get back to Atlanta and Mellie. "Son," he tells Skeet," school's starting up in a couple of weeks. Better get yourself packed and make your goodbyes."

In the days before his father beat a path to Bateaux Bay, Skeet had presented his case to Sable. He got her alone one morning while Leela was busy writing. He needed to get Sable's answer before taking up what he had in his mind with his dad. Skeet had learned plenty about court room strategy from listening to his dad. Good lawyers, those who won their cases, knew the answers to their questions before questioning a witness in court. If he had any chance of winning his argument, he needed Sable on his side.

Skeet found Sable in the backyard garden. She was on her knees routing out weeds between rows of vegetables. He knelt beside her.

"Auntie Sable, I thought I'd find you here. Want some help?"

Sable looked up, surprised and pleased. "That'd be nice, Skeet."

He went about pulling weeds, letting companionable silence flow between them. After a time, he began his spiel.

"Auntie, you and nana Vernell have been so good to me this summer. You've treated me like a son. Since my mom passed away, it's been, um, difficult. I've had a hard time adjusting. My dad's good to me. Mellie too. They're going to be married soon, and well, they have each other," he sighs, audibly.

"I'm deeply sorry you've lost your mom, Skeet. I don't know Mellie, but your Dad speaks highly of her."

"Yes, she's a real nice lady. With the two of them working so much, they don't have much time for each other, let alone time for me. Oh, I'm not complaining," he quickly adds. "They do their best, you know. It's just that, well, I've been happy here, happier than I've been in a very long time. Leela, she's my sister now."

"Skeet, we've been happy to have you with us. I know Leela will miss you as we all will."

"Auntie Sable, I, um I was wondering, would you be *against* me staying here for a bit longer?"

"Skeet, of course not. You'll always be welcomed here for as long as you need." Sable put an arm around his shoulders, her mothering instinct welling up in her eyes.

Skeet hugged her back. "Auntie Sable, you're the best auntie in the whole world. I'll talk to my dad."

Later, when Bass and Skeet approach Sable, she is dumbfounded to find herself agreeing with Skeet. His eyes, so like Leela's, hold a plea.

"We, um, certainly have the room, if you're okay with Skeet staying for the school year. I'm certain Leela will be excited. They've grown so close this summer."

Skeet doesn't waste anytime cajoling his dad. "It's just for a year, Dad, you know, until you and Mellie get settled and all."

And that was that.

Leela, who'd known about the plan all along, skids into the kitchen.

"Thank you, Uncle Bass, thanks Mom. Isn't it wonderful? We're gonna have a great year together! We'll look after each other, won't we Skeet?"

"That's the plan, Cuz." The duo snatches a couple of apple fritters from the counter before taking off. They leave two stunned adults in their wake. Sable's argument about Leela not being safe, evaporates. There'd be no more talk about leaving Bateaux Bay.

Vernell, having seen Skeet and Leela conspiring, shakes her head. "Appears the two of you been railroaded," she smirks.

"Looks like it," Bass grinned. "He's gonna be one hell of a lawyer someday."

Thirty-Six

༺ THE TRUNK ༻

All for one and one for all.
~ Alexander Dumas-The Three Musketeers ~

For sneaking out of the house the day of the fire, Leela and Skeet remain grounded until the start of the school year, two weeks away. They didn't seem to mind their confinement, which caused Sable to question whether the grounding was, after all, a consequence.

As it was, Finn came by most days. Izzy and Ham had visited several times.

"What we got here," Vernell had quipped, "is a damn revolving door. Ain't no punishment at all, is what I'm saying." Sable took her mother's remarks in stride. She tended to agree, although she hadn't been inclined to stop the visitations. Skeet still mourned the loss of his mother. Leela was steadfast in her indifference to her father. When the divorce papers came through, he'd signed them giving Sable full custody. He'd enclosed a sealed letter to Leela.

"Nothing he has to say will change anything," Leela had tossed the letter on the table. "I don't need to read it." Sable left the letter on the table in the hope Leela would change her mind.

Later, Sable finds the letter torn into small pieces. Sable shakes her head, her heart panging for her daughter. Dale hadn't been a bad father, just an indifferent one. Sable tosses the pieces into the garbage can, hoping her daughter will confide in her when she's ready. Sable goes about getting lunch ready. Laughter from the up-stairs landing echoes down the stairs. Those two, what a pair they make, Sable smiles to herself. Anyone would think they were truly brother and sister they way they tease each other.

As she listens to the children's laughter, and the hum of Ver-nell's sewing machine, Sable feels a contentment she hasn't known since she left Bateaux Bay to marry Dale. The years she and Brick had spent apart, and the heartache they'd both nursed, is in the past now. Sable checks her watch. Brick will be here soon. Her heart kicks up in anticipation. They see each other every day now. She doesn't know what her future holds, except for the sure knowledge he will be in it.

Sable goes to the stairs, calls out, "Leela, Skeet, lunch will be ready soon."

"Okay Mom. We'll be down in a bit." Leela called from her upstairs landing.

Leela and Skeet whisper as they make their way to the attic door.

"There are no ghosts in the attic, Skeet. I've been in there a couple of times. Izzy too."

"Course not, I was just kidding. Granny Vernell said the floor is rotten. We might fall clean through, she told me."

260

"She says that to keep us out, is what I think." Leela brushes away his worries with a wave of her hand. "Listen, there's so much stuff in there, all kinds of pictures and papers and trunks. It's the trunks I want to open. I think there might be things about Eulie. Maybe a journal or papers about where she went and what happened to her. Come on, Skeet, this is important. They won't hear us, not with granny sewing and mom in the kitchen. It's perfect timing."

"Fine, but just until lunch is ready, okay?"

"Deal. Let's do this." Leela, flashlight in hand, goes up the steps into the gloom of the cavernous attic. The noon sun sends a shaft of dusky light through a single arched window. Shadows crawl along the walls.

"Follow me, Skeet. Step where I step."

"Wow, this place is loaded with stuff. It could take weeks of looking to find anything."

"Time is what we've got, Skeet."

"Right. Um, where do we start? I mean, there's boxes and old trunks all over the place." Skeet takes one nervous step after the other in order stay close to Leela.

"We should start at the back and work our way forward. Look, there's two big trunks near that old dresser," she says, shining the flashlight on them.

"Hey, Leela, there's a small sofa over there. It'd be great for my room, you know, like for a reading nook or something. Think your mom or granny would mind?"

"Nah, they'd probably get Brick to help us get it to your room. See, all kinds of good stuff in here." They wend their way to the back wall stepping over and around boxes and miscellaneous pieces of discarded furniture.

"Here, you hold the flashlight." Leela kneels by the first trunk. "This is an old steamer trunk, I think. See the rounded top." She tugs at the leather strap, pulling it through the rust encrusted clasp. When she tries to open it, the hinges don't budge.

"I bet they're all like that. We gonna need some oil to grease the hinges, Leela."

"Yep, and I came prepared." Leela digs out a tin of oil from her jean's pocket. This is from granny's sewing box. It's for her sewing machine."

After applying the oil, Leela works the top open. "Shine the light here, Skeet."

She rummages through layers of musty smelling clothing.

"These are ancient, like from a hundred years ago." Leela holds up a brocade jacket with split tails and a linen shirt with puffy sleeves and ruffles at the cuffs.

"Hey, I'm thinking Halloween costumes, Leela." Skeet laughs. "Except we gotta get that smell out."

"Nothin but men's stuff in here. Let's try the other one." Leela gently lowers the heavy lid.

They go through the same process with the other trunk, finding women's gowns, coats and shawls.

"Gosh, girls sure were tiny back then," Skeet remarks. "You might be able to squeeze into one of them. That is if you cut back on those fritters, Leela."

Leela rolls her eyes, smirking at him. "Well, the men's stuff is too big for your itty-bitty, skinny self, Skeet. So there." Leela says, sitting back on her heels.

"Let's go, Leela, I'm hungry. It's stuffy and smells weird back here."

"All right, but we're coming back tomorrow." Leela lets out

a long, disappointed sigh. She's getting to her feet when she hesitates, pointing to a small trunk tucked beneath the eaves.

"It's a child's trunk, Skeet, won't take but a minute." Leela drags it out. Its top is flat and bound with leather straps and bronze buckles. One strap is shorter than the other. A ragged cut is along its edge. She oils the hinges, slowly working the lid until it eases open.

"Whew, it smells funny," Skeet wrinkles his nose.

"Yeah, sort of does smell icky, Skeet." Leela pokes at the bundle within. "Hmm. Something hard and narrow had been wrapped up. Could be a journal."

Leela pulls at the yellowed material dislodging a purple object.

"Skeet, it's a star, a Eulie star. What's it doing in here of all places?" She examines it, turning it over in her hands. "There are markings, Skeet. She's marked it. Why?"

Handing it over to Skeet, she pulls away more of the material, keeps pulling until a round, wizened face is revealed. "Oh, what is this? A baby doll?"

"Yeah, a pretty scary looking doll." Skeet leans in close for a better look, while Leela unwraps more layers of cloth. Tiny hands are exposed. One little hand is bunched in a fist, the other is splayed open.

"Skeet, I've never seen a doll like this. The eyes are all sunken in."

"So, we've found ourselves a mummified doll. Who'd have thought, huh?"

"Oh, oh," Leela drops the bundle, scoots back from the trunk.

"What?"

"Skeet, it's, it's not a doll. It's a dead baby!"

"That's not funny. I'm already freaked-out enough, Leela."

"I'm not kidding."

Skeet sinks to the floor next to her. "A real dead baby? You sure?"

"Pretty sure. Let's put it back."

"What? I'm not gonna sleep being so close to a dead baby. We gotta tell your mom."

"Right, I know you're right. Oh Skeet, it might be Eulie's baby. Poor Eulie. No wonder she didn't write about it in the mural. The white star she made was for her baby who died." Leela's heart breaks for the girl. Then a darker thought comes to her. "I bet they wouldn't let her keep it, so they killed it."

"They murdered a baby?"

"Think about it. Why else would it have been hidden here instead of being buried? It was probably Caroline who did it. She hated Eulie."

"Well, they're all dead and gone, long gone, Leela. Come on, we can't have a dead baby in the attic. We gotta tell your mom. So much for lunch. I think I'm gonna be sick."

"Help me with the trunk, Skeet."

"Uh, no way. It's a crime scene. My dad says never mess with a crime scene."

"Right. I forgot. Let's go." Leela takes the purple star from Skeet. "This we keep. It won't mean anything to the sheriff anyway, and I want to see if Eulie wrote something on it."

"Okay, guess it won't make any difference being that they're all dead and gone," Skeet quickly agrees," eager to get away from the dead baby.

"Skeet listen to me," Leela grips his arm. "We can't tell them we think it's Eulie's baby. No one knows about Eulie, except all of us. If we tell them they might take the tracings for evidence. They might take the stars and the flower painting. It's our secret. We can't tell them, not yet.

"Yeah, they probably would take all of it for evidence."

"We tell them what we found. We don't know anything about whose baby it might be, right?"

"Right," Skeet agrees."

Leela tucks the wooden star into her overall's pocket.

When they get to the kitchen, both Leela and Skeet are pale-faced and nervous.

Sable and Brick are setting the table for lunch. Vernell is at the stove.

"Um, Mom, we, um, have something to tell you." Leela says, unable to stop the tremble in her voice. All at once, the shock of finding the baby and the heartache she feels for Eulie surge through her.

"What is it honey? What's wrong?" Both Sable and Brick cast worried glances in their direction.

"Good Lord," Granny Vernell says, "the two of you are white as sheets."

Thirty-Seven

Oh boy, the town will be in an uproar.
~ Granny Vernell ~

"It's a mummy, a dead baby mummy," Skeet spits out. Leela rolls her eyes at him, clears her throat. "What he means is, we found a dead baby in one of the trunks in the attic."

"Ain't nothing but old dolls up there," Granny Vernell snickers, waving them off with her spoon.

"No, granny, it is a real dead baby. Mom?" Leela appeals to her mother. Sable looks to Brick.

"Show me what you've found," Brick says.

Later, when they return to the kitchen, Brick looks to Sable. He's a shade paler than when he left the table. "We better call the sheriff, Sable. It, ah, it looks to be a dead baby in one of the old trunks.

The stirring spoon granny Vernell is holding clatters to the floor. She follows, hitting the floor hard enough to shake the kitchen table.

267

"Ma, Doc Henderson is here. He's going to check you over. You fainted, Ma," Sable says. She sits by her mom on the couch. Brick had carried Vernell to the living room, placing her on the couch. Sable applies a cold, damp cloth to her mother's forehead, while Doc Henderson checks her vitals.

After the doctor assures Sable her mother is fine, Brick calls Sheriff Humphrey. The sheriff arrives with the county's coroner and two deputies. Leela and Skeet are quiet as mice, huddled together in the over-stuffed chair by the fireplace. Sheriff Humphrey eyes them suspiciously when he arrives. "I'll have a word with the two of you in a bit. I'll be taking your statements." He and the coroner head up the stairs behind Brick.

"They better watch where they step," Skeet whispers to Leela, "big as they are, they might fall clean through and end up hanging from the ceiling."

Leela covers her giggle with a cough. "Shush, you'll make me laugh and we've got to be serious when the sheriff talks to us."

"I'm seriously hungry, aren't you?"

"Not even a little. How can you be hungry at a time like this?"

"Dunno. I get hungry when I'm nervous."

"Well, it'll probably be awhile before they come back down. Lunch is still on the table, I bet."

In the kitchen, Skeets helps himself to fried ham, green beans and a dollop of grits swimming in butter. "Ya know, I'm going to end up either loving grits or hating them. Whichever. But do we really have to have them at every meal?"

"Shush, granny will hear you," Leela warns. She pours sweet tea in a glass, turning her nose up at the meal.

"What do you think they'll do with the baby, Leela?"

"I don't know, though it's pretty obvious the baby died a

very long time ago. They'll do an investigation, I guess. Skeet, you know this will be in the paper. Your dad's gonna find out."

"I'm going to call him tonight and explain. "No, not about Eulie," Skeet is quick to allay her fears.

While Skeet is chowing down, Eulie sips her tea, her thoughts on the baby and who might have ended its life. Was the baby truly Eulie's? Had it died of natural causes or had the baby's life been snuffed out? Was Caroline cruel enough to murder a baby? From what Eulie wrote, it was clear she hated Eulie, hated her with a passion. But why? Why hate someone who was a mere slave? Then there was the star Eulie made for her baby, naming him Simon Amadi Stone, and assigning Seamus as the father. She'd written that Amadi meant *free man*. Did death make him free? Or had she taken the baby with her when she ran. Maybe the dead baby in the attic wasn't Eulie's baby at all. It could just as easily be some other slave's dead baby.

"Maybe it's not her baby, Skeet." Leela states.

"Huh?

"I mean, how do we even know it's hers?

"We don't," Skeet points his fork at her.

"You know what I think? I think Eulie would never leave her baby behind, dead or alive. She wouldn't leave her baby in a trunk, she just wouldn't." Leela says this with the surety of someone who knows another's mind. "I know Eulie's heart, Skeet. She would die before leaving her baby in a trunk.

"I can believe that. So, what do we do now?"

"We trace the star, Skeet," Leela pats the star in her pocket, thinking Eulie might have named the mother and possibly, the father. Then we keep searching, Skeet. There must be records of the slaves who lived here. We need to fine those records."

"Oh boy, the attic again?" Skeet swallows hard.

"Where else, Skeet."

"Just so you know, if we find another dead baby, I'm out of here."

Thirty-Eight

❧ A TIN BOX ❧

I want to believe Eulie made it to freedom.
~ Leela ~

Later that day, after the sheriff and the coroner have carted the trunk and baby away, and after Sable has determined Leela and Skeet haven't been scarred for life by the shock of it all, the cousins sneak away to Leela's room.

"Lock the door Skeet, mom's liable to come check on me again."

With their heads together, Skeet holds the tracing paper over the star while Leela rubs the pencil's tip over the markings. Words emerge.

Simon Stone 1851

Leela shakes her head. "This is strange, Skeet. Simon Stone, my great, great, grandfather was born in the same year. At least, that's what's in the family Bible. Caroline Clayton Stone was his mother. And obviously, he lived."

271

"Looks like there were two babies with the same name and one of them was murdered and hidden in a trunk. I mean, if it wasn't murder, why hide the baby?" Skeet pronounces.

If this is Eulie's baby, why would she write this? The star from the church says she's the mother of Seamus' baby, Simon Amadi Stone. It doesn't make sense."

"It's a mystery, Leela. I don't know how we solve a hundred-year-old murder, do you?"

"We keep looking for evidence, Skeet, that's what we do."

Leela and Skeet are warned to stay out of the attic. It seems Sheriff Humphrey wants to continue his investigation. This warning did not in any way deter Leela from insisting they pursue their own investigation.

"Who knows what the sheriff and his deputies will take. It won't mean a thing to them, Skeet. Whatever they find will just end up in a box in the courthouse basement."

"We better wear gloves just in case they dust for prints." Skeet announces.

"As in fingerprints? That's crazy. Do they think somebody put the baby in the attic recently? I mean, who would put a hundred-year-old baby in our attic?

"Just saying."

"Guess we're wearing gloves. There are rubber cleaning gloves under the kitchen sink. We'll go tonight when granny and my mom are asleep. If there's anything important to be found, we need to fine it first."

"Okay, but you'll be opening up the trunks by yourself. If there's anything dead, I don't want to see it. I'm going to have nightmares about that mummified baby, Leela."

"I doubt there are more, Skeet. Come on, it was a baby, a

little baby who never did a bit of harm to anyone. But, if you want, I'll check each trunk first, okay?"

"I'm an artist, ya know. We are more sensitive to, um, grisly things. Especially a mummified baby."

"Fine. I get it. You're a sensitive artist. Well, I'm going to be a writer, a journalist. It won't bother me one bit to write about grisly things like—*murder.*"

"Are you sure we're related?"

"Ha, ha. So now you're a comedian."

"Sorta am, ya know," he grins.

"Think you can stay awake past midnight, Skeet?

Of course. I'm workin on stuff, ya know, my art."

"Good. I'll whistle at your door. I'll bring my flashlight, you bring yours."

It's after midnight before Leela is assured her mom is asleep. Vernell's snoring is so loud it reaches upstairs. Leela, her tote bag slung over her shoulder, pads barefoot down the landing to Sheet's room. "Hey," she whispers at the door. She waits, but there's no rustle of sound from his room. Leela mimics the rasping call of the crow. She tries the door, the knob twists. She finds Skeet at his desk, his head between his arms. He's snoring.

"Hey, hey," she whispers, shaking him lightly.

"He startles. "I'm awake, I'm awake."

"Shh... come on, let's go."

The moonless night renders the attic pitch black. The beams from their flashlights carve tunnels of light into it.

"I'll go to the back. You search over by those portraits." Leela points her light in that direction.

While Leela is searching through the trunks and old dressers, Skeet is sorting through yellowed papers he found in tin box.

"Leela, come over here. I think I've found a couple of death certificates signed by a doctor and a man who signed off as a magistrate."

Leela wends her way slowly to him. With both their flashlights honed on the papers, Leela eyes the faded lettering. "This one is about Caroline," Leela says. "Look at the date. She passed away during the Civil War. And see, there are more. This box looks to be full of death and birth certificates. We can match these up with what's written in the family Bible, Skeet."

"You find anything?" Skeet closes the lid, tucks it under his arm.

"Not sure if it's anything important. I found a leather pouch with what looks to be old letters. We'll take this stuff to my bedroom. We'll go over all of it tomorrow when my mom and granny are gone."

The next day, while Sable is at the library and granny Vernell is off doing alterations, Leela and Skeet spread out the papers and letters on her bed. Skeet is sorting the certificates by chronological dates, while Leela looks through the letters.

"Skeet, this is a letter from Joshua to Silas. Oh, I can't believe it. A letter from Joshua." Leela smooths out the crinkles. The paper is wafer thin, the ink blurred, but legible. Leela scans the letter. "It's dated October 1851. That's the same year Eulie gave birth to Amadi. He's says the package is in Philadelphia and that the package will be going to New York."

"A letter about a package?"

"It might be code. He wouldn't say it was a runaway slave. They used codes during the underground railroad. Maybe it's a code about Eulie."

"Or it could be about a package, Leela. Don't get your hopes up thinking it might be about Eulie."

"I'm not. I won't. Don't you want to know if she made it to the free states?"

"Yeah, course I do. Look, here are the records from 1850 to 1891. Here's one from the Confederate army. It states Seamus Miles Stone died June 5, 1862. And that he fought bravely and died on the field at Tantler's Creek in Pitt County, North Carolina. Attached is a letter he, apparently, never finished." Skeet reads the letter, *"Silas, the battle has been raging all day. It pains me to write that I am uncertain anything has been gained or not."*

"I hate to bad mouth a dead guy, but I think he got his just desserts for what he did to Eulie." Skeet says, putting the letter and certificate aside.

"Silas lost his only brother and his wife within a few years of each other. At least he had his daughters and his son, which, if you think about it, is a darn good thing or we wouldn't be here. Silas died in 1867, and according to what is written in our Bible, he never remarried."

"Leela, are we done now? We've been through everything in the attic. If we can't find anything about that baby, I doubt if Sheriff Humphrey and his deputies will either."

"I know. It's disappointing. It's like Eulie vanished into thin air, except for what Joshua wrote. I want to believe she made it to the free states because if she'd been sold, there'd be a record of it. I've looked through all of Silas' bills of sale and there are records of other slaves, though nothing more about Ozee and Zina." Leela returns the letters to the leather pouch.

"That's that, I guess. At least we know what happened to the rest of the Stones. That's something, anyway." Sheet places the tin beneath Leela's bed.

"There's one more thing. I found something, and well, I've

been saving it as a surprise for you." Leela grins, her violet eyes shine with excitement.

"Really, a surprise for me?"

"Yep." Leela pulls out a box from beneath her bed. Opening it, she takes out a gray pestle and a stone bowl with a crack along its side. The bowl has the residue of dark stains inside it.

"It couldn't be, could it?" Skeet's eyes widen in disbelief.

"I think this was Eulie's. Look at the stains. She used it, don't you think, to crush plants to make her colors."

Skeet takes the bowl. He cradles to his chest it as if it were a thing alive. "Where, when…?"

"I found it in one of the trunks. You didn't want to look, so I thought I'd keep it as a surprise."

Later that day, granny Vernell stomps into the kitchen, a newspaper stuffed under her arm. Leela and Skeet are helping themselves to granny's peach pie.

"Lord have mercy, the town's in an uproar. Everybody's talkin' about that dead baby. Look," she tosses the paper on the kitchen table. Got pictures of the poor thing and our house. Good Lord, the news' folks are sure to beat a path to Bateaux Bay. Lord, they'll be campin' out in the front yard. You mark my words."

Thirty-Nine

꧁ THE HEADLINES ꧂

Secrets have a way of making themselves known.
~ Leela ~

The backwater town of Bateaux Bay is not prepared for the onslaught of media attention. Scores of reporters from Savannah and Atlanta had descended. Sheriff Humphrey basks in the limelight. Photographers come at all hours of the day and night, their flash bulbs trailing like shooting stars. Sable refuses to allow Leela and Skeet to give interviews. Sable made one statement through the Sheriff's office. Brick ferries necessities from the grocers. Sable takes off from her work at the library until the furor dies down. The gossip, however, will linger on long after the reporters and photographers have gone.

Headlines like: *Mystery of the Mummified Baby*, and *Hundred-Year-Old Baby: Whose was it?* continue for weeks. According to the coroner, the baby had died, cause unknown, over a hundred years ago. The unwelcomed notoriety is visited upon anyone related to the Stone family, which included the Clayton's, the Franklin's, the Devlin's and several less related families. Leela considers it just desserts for Darla and her mother, Luanne, to be subjected to the same scrutiny as her family.

In the middle of all this, Leela is having her birthday party as planned. She stands before the beveled-tilt mirror eyeing her reflection. She smooths the folds of her pleated skirt which falls to just below her knees. Her blouse, a soft hue of violet, heightens the color of her eyes and picks up the colors in the madras material of her skirt. It's feminine, she thinks, without being too girly. Leela had picked out the material as well as the pattern, a new Butterick from Woolworths. Leela's school clothes for the year had been a collaboration between granny Vernell, Leela and Sable. Leela insisted on there being no pinks or frills. It wasn't her style, she'd explained to her grandmother, who, after seeing the stubborn jut of Leela's chin, relented.

Leela, pleased with her reflection, twirls in a circle. The pleats swirl around her knees. Over the summer, she'd filled out with subtle curves in all the right places. She'd even gotten control over her wayward curls. Her mother had bought her big rollers and a can of hairspray guaranteed to reduce frizz. Her shoulder length hair is combed into a smooth pageboy; it glints copper in the sun. She is ready. She is having a party. Her first ever. The enormous dining room, which hasn't been used in a generation, she's decorated with paper stars and flowers from the garden. She's made tiny sandwiches and chocolate cupcakes dotted with sprinkles. She's told her mom and granny not to bother with a cake.

Even in the August heat, Leela keeps her windows cracked open for the birds. She's scattered seeds and berries along the sills for Rogue, the red tipped blackbird and Sweet Pea, a white tipped mockingbird. The two are among her regular visitors. She whistles Rogue's call notes: *Kong-la-ree-o-ka-le*. Sweet Pea shows up first, echoing Leela's call. "Oh, so you're back for another free meal, are you, Leela smiles as the bird perches on the sill, unafraid. Leela whistles the melody to *Love me Tender*. The mockingbird picks up the tune.

Hearing familiar voices echo up the stairs, Leela checks her appearance one last time before heading downstairs. Her mom and granny have agreed to made themselves scarce, both are off visiting friends. Skeet, his buzzcut grown-out, has slicked back his hair in an imitation of Finn's ducktail. He's chatting with Izzy and Ham in the entrance hall. Finn shows up next with Ishmael.

"We come with presents for the Birthday Girl," Ham says, giving Leela a hug.

"You guys, really. You didn't need to buy stuff for me. I'm just glad you're here. Come on, let's go into the dining room. Skeet and I decorated it." She motions for them to follow her. When she gets to the table, she takes a step back.

"W-hat?" she sputters.

In the center of the table is a black typewriter topped with an enormous red bow. It's an older model, a manual. Leela had seen a similar one while shopping with her mom. She'd spent time admiring it, though she hadn't thought her mother had noticed. A sheet of paper in the carriage reads: Happy Birthday, Leela. Love Mom, Granny and Brick.

"Wow, Leela, now you'll be able to write your stories like a professional." Skeet pats her on the back. The others gather around. "That's a beauty," Finn slides over. Putting his arm around her, he presses a kiss on her cheek. Leela presses her fingertips to her eyes. She won't cry, she won't.

"Hey, we got goodies here, folks. Chocolate cupcakes, sandwiches and chips. Let's chow down before the big opening of presents." Skeet, as usual, is governed by his stomach.

"Not so fast," Ham holds Skeet back. "The Birthday Girl gets a song!" With Ishmael in the middle, the other four take their places next to him. Izzy hums a note and the group sings the happy birthday song to Leela. Tears come. She can't stop them. The joy she feels at having these friends overwhelms her.

"Chow time," Skeet breaks up the group. Everyone gathers plates and soft drinks. Smiling through her tears, Leela takes her place at the head of the table. Skeet regales the group about what it was like to find a dead baby and about the grilling both he and Leela had gotten from the sheriff.

Izzy presses her hand to her stomach. "Ugh, please no talk about dead, mummified babies until we've eaten, okay?"

"Right, but I'm spilling the details later to the guys." With a wicked grin on his face, Skeet stuffs a wedge of sandwich into his mouth.

"You to do that," Izzy shudders. She takes her plate and goes to sit by Leela, who is admiring how especially beautiful Izzy looks today. The cornflower blue dress brings out the blue in Izzy's eyes. Leela notes the frills on the bottom of the dress and the tiny white bows that cover the buttons. Her lips curve into a knowing smile. It had to be one of granny Vernell's creations. Since the church fire, granny Vernell has softened her attitude toward Izzy and Ham.

Leela casts a warm gaze around the table where her friends sit. All the boys have dressed for the occasion. Ham wears a white dress shirt, black pants and a red tie. Finn's outfit is similar, though with a striped red and blue tie. Ishmael has gone all formal with a jacket, vest and yellow bowtie. When Ishmael is sitting, hands clasped to his chest, he looks normal, even handsome. If only, she thinks, there was some kind of medicine to help him.

In her mind's eye, Leela imagines her friends all grown-up. She wonders what their future selves will pursue. Skeet, an artist, no doubt. Ham, a lawyer championing Civil Rights. He'd come back from his trip to Washington D.C. all fired up about the work Dr. King was doing. The Million Man March had done more than dazzle him. It had set him on a path far from Bateaux Bay. Izzy, Leela thinks, will probably manage a bakery. Ishmael will continue to garden, though perhaps they'll take him on as head gardener at the courthouse—it could seriously use improvement. And Finn? She imagines him flying planes. He's slated to be captain of the football team this year. He said he was hoping to get a college scholarship. Would she even know him say, ten years from now? Her heart pangs at what the future holds for all of them. Leela makes a promise to herself. She will stay in touch with her friends, no matter what.

"Time for presents," Izzy calls out. She's appointed herself as the official presenter of gifts. "This is from Skeet," she says, setting the small, hand-painted gift box in front of Leela. Opening the lid, Leela sees a miniature painting nestled on a mound of cotton balls.

"Skeet, this is me. You've painted me." Leela lifts it from the box. "When did you do this? It's incredible. I love it." Leela beams at him. Skeet ducks his head at her compliments. Finn peers over her shoulder. Soon the rest are admiring it.

281

"This one is from Ham," Izzy says, giving Leela a rectangular box covered in bright yellow wrapping paper. A matching crotched flower rests on the top.

"My mom made that for you," he says.

"Please tell her thank you for me," Leela says, pulling at the wrapping paper. Inside the box is a beautifully tooled leather journal. Thank you, Ham."

"It's a proper place for all your poems," he says, giving her a quick hug.

And the gifts keep coming. Izzy's gift is a recipe book entitled: Easy Recipes for the Beginner Cook. "I'll need this someday, Izzy. Granny Vernell has about given up on teaching me. I burn nearly everything I cook." Leela grins.

Finn hands her a small box, professionally wrapped. Inside is a silver charm bracelet with an enameled blue bird dangling from it. "Finn, I love this. I've always wanted one." Leela, in an uncharacteristic move, reaches around his neck, pulling him down for a kiss. The kiss lingers.

"Break it up you two," Skeet makes a gagging noise.

"Two more gifts, Leela," Izzy says, bringing over Ishmael's gifts. Leela had thought he might bring her a lovely bouquet or a potted plant, not two brightly wrapped packages. The first is the size of a book. Leela unwraps it. Her jaw drops. She sputters, unable to get the words out. Skeet takes it from her. "Oh my God. It's a journal, an old one by the look of it. And it's filled with drawings." Skeet looks to Ishmael. "This can't be, I mean, it isn't, I mean, hers?"

"Y-yes. Eu-Eulie's j-journal."

"H-how," Leela has finally found her voice. "How did you come by this, Ishmael?"

"From D-Delia." Ishmael holds a letter in his hand. Leela reaches for it. Ishmael shakes his head. "Y-you o-open g-gifts f-f-first."

"I d-don't understand. How did she, I mean, when did she…"

"Just open the other gift, Leela." Skeet shoves the package at her. Still stunned by the journal, Leela can only stare at the package in her arms.

"Ah, anytime now, Cuz." Skeet mutters as the others gather around.

"Okay, okay." Leela places the package on the table. From the shape and feel of it, Leela thinks it might be a portrait. Her fingers numb with excitement, she peels back the flowered wrapping paper. Her breath hitches when she sees the rich colors, Eulie's signature style. "Oh, oh, it's so beautiful," she breathes out. The others echo her words. The group gazes at it in wonder, so life like is the rendering. It's a portrait of a pair of hands. One hand is holding a flower, a white rose in full bloom. The other hand holds a bud, dark and wilted.

"Those hands, they, um, look really real, you know." Izzy shudders.

"Right, like the hands are holding out the flowers to us." Finn adds.

"Ah, hey guys, I bet there's a meaning here. Eulie's telling us something. I'm the resident artist, ya know, and I think this is a message." Skeet runs his fingers over the white rose and the dark bud.

"Don't touch anything. I'll be right back," Leela says, coming out of her daze. "I'm going to get the tracing papers," she calls out over her shoulder.

"Okay, resident artist, what do you think she's trying to tell us?" Ham quips.

"Well, it seems like the roses might be symbolic, right? Like one rose is alive and the other is, well, dead?"

Forty

I confess my sin.
~ Eulie ~

After placing the tracing paper over the painting, Leela's fingers tremble slightly as she rubs the tip of the pencil over the white rose. The others gather around her. Letters spell out a name.

"Simon Amadi Stone," Leela reads. "This represents Eulie's baby. If the white rose is symbolic of life, does this mean Eulie's baby lived? The star we found on the dead baby in the attic said Simon Silas Stone. It doesn't make sense because we know Simon lived."

"And Simon Amadi's star was in the church with the other children, the ones who were lost or maybe died." Skeet shakes his head.

"I think it means that the dead baby in the attic wasn't hers." Ham says.

285

"But why would there be two stars with the name of Simon?" Izzy asks.

"Leela, why don't you finish the rubbing. See what she's written on the bud," Finn's calm voice settles over the group.

Ishmael pats her shoulder. "F-finish Le-Leela."

Leela's fingers visibly tremble now as she traces over the dark, wilted bud.

"Simon Silas Stone," Leela's fingers go numb, the pencil slipping from her fingers. "But—but he didn't die."

"Hold on, Leela, think about this, Amadi's star from the church was white while all the others were purple. And the dead baby in the attic's star was purple like the others in the church. So, maybe purple means dead or lost, while white mean life," Skeet says.

"The white rose is blooming, and the bud is obviously dead. So, if Simon Amadi, who we believe is Eulie's, lived, then it means Simon Silas Stone…" Leela's eyes widen, "It has to mean Silas' child died." She looks at Skeet, then looks at the others. "But, Simon lived, my great, great, grandfather is Simon Silas. How, I mean, what happened? Were the babies switched because one of them died. Who did the switching and how did one of them die? Would Silas or Caroline have taken Eulie's baby if theirs died?"

Finn's arms encircle Leela, pulling her close.

"If we go by the evidence, by Eulie's painting and the stars, Simon Amadi is Simon Silas," Skeet pronounces. "Which means, we, you and me, Leela, we're the descendants of Eulie and Seamus? Right?"

Leela, returns his look, saying, "I can't see it any other way."

Ishmael holds out the letter from his grandmother. "Y-you r-read L-Leela."

"Oh, yes, I'd forgotten." Leela, her breath coming quick, takes the letter from him, though her mind swirls with thoughts of Eulie and the babies. What had happened? How did this come to be? She envisions Eulie in her mind. Eulie vowed her child would never be a slave, no matter what she had to do. Did she switch the babies? Did she have something to do with baby Simon's death? Eulie, oh, Eulie, what happened?"

Forty-One

I fear nothing. I hope for everything. I am free.
~ Eulie ~

After closing the room's door behind her, Eulie stood in the darkened hallway with her newborn babe asleep at her breast. Her babe breathed deeply, his chest rising and falling with ease. Her own breath stilled. She keened her ears for the sounds of stirring. The house remained still and quiet save for the pitiful whimpers of the babe in the nursery below. She padded barefoot down the stairs to the landing of the second floor, a place Eulie had not been since the day of her arrival. She crept along, fear pounding at her temples. The babe's room was lit by the moon as her room had been. Eulie softly crooned the sweet calls of the gray trembler. Caroline's babe quieted as she entered the nursery.

On the far side of the room, the wet nurse stirred on the cot causing it to creak at its joints. Eulie, not daring to breathe, stood as if her body had turned to stone, though her heart was near to bursting out of her chest. Eulie waited, time an endless measure of her desperation, until she was convinced the rhythmic snoring meant the nurse was deep into her slumber.

Eulie went to the cradle. The babe's eyes were wide open, his tiny hands clenching at the air. As if she were in a dream sleepwalking, Eulie laid her babe next to Caroline's. Except for the wheezing in his thin chest, the babes were alike as twins, both having broad foreheads and tuffs of reddish-brown hair. Eulie picked up Caroline's babe. He whimpered. She pressed him to her breast. He cried out. Fear raced up her spine. She cast a glance at the wet nurse who rolled over onto her stomach. Eulie placed her hand over the babe's nose and mouth to quiet him. With one last look at her sleeping babe, she backed out of the room. After she retraced her steps to the third floor, Eulie lifted her hand from the babe's face. He made no sound. His thin chest did not rise and fall with breaths. She blew air into his little mouth. Still, he did not breathe. She thumped his chest. Still his heart did not resume its beats.

Eulie went numb. Her body acted on its own. It was as if another person dwelled within her. She went back to her room. She laid him on her bed. Her paints and solvents were in clay pots by her worktable. She mixed vinegar and linseed oil. She doused his body with the mixture before wrapping him tightly in the sheet from her bed. She emptied the small trunk by her bed to use as his coffin. She tucked him inside, covering his face with the ends of her sheet.

To Eulie, he'd become another lost babe. Lost to the world. She went to her worktable. There she took one of the cutout stars she'd used for the babes in the church. Eulie bent to her task, inscribing both his name and his mother's as she had done many times before. She swiped a thin layer of purple paint over what she inscribed. Within the folds of the sheet, she placed it over his silent heart.

There was nothing now for her to do but hide him, hide him where he would not be found, God willing. The attic was by her room. The trunk was small, and he weighed so little. She carried it into the attic. The full moon sent shafts of light into the dark, cavernous place. She placed it far into the back beneath the eaves. On her knees before him, she prayed his soul would rise to heaven. Though on her soul, she prayed for the Lord's mercy.

She had done what she had done. Her son was safe. Her son was free. What caused Eulie the most terrible anguish, what cleaved her heart was what had befallen Silas' babe. In her fear, she had caused his death. Her plan had been to take Caroline's babe with her, to keep him as her own if she made it to the free states. If she was caught, she would keep him until he was taken from her, sold to the highest bidder. She had meant to trade one life for another. That Silas' child might become a slave instead of her child was to her mind, an inevitable choice.

Closing the attic door behind her, she was down the servant stairs and out into the garden before realizing she'd left the travel bundle behind. Her supplies and her journal were inside. Returning was not an option. With the moon guiding her, she ran for the church in the piney woods. She had one more star to paint, one more star to mark. She would leave it on the alter for them to put on the ceiling with all the others. When she finished her task, she left the church, going deep into the piney woods. She did not know where to run, so she looked to the heavens and followed the North star.

Eulie hoped Dory would wait for as long as possible before revealing she was gone. Perhaps she had a day at most before the hue and cry went out. Then they would come for her, hunt her down as if she were an animal. She was beyond caring. She had saved her son, at a terrible cost, but he would live as a free man.

She had no destination, for there was none and not a soul to welcome her. And she found no fault in this. She ran under the stars and at dawn had shimmied out of the long-sleeved blouse and skirt that swished at her ankles. These had been a gift from Joshua, who had been her mentor. She folded the blouse, tucking it inside the skirt along with her brogans and looped it over her shoulders.

Clothed in a thin cotton shift, her skin, the color of pale cream in coffee, glistened with her efforts. She cradled her arms to her chest as she had done when last she'd held her babe. Was it just hours ago? Her fingers, stained from the paints she'd labored over for so long, had caressed the curve of his round cheek. He'd opened his eyes upon hearing her voice. They were a babe's blue or nearly so save for a faint coloration of violet within the iris. The mural in the sewing room, she bequeathed to him though, God willing, he would never know how it linked her to him. It gave her comfort to know his gaze would fall upon it for years to come, and his children's children as well.

Eulie ran beneath the stars, kept running even as the sun rose pink and gold in the sky. She had nothing but her freedom, needed nothing but the air filling her lungs. She was as fleet as a deer, bounding and leaping. She was young and lithe and strong of limb. She sang to the beats of her heart, chanting the rhythms of the old songs, the songs of the sugar isles. Her throat, her heaving chest erupted with laughter. The sun, filtering down through a filigree of leaves, of pine needles, anointed her dense, coppery waves with its warmth. Her bare feet pounded the loamy soil and lichen covered stones. She was unaware of the fine droplets of blood she left behind with each foot fall. She did not feel the blood seeping down her thighs. She ignored the pain in her womb, the throbbing there. The birds sang their morning songs. She sang with them in a voice sweet and clear. She sang the call notes of her island, the island of flowers. She sang the sweet notes of the gray warbler.

The braying of hounds, some distance behind her, scattered the birds from the trees. It was no matter to her. She would run until her legs gave out, run until her heart burst within her chest. She would not go back. She would never again live as a slave, owned by another. She would end her life before letting them take her. There were branches aplenty, and ample cloth to wrap around her neck.

Forty-Two

You must face the dark secret in your nightmares, Leela.
Only then will you be free.
~ Granme´ Delia ~

Leela wipes nervous moisture from her hands before unfolding the letter. Attached to the lined writing paper is a crinkled sheet of yellowed paper. Leela puts it aside to read what Granme Delia wrote. Scanning Granme´ Delia's words, Leela takes a deep breath. "The first part is addressed to me," Leela looks up at the group.

"Read all of it. We want to hear it," Skeet hollers.

"Fine. I'll read all of it," Leela narrows her eyes at him. With nerves trembling her voice, she reads Granme´ Delia's words. *Leela, my family has awaited your arrival for many years. Your newly awakened voice has power. Use it well. One day you will tell Eulie's story, of that I am sure.* Leela pauses, looks away from the group.

295

"What's wrong, Leela?" Izzy asks.

"The next part, well, its personal." Leela knits her brows.

"You don't have to tell us, Leela." The hard edge of Finn's voice stops Skeet from speaking out. Leela offers Finn a grateful look.

"Granme´ Delia goes on to say that she is the great, great granddaughter of a slave name Dory." Leela's eyes light in surprise. "Eulie mentioned Dory in the mural. She was a house slave while Eulie was there."

"Wow, that's something, Granme´ Delia being related to Dory." Skeet pipes up. "Hey, that means Ishmael is too." He slaps Ishmael's back.

Leela continues reading. *My family has been in possession of this painting and Eulie's letter since the end of the Civil War. Eulie wrote to Dory, saying a descendant of the Stone family, a girl who talked with her hands, was to be given the painting. We, the Fields-Dubois family, have waited these many years to do so."*

"She means you, Leela." Skeet marvels. "How did Eulie know?"

Leela, shaking her head, takes a deep breath and sets Granme´ Delia's letter on the table. Eulie's letter is fragile, yellowed and crinkled with age. It appears to have been folded and refolded by many hands. Leela gently smooths it. "Here goes," she says to the others. "Eulie wrote this. I recognize the shape of her letters. It's dated the twenty-fifth of the January, eighteen sixty-eight, Harlem, New York."

"New York? Eulie made it to New York." Skeet slaps the table in his excitement.

Leela shushes him. She reads Eulie's words.

Dory, sister of my heart, it is my hope you have not despaired of me. It is now, during this time of reconstruction after the war, I'm able to get this correspondence to you. Joshua has taken on the service of its delivery. I trust no other. It has troubled me these many years for you not to know of my whereabouts, or if, indeed, I lived. These words are for you alone, though I understand if you require help from a trusted friend or family member in the reading of this missive. Dory, the last night we spoke, I gave birth. This you surely assumed as I left the result for you to dispose. After you told me I had been sold, I had no choice but to run. I followed the North Star. Dory, my child lives and has always breathed freedom. More than this I cannot reveal, even to you, sister of my heart.

Late in the afternoon of the next day, the braying of hunt dogs filled me with despair. When I heard the rumble of a wagon, faint hope rose inside me. Following the sound, I made my way to it. Two Negra men drove the wagon. I presented myself to them in the hope they would hide me. They were free men on their way to Savannah. I asked if they knew a man by the name of Carter, Joshua. They knew of him. When we arrived in Savannah, I prevailed upon them to take me to the boarding house where Joshua and I had stayed. Tansy, one of the maids who is a free woman, took me in. Joshua kept a room there while doing his work for Silas Stone.

A white man, whose name I was never privy to, contacted Joshua. It was through this man I made my way to the Free States. I cannot tell you how, except to tell you it was a dangerous and arduous journey. Many of the safe houses that harbored me were owned by white families. They risked their lives for me and for those who accompanied me.

As for my beloved Ozee, I have had no word of him these many years. Joshua related to me he ran soon after his arrival at the plantation. I wake in nightmares for I fear harm came to him. Yet, the love I have for him is alive in my heart. In my village, it was believed you cannot be in love with the dead. So, as my love lives, he lives. For this, I thank God.

After the war ended, Zina and her grown children came to live with me. Joshua had always looked to their welfare. She took Joshua's surname as I have. In the past year, Zina has taken ill. The doctor says her life may not be a long one. I remain to care for her until she is called to heaven. It is my desire to one day return to Bateaux Bay. I have missed you so.

Dory, I entrust you with this letter and the painting. Joshua told me his grandmother, Imani, foresaw the future. She told of a girl who talked with her hands. She said this girl will be a descendent of the man who sired me. It is to this girl I bequeath the painting Joshua brings to you. It will come as no surprise to you what we both suspected. Silas Stone is my father. Joshua confirmed this after Silas' passing.

Until the fates bring us together again,
Yours eternally, Eulie Carter

Forty-Three

We don't see things as they are, we see them as we are.
~ Anais Nin ~

After Leela finishes reading Eulie's letter to Dory, her eyes blur with unshed tears. "It's true then, I am Eulie's descendent. Which means all of the Stones from Simon's time, are her descendants as well. I want her story, our story to be told. I've started writing it. I'll send it out into the world."

"Hold on, Leela. I admire Eulie, I do," Finn says, taking her hand. "She survived a terrible time, so don't take this the wrong way, okay? If word gets out, it won't be easy. Lots of people here are blood relatives of the Stone family. It won't matter to them how long ago it was. They will deny it or worse, they'll strike back somehow."

"I don't care, she's..." Leela begins.

"Finn's right, Leela," Izzy interrupts. "The Klan will seek revenge. It's what they do."

299

"You don't know them, Leela." Ham adds. "They've never gotten over losing the war. There's bad blood, even after all these years. They blame us, the coloreds, though God knows why. We had no say in any of it."

"Leela, Cuz, I think they have a point. Maybe we should keep what we know to ourselves. At least for now, right?"

With visions of burning churches in her mind, Leela sinks into her chair. The idea of someone burning down this house, and along with it Eulie's mural, horrifies her.

"Right, I know all of you are right," Leela says, resigned to what she knows is true. "What I don't understand is why there's so much resentment, so much violence still for what happened so long ago."

Finn shrugs, shaking his head. His eyes are filled with understanding for her dismay at what no single person can change. "People hold on to the past, to their grudges, Leela. I guess we, I mean our generation, we need to bring about the change."

Ham eyes light up as he takes in Finn's words. "It's us, we have to change things."

"Okay, here's what we're gonna do for now, cause we're here and now," Skeet says, surveying the group. "Let's make a pact, y'all, a secret pact. "Like we promise not to speak a word of this to anyone, and I mean, not your momma, your papa or your best friend, not until the day Leela's story is out in the world. Agree?" Skeet's intense gaze goes around the table.

The others nod, casting their glances around.

"Thought you would," Skeet raps the table with his knuckles, clearly enjoying his moment of leadership. "Still, it ain't a done deal until we make it a document, signed, sealed and delivered. I'll write it and we all sign. "Agree?"

The others exchange surprised glances, though all nod.

"Okay, sit tight while I write this up."

"L-Leela," Ishmael edges close to her. "Eulie b-buried h-here."

"What do you mean, buried here, Ishmael?"

All heads swivel to Ishmael.

"S-S-she in c-c-cemetery. D-Delia knows."

"Eulie actually came back?"

Ishmael bobs his head.

"Will Granmé Delia talk to us about it?" Leela clasps her hands, excitement building in her chest.

Ishmael, bobbing his head, answers with a lopsided grin.

"Now, can we go see her now?" Leela stands, ready to go.

"Whoa, folks. Y'all sign first, then we go." Skeet waves a sheet of paper under their noses.

Before they leave for Granmé Delia's, Leela hides the letters and Eulie's painting in her bedroom. The space beneath her bed is crowded now with all things related to Eulie. She scribbles a note to her Mom, letting her know where they've gone.

Leaving the remains of Leela's birthday party behind, the group heads to Ishmael's house. Leela's mind swirls with questions. When did Eulie return? Did Ozee live? Did he come back for her? When did she die?

Leela considers what she does know. Eulie wrote her letter to Dory in 1868, after Silas' death in 1867. Caroline was dead, had been dead. So was Seamus. There wouldn't have been anyone who knew her; no one left to recognize her, except Dory. No family member would have been alive to connect her with the Stones. She'd been kept isolated in the room. Eulie's returning to Bateau Bay begins to make sense.

Granme´ Delia is waiting for them. Scents from Ishmael's flowering garden waft inside. The living room is sparse, though comfortably furnished. Soft drinks and snacks are set around her table as if she's been expecting them. Her face brightens when they enter, though her pale gaze lingers on Leela. She gather's Leela into her arms, whispering, "Daughter of my heart, I have waited for you. Now my tired bones will soon find their rest.

"Oh," Leela's eyes smart. She hadn't seen Ishmael's grandmother since the day of the gathering. Then, she'd not realized how old Granme´ Delia was. The white braid is wrapped around her head. To Leela it looks like a halo. Her brown face is thin, exposing sharp angles and wizened skin. Her clothes fall like leaves around her frail body. Yet, there is a glow around her, something other worldly.

"There is a time for all of us, Leela. The Lord will call me when it is my time. I have fulfilled my destiny. One day, you will fulfill yours. Now, you have questions needing answers." The elderly woman gestures for the group to sit at the table. When they've settled, Granme´ Delia speaks.

"Eulie Carter returned in the fall of 1884, seventeen years after Silas' death. Her son, Simon, would have been sixteen when Silas passed. When Eulie returns, Simon is thirty-three and married with children. We know of some of her doings from a journal left by Dory's daughter, Juliet. Eulie stayed with Dory for an unknown length of time, though it is clearly written in Juliet's journal where Eulie spent the duration of her life. She lived and died of old age at Stone House."

Leela gasps. "At Stone house? There's no mention of her death in our family Bible."

"Leela, my child, it would be highly unusual for colored help to be mentioned in the Bible of a white family. Perhaps there is

302

a mention of her in a last will and testament. Your grandmother or another relative may have your family's old wills in their possession."

Leela shakes her head. She can't imagine granny Vernell keeping a colored person's name in her Bible.

"My dad might have them. Him being the family lawyer and all." Skeet, who hasn't taken his eyes off Granme´ Delia, whispers to Eulie, "Blind, Leela, I think she's blind."

"Shush," Leela elbows him, though suddenly she realizes he's right. Granme´ Delia's eyes are clouded, yet she seems to see as well at the rest of them.

"We know Eulie and Dory remained friends during their lifetimes," Granme´ Delia continues. There is frequent mention of Eulie in Juliet's journal over the years. Eulie did not marry, nor did she have another child. Eulie is buried in the white only cemetery, which would have been considered a blasphemy and illegal at the time. Even now, there are no coloreds buried there."

"Where is Dory buried," Ham asks.

Dory, Juliet and other family members are buried in the colored cemetery. We've done our best to keep it up, though time and weather have taken its toll on most of the markers. Ishmael and I are the last of Dory's line—many have gone from here and have forgotten where they come from, as my daughter, Monique, has." Granme´ Delia rises from her chair and goes unerringly to the glass fronted bookcase on the other side of the room. Her hand flutters over the books there before retrieving a leather-bound journal. It's worn thin with use and age. "This is Juliet's. I know she would want you, Leela, to be its next keeper as I have been and my family before me."

Leela takes the journal, cradling it in the palms of her hands.

Skeet, looking a bit slighted, asks if there are any paintings she'd left.

"No child, if she ever painted again, we have no knowledge of it. It might be possible to locate Zina's descendants. If Eulie painted during her time in New York, her descendants might know of it. Eulie and Zina took the surname of Carter, after Joshua. Though Eulie changed her surname to Clark when she returned to Bateaux Bay. I assume she did so as not to be linked to Joshua. I do have something special, however, a photograph taken in 1884, a daguerreotype. It pictures Eulie and Dory. They both would have been about fifty or so at the time. Leela, open the journal. It's inside."

Leela, stunned by this, opens the journal. Attached to the inside cover is a sepia toned photograph. It is yellowed with age, though still remarkably clear. They all gather around Leela.

"Geez, she's beautiful," Skeet breathes out.

Eulie's eyes seem to gaze afar, as if she's looking into the future the way she'd done in the mural. Except here, she's smiling. Skeet is right. She is beautiful. Her violet eyes, so like Leela's own, are set in a perfectly oval face. Her lips are well-shaped and full. Her nose is straight with a slight flair to her nostrils.

"She's um, well, she looks almost white," Ham says.

"She's a quadroon. My momma told me many of us are mixed. Some more than others.

"Yeah," Skeet quips, "like you with your pretty blue eyes."

Izzy brings her hands to her face, her light brown skin glowing pink.

"I take after my dad. We're both black as night," Ham grins.

"Eulie's painting of the hands with the bud and the rose, as you've discovered, is her confession." Granme´ Delia takes Leela's hand in her own. We may never fully understand what happened. It is my belief Silas' child died by a sudden mishap, or illness. Eulie, as you've come to know her, did not have it in her to hurt a child. It is clear, though, she alone could have switched the babes soon after their births. I see what is in your heart, Leela. You've promised to tell Eulie's story, and you will. Someday. This is not the time. You will know when it is. It is my hope the Lord will keep me upright until you do."

"Thank you, Granme´ Delia, for keeping Eulie's letter, for her painting. Ishmael is my cousin. I'm proud to say he is, my mom too. We love him. He is part of our family."

"You bet he is. My dad knows too." Skeet pipes up.

"Of *your* love, I have no doubt." Granme´ Delia settles back in her chair, a long sigh escapes her lips. "Go now children. I'm tired. Come back anytime. Ishmael, my dear, take the children to the cemetery. Eulie's headstone is there."

One by one, the group stops by her chair, bending down to kiss her cheek. Leela wraps her arms around Granme´ Delia, whispering to her. The old woman whispers back.

When the group gathers outside on the stone path bordered by Ishmael's flowers, Skeet asks Leela what the whispering was all about. "Come on, Cuz, what's so secret?"

"Skeet, it's nothing really. Just about some bad dreams I've been having.

"Yeah, I have 'em too, sometimes."

"But I have the same one over and over. It's sort of scary."

"So, what does she think you can do about them?"

"Well, Granme´ Delia thinks I need to try to remember this nightmare. She says not to be afraid of it. Whatever happened was a long time ago."

"Okay, so how do you try to remember it?"

"I don't know." Leela shakes her head, an expression of worry etched on her face.

"How about hypnosis? I have a book on it."

Finn rolls his eyes at Skeet before pulling Leela aside. "Ready to see where Eulie's buried?"

"Yes, I want so much to see it. I'm going to read the journal. Maybe there's something Juliet wrote that will explain why she lived there. The only thing that does make sense is that she wanted to be near Simon and his children."

Finn and Leela trail behind the others after they leave Granme´ Delia's house. Finn pulls her close. "I'm a pretty good listener. I mean, if you want to talk about—anything."

Leela threads her hand through his. "Thanks, but I really don't know where to start. I'll figure it out. Granme´ Delia, she said I won't be really free of my nightmares until I let myself remember."

"Are they very scary?" Finn pulls her hand to his chest.

"Yes, the same one over and over. In the dream I'm a little girl. I run and run looking for my mom. And then I see my dad and he's really angry. When I wake up my heart is pounding. I can't' go back to sleep afterwards."

"Leela, maybe this dream is about something that did happen. Maybe you should ask your mom."

"I will. I've never thought it might be from something, you know, real that happened."

On the way to the cemetery, Leela thinks back to her childhood. A vague memory flits through her mind. A queasy feeling settles in her stomach.

Forty-Four

When I was little, I became scared of what I'd seen;
afterwards, my words came out wrong.
~ Leela ~

Memorial Gardens is as much garden as cemetery. Masses of flowers and shrubs border the entrance. A narrow gravel path wends past family plots. Towering white oaks and willows shade much of the area. Birds flit from trees and headstones. Many of the headstones they pass are elaborate. Marble and brick mausoleums rise up here and there. The group gathers around the Stone family's plot, which is large enough to hold the entirety of Silas Stone's descendants. Intricate wrought iron railings encompass it. Skeet and Leela exchange meaningful looks.

"Don't know about you, Cuz, but I don't plan on resting my bones here. How about you?"

"Only if I die a spinster. Then I'd like to be near Eulie. I don't know what my mom wants. I should ask her. It's a pretty place. I

307

think Eulie is happy to be near her loved ones."

"It's a beautiful resting place," Izzy says to Leela. "Looks like it's been well cared for over the years."

"That's granny Vernell's doing. She told my mom she has a caretaker keep it up."

Ham scans the beauty of the white cemetery with a jaundiced eye. "The old colored cemetery needs work. Any volunteers?"

"I'll help," Finn says, he catches Leela's gaze. "Me too," she echoes. "We all will," she looks to Skeet.

"Okay, count me in, but after this, I'm done with cemeteries. Pretty or ugly, these places give me the heebie-jeebies." Skeet steps up to the wrought iron gate, tugging at it. It swings open on well-oiled hinges. One by one the group files in. Ishmael places white lilies from his garden on Eulie's grave. Her small head stone is nestled between the large granite monuments of Simon and Sawyer Stone. It reads:

Eulie Ami Clark, Beloved Nanny. 1835-1931

"Geez, Eulie lived to be ninety-six," Skeet shakes his head, awestruck.

"I think my mom would have been around three years-old back then. I'll have to ask her if she remembers her."

Skeet side-steps graves, stopping to read headstones. "Look, can't miss Silas' head stone. His is enormous. There's Caroline's, and Seamus' looks to be a marker, not a grave. Guess they never did get his body."

"Sage is not here either, just a marker. But Savannah and her babies are here. And my grandfather Samuel's is the most recent. I was a baby when he died." Leela adds.

"My grandfather, Seymore, isn't here either," Skeet says. I guess he's buried in Atlanta near my granny, Alyce. My dad doesn't like cemeteries. He's never taken me to see their graves. My mom is, um, she's buried with her relatives in Savannah."

The group walks between the headstones, reading the dates and memorials. Before they leave, each goes to Eulie's headstone touching it with reverence.

"Okay, y'all, I think we still have a birthday to celebrate. How about we head over to McCrory's Pharmacy and have him make us some Root Beer Floats?" Skeet wiggles his eyebrows for emphasis.

That evening, while Vernell is watching I love Lucy, Leela pulls her mother aside.

"Mom, I um, I was wondering if anything unusual happened when I was little. Did I act strange, I mean different than usual?"

"Strange? Of course not, honey. I do remember you were very quiet when I came home from the hospital. I was there for a several days when I had my appendix out. I thought you were angry at me for being gone. You wouldn't speak for days. Come to think of it that's about when you began to stammer. You were six years old; I believe. You were a stubborn little thing. I couldn't get you to talk until I bribed you with ice cream."

"Who took care of me while you were gone?"

"Your dad, of course. He insisted. I think he wanted some alone time with you. He'd never spent much time with us. He was traveling a great deal then. Why do you ask?

"Oh, no reason. I just remembered dad and me together. That's all."

"He tried to be a good dad, though some men aren't meant to be dads, I guess."

Later that night, while Leela is at her desk practicing on her new typewriter, she thinks about what her mom told her. Whatever had happened, happened while her mom was gone, and she was alone with her dad. It fits with the dream. In the dream, she's searching for her mom and her dad was so angry. All at once, Leela realizes it was her he was angry at. What had she done? Leela closes her eyes, sifts through her earliest memories. She remembers playing with a favorite doll, Chatty Cathy. She was sitting in the living room, the doll between her legs. She pulled the string over and over to make Cathy talk. She remembers getting up, dragging the doll behind her, searching for the voices she heard. She remembers calling out for her mommy.

The memory ends in a blur. Try as she might, she can't get past that blur. Rubbing her tried eyes, she leaves the desk to get ready for bed. After her normal ritual of toothbrushing and face washing, she crawls into bed. Yawning deeply, she drifts off, thinking of her birthday, and of everything she learned about Eulie. When sleep comes, it draws her into the past.

She's walking down a narrow hallway. She feels the carpet beneath her bare feet. In one hand she's dragging a doll. She hears sounds, voices. She goes toward the sounds. Her little girl voice is plaintive, calling out for her mommy. She reaches up on tiptoe, turning a knob. The door swings open. Mommy and daddy are on the bed, but it's not mommy. Mommy doesn't have red hair. Mommy's hair is brown. Daddy jumps from the bed. His face is ugly and red. He's yelling at her. He grabs her arm. He's hurting her arm. He drags her away, still yelling. He tells her she's a bad girl. He says bad girls who tell things to their mommies are sent away. He says bad girls go to an orphanage, away forever from their parents.

Leela wakes up, her heart pounding as usual. But this time she remembers why. She'd been afraid of being sent away to an orphanage. She must have been afraid to talk, afraid daddy's secret would spill from her lips. That's when her words came out wrong. Leela balls her hands into fists. He was a monster to threaten her in that way. He caused her the pain she suffered growing up a stutterer. Granme´ Delia said not to hold hate in her heart, but how can she not?

Leela goes to the mural, as she often does to seek solace from a girl long dead. "Eulie," Leela whispers to the girl, "why did you come back? Why did you choose to live at Stone House? How did you forgive all that had been done to you?" Leela shakes her head. The answers to her questions are long buried. "Eulie," Leela says, "it's enough to know the Stones had cared about you. They must've truly come to love you, Eulie, because they marked those words for all the world to see." Leela presses her fingertips to the figure of the young girl in the cane field. "Night, Eulie."

Leela goes back to bed, curling up with thoughts of Eulie, of her life and the mysteries surrounding it. She wonders about her own life, of all that is yet to come. One thing she knows for sure, no matter what the future holds, she will always have her friends.

Forty-Five

I have loved and been loved.
I have been blessed in abundance.
~ Eulie ~

JULY 1884 BATEAUX BAY

The mid-morning sun hinted at the heat soon to follow. The sidewalks, shops and streets bustled with activity. Patrons scurried to do their business before the heat and stifling humidity encompassed the day. Impatient shoppers made foolhardy dashes between carriages, wagons and skittish horses. Eulie, wearing the plain dress and smock of a colored maid, was jostled and shoved aside by those on the sidewalks. None begged her pardon.

Even so, Eulie kept pace behind the two women and children she secretly followed. A slow smile creased her cheeks as she observed the goings on of the two boys, twins, who struggled mightily against the hands of the women who held them in check. These children were the reason she'd returned, the reason

313

she'd left her comfortable lodgings in the Harlem borough of Manhattan. The boys were Simon's children. The women, finely attired, were Isabel, Simon's wife and her younger sister, Yvette Franklin. Simon had married young. By the time he was thirty-three, he'd sired the twins, Sawyer and Sage, and had an infant daughter, Savannah.

When Zina passed away, Eulie returned to live with Dory. She changed her surname from Carter to Clark, feigning widowhood. She feared Joshua's surname would be linked to Silas and hers to Joshua, who'd been his manservant. Often, a vision of Ozee blossomed in her mind, causing her heart to ache with sorrow. He was the ghost who haunted her dreams. The carved bird he made so long ago was nestled in her pocket. She thought him truly a ghost because she no longer felt his living presence as she had years ago. What could have been between them was never to be. Still, she clung to the love he'd offered.

What had burned in her heart all these years was her desire to see her son, Simon, and his children. Despite Dory's misgivings, Eulie had offered her seamstress services to the Stone's housekeeper, Nola. The irony here did not escape her. Still, she would willingly labor at whatever task they required in order to have even a glimpse of Simon and the children. The housekeeper, Nola, who had been born in the New Orleans, spoke French Creole, Eulie's native tongue. They'd bonded over their shared language.

Eulie kept the women and children in her sightline. She eyed Isabel's sister, Yvette, with mounting concern. The girl was a flighty sort; she batted her eyes at every young male who tipped his hat in her direction. Sawyer, the more irascible twin, took this opportunity to wrest his hand from her grip. Eulie sucked in a horrified breath when he leapt away from Yvette, dashing blindly into the street. Eulie dropped her satchel of mending, her heart lodging in her throat as she chased after him. With one hand, she grabbed the back of his short jacket, flinging him toward the sidewalk a moment before a carriage surged upon him. Eulie's skirts were caught in the wheel spokes. She was dragged some distance before the driver was able to reign in the horses.

Knocked senseless, she awoke with blurred vision. Pain radiated down the left side of her body. Her left arm, wrapped tightly from wrist to elbow, hummed with pain.

"Shh, *Ami*," said a voice she recognized.

"N-Nola," Eulie managed, blinking away her blurred vision. She tried to move, grimacing as intense pain flashed through her."

"*Non, me petit Ami*, you must stay still. Doctor Blaine insists you not move until he returns." Nola pressed down gently on Eulie's chest.

"She's awake?" A deep male voice inquired. Eulie's gaze shifted to the man standing over her.

"*Qui*, Master Simon, though she be in some terrible pain, I fear."

Eulie's heart paused a beat, then her heart lunged forward, racing. Simon bent over her, lowering his face close to hers. She'd had glimpses of him now and then. Times when he'd turned a corner, times when he strode by, his face turned in conversation. Pride would burst within her to see how handsome he appeared, and how affable he seemed with those of his acquaintance.

"Mistress Clark, my wife and I have prayed daily for your recovery. We are truly indebted to you for saving our son's life.

Had you not stepped into the path, flinging him aside…" He clenched his jaw, holding back his emotion.

Isabel stood next to him, her eyes welling with tears. "We insist you remain here, Eulie, until you are well mended. Word has been sent to your friend, Dory Fields. She sends her concern and is intent on visiting you when you are able. You must rest now. Doctor Blaine will return tomorrow.

Thus, began Eulie's extended convalescence. Weeks turned into months. She hobbled about insisting she be put to good service. Her broken left hip had ill mended, leaving her unable to walk without a cane. She became a fixture, mending clothes and brewing healing concoctions from herbs in the garden. The same garden where years before she'd been attacked by Seamus. The memory of that night, Eulie buried deep within her mind. Over time, the family came to depend on her, not only for her sewing skills and her knowledge of healing herbs, but for the calming effect she had on the children.

The children marveled at her bird calls. Nola had taken to addressing Eulie as *Ami*, friend. Soon, she was *Ami* to the children. They followed Eulie around, tugging at her skirts. They often gathered in Eulie's room by the kitchen—a former large storage pantry turned bedroom which suited Eulie fine. Stairs were beyond her and would be for her lifetime.

"Ami," Sage begged, "do the blue jay, I want to learn."

"No, Ami, do the screeching hawk," Sawyer insisted, punching is brother in the arm.

Simon, upon seeing Eulie's fine script—Joshua had made her practice until her fingers had ached—called upon her for some of his correspondence. When he inquired of her past, she told him she'd been born free in France and had traveled as a maid to England, to the Caribbean and then to New York. There she'd married and followed her husband south. Her deceased husband, Mister Clark, had been a friend of Mister Fields, Dory's deceased husband. The two widows shared a laundry business. This fabrication fell easily from her lips. It was part of the story she'd told during her life in Manhattan. She never spoke about her livelihood as a painter in New York. Dory alone knew Eulie's past.

Months turned into a year, then two as Simon's family came to regard her as a member of their household. She refused re-numeration, declaring her room and board sufficient to her needs. He insisted, putting money aside for her. Eulie, now referred to as *Ami* by all, considered herself blessed beyond her wildest hopes. She thanked God daily for this wondrous gift, though it was not without retribution for her sin. The constant pain in her hip and her infirmity were both a blessing and a reminder of the small trunk beneath the attic's eaves. Often, in the midnight hours, she quaked with fear of its discovery, of the little body inside and of the star with Simon Silas Stone inscribed upon it.

There were times when Simon shifted his gaze, eyeing her speculatively. "There is something familiar about you, Ami," he'd said more than once. Those words froze her heart. She worried others might see the resemblance between her and Simon. It was there in the shape and color of his eyes, and in the curve of his full lips. On her island, it was said that blood will tell. And so, it was Simon who sought her company. He was curious about her time in the Caribbean. He never mention his mother, Caroline. Gossip had it they had not been close. Eulie did not doubt this. Caroline had not been a nurturer, not even to her young daughters.

317

In this way, many years sped by. Simon's children grew into adults, still attending to her as if she were a beloved relative. When Isabel died of a sudden illness, Simon aged dramatically. "Ami," he would say, "come to the parlor, I have news of Sage." Or, "Ami, let us take the carriage to visit Savannah and her new-born." The two would often be found in the library, heads bent together, discussing his business and books.

When Simon passed away at sixty-one, Eulie was by his side. Her grief consumed her. She wore a widow's black until the end of her days. During this time, she wanted nothing but to lay her head down and join him in heaven, God willing. Though God, it seemed to Eulie, intended for her to live on, for he had granted her a hearty and hale constitution.

Sawyer, who had been born hours before Sage, inherited Stone House and the family's shipping business, which suited Sage fine. He had a desire to travel, finally settling in California. Sawyer was the image of Simon, though his temperament had little changed since his boyhood. He was stubborn and impulsive. The rest of the household looked to Eulie, who at seventy-seventy was the only one able to tamp down his mood swings.

Sawyer's wife, Laura Lee Hodges, bore him two sons, Samuel and Seymore. Eulie became as a grandmother to them. She'd taken to sitting in one of the veranda's rocking chairs on fine days. The boys, Samuel and Seymore, at her knees begging for a story or for her bird calls.

"Ami," Samuel demanded, "teach me more bird calls."

"No, Ami," Seymore said, nudging his brother, "tell us the story of the bird who lost her song."

Sawyer was in his early fifties when he suffered a heart ailment that kept him at home, much to Laura Lee's dismay. She counted on Ami to keep him occupied with correspondence and other business matters. Sawyer's boys went to university, Samuel into business as he would inherit the family's shipping concerns, while Seymore studied architecture. Seymore would eventually take up residence in Atlanta as a commercial builder.

Eventually, Samuel, the eldest of the two boys, married Vernell Dawson, a farm girl he'd met in Alabama. By then Eulie was ninety-two-years old. She spent her days on the veranda telling stories of times long past, stories so far-fetched as to not be taken seriously. Stories of planting cane stalks, of maroons and overseers with their cracking whips and braying dogs. She told of slaves being thrown to the sea and of children lost from their mothers. Vernell rolled her eyes at these stories, insisting Ami had gone senile. Vernell had never taken to the old colored woman whose skin was almost as light as Vernell's. So, when Vernell was finally delivered of a child, a girl they named Sable, she kept the babe from Eulie. Yet as Sable grew, she gravitated to Eulie, as all the Stone children had done.

On a warm spring day in 1931, Sable, an energetic three-year-old by then, begged Eulie to draw her pictures. They were on the veranda, Eulie in her rocking chair with Sable on her lap. Eulie sketched her island birds for Sable. Eulie would whistle a bird call and Sable would guess which bird by pointing to it. It was Sable's favorite game.

"Ami, do another, do another," Sable said, placing her little hands on Eulie's cheeks.

Eulie whistled a bird's call. "Whose call is this, Sable?"

"Warbler's call, Ami." Sable proudly pronounced, pointing to the gray warbler.

"Yes, so it is, my clever girl," Eulie laughed, placing a kiss on Sable's soft, round cheek.

Eulie, feeling the weight of her days, said to Sable, "Let me rest for a bit, dearest." Eulie slipped her hand into her smock's pocket, wrapping her fingers around Ozee's bird. It comforted her, calmed her heart which had taken to skipping beats. She closed her eyes, smiling as memories of Ozee flickered behind her eyelids. Sleep came on a whisper of wings in Eulie's ears. She breathed in sweet, island air. A figure emerged on the beach; his hand raised in welcome. Ozee's arm curled around her shoulders. She rested her head against his broad chest. "You are here," she said, smiling through happy tears.

"I've always been here, waiting for you, he said."

Eulie's head lolled against the back of the rocker. Her body slumped in the chair.

"Ami, Ami, wake up." Sable, impatient for their game to resume, pushed at Eulie's shoulders. Still, Eulie did not wake. The little girl pushed and prodded at Eulie chest. "Ami, wake up. Play with me, Ami." Sable's lips trembled. Even at her tender age, she sensed something was terribly wrong with her Ami.

"Papa, Papa, Ami won't wake up," Sable cried out, slipping from Eulie's lap.

Samuel rushed from the library to the veranda. He knelt by Eulie, pressing his ear to her chest. She was frail, her bones as hollow as a bird's. He carried her to the parlor, placing her on the settee. Gently, he laid her hands over her chest. "Ami," he said, his breath hitching.

Sawyer came shuffling out from his first-floor bedroom. Like Eulie, he hadn't been able to negotiate stairs for some time.

"What's Sable carrying on about, Sam," he said, coming to the parlor. When he saw Eulie on the settee, he paced a hand to his heart.

"It's Ami, Pa. She's gone, Pa."

Sawyer, who'd known Eulie longer than his own mother, sank to his knees, "Ami, oh Ami." Samuel helped his father up, guiding him to a chair by the settee. Sable, seeing the sad faces of her father and grandfather, set up a wail of her own. "Ami, Ami, wake up," she cried out.

Vernell, coming in from her sewing room, stamped her foot at the entrance of the parlor.

"What's all this darn racket about. Scared the breath outa me. Sounded like somebody up and died," Vernell, arms akimbo, barked out.

"It's Ami, she's passed on." Sawyer held Ami's limp hand his. Samuel knelt by his father.

"Oh, good Lawd, she was just an old, colored woman. And senile to boot."

"Hush your mouth, Vernell," Samuel snapped at her.

"If Ami had color in her, it was way back. Don't matter now," Sawyer narrowed his dark violet eyes at Vernell. He'd never cottoned to the woman. Didn't know what Sam had ever seen in her. "I'm having her buried next to my pa. He'd want that and so do I," he said.

"Ami will rest peacefully next to Grandpa Simon," Samuel said.

"What you talkin' about? She's colored. Colored don't belong in a white cemetery. It ain't even legal." Vernell stamped her foot.

Sawyer clenched his jaw. "She's white if I say she is, Vernell. You say otherwise and you'll have me to deal with."

Vernell pinched her lips together. She backed out of the parlor, shaking her head, muttering, "Damn nigger lovers. My folks be turning in their graves."

Forty-Six

❧ STONE HOUSE ☙

The past is a living thing, shaping our destines,
shaping our very selves.
~ Leela ~

JULY 1977 BATEAUX BAY, STONE HOUSE

Death is on Leela's mind. Has been on her mind for the
entire six-hour drive from Atlanta. Five years ago, she'd
returned for granny Vernell's funeral. Now, here she is for yet
another, Granme´ Delia's. During her last visit, she'd been welcomed with open arms. But this time, well, she has no illusions.
Except for a handful of close friends, she's about as welcome as
a hurricane. She's put the town on the map, and in the town's
opinion, not in a good way. She might as well have set the town
on fire with the publication of her award-winning novel, *A Single
Drop of Blood.* Still, the glut of tourists drawn to the notoriety
have, no doubt, added to the town's bottom line.

Leela hadn't gone unscathed. Along with her recent celebrity
status came the hate mail and disturbing anonymous phone threats.

One particularly nasty call was from a voice Leela would never forget, Darla Devlin. She'd threatened to sue Leela, saying her book was full of lies, and that the only 'nigger' was Leela herself. She said Leela would pay, one way or another. Leela called her out, exposing her for the coward she was. After that, Darla never called again, though other voices called, their veiled threats left Leela nervous, but not for herself. Her worry was more for her family's home, Stone House, and for the dear friends she'd left behind.

Shaking off the memories of those calls, she takes a sip from her water bottle, eyeing the dark shimmers of superheated air rising from the asphalt. It filters up through the Mustang's vents competing with the air conditioning she's put on full blast. The pungent odors of slash pine and sap give way to the tang of brine and marine life as she nears her destination. The monotony of nothing but towering pines and scrub palmettos along the stretch of flat miles had her blasting the volume on her tape deck for the past two hours. She'd been near to dozing off more than once.

When she finally enters the main hub of Bateaux Bay, she switches off the tape deck. The town is a veritable time capsule. Main Street with its narrow sidewalks and rows of brick and glass fronted shops have not much changed since she was a teen. And even then, it had retained much of its pre-Civil War past.

Skirting the park and the pier, she turns onto a sand and oyster shell road which leads to a rise of bluff overlooking a wide, sun-kissed bay, and her destination. She parks along the sandy shoulder near the house. A sign perched by the driveway, a new addition since her last visit, reads: *The Stone House Bed and Breakfast*. As part owner, she had agreed to the concept, though she'd had her doubts. Yet, here it is, a house with a nary a stone and rooms to let, save for one. She'd been told that room is viewed behind velvet ropes.

Prosperity, it seems, has come once again to Stone House. Has truth finally set it free from its secrets?

Leela walks down the sloping drive to the repainted and re-purposed veranda which is now an alfresco dining area. Board and batten siding gleam with fresh white paint. The shutters are a vivid blue to match the bay. The roof no longer sags. She is glad to see they've left the massive front door untouched. Hewn of heart of pine and fossilized by over a hundred years of sun and storms, it carries the memories of all who have passed through it. The scent of azaleas and roses mix with the sharp tang of fresh paint. Yet all the fresh paint in the world cannot disguise the scents of other days. Days of lemon oil and ash soap on wide-planked floors. Days of the toil and sweat of those who labored here. A time when women wore wide hooped skirts of silk and taffeta. A time when men mastered the land and the yoke of slavery. There are many who wish to bury the past. Leela is not among them.

She hesitates at the rise of steps to the veranda, taking it all in. She smooths back a wayward curl. She notes a slight tremble in her fingers, her heart kicking up in anticipation. Will *he* be among those who gather inside? Closing her eyes, memories of her time at Stone House wash over her. She'd been fifteen, a solitary girl, a girl with no words. A girl who hated the sound of her own voice.

Leela steps up to the veranda. How much has changed, she muses, since the day she and the others made their pact. They'd been kids; their futures yet to be written. Each had promised to keep Eulie's secret until Leela had written her story. They kept that promise, and promised too, that their friendship would always bind them.

Finn had left for college by the time Leela was a senior. When she, Izzy and Ham graduated, Skeet was left to hold down the fort at Stone house, supervised by her mom and Brick, who'd married soon after Leela had turned sixteen. Skeet had decided to stay and finish high school in Bateaux Bay. The town had grown on him, he said, but most of all, he liked not having to play football. He visited his father and Melanie during the summers.

Over the years, they'd kept in touch with phone calls, letters, holiday cards, invitations to graduations, to weddings and baby showers. Granny Vernell's funeral five years ago had brought them together, all but Finn. He'd been drafted right out of college in '67, his dream of becoming a jet pilot was realized in the US Air Force. He'd called her in April of '75, right before the fall of Saigon. His voice was deep, deeper than she remembered. He couldn't tell her much, but through her newspaper contacts in DC, she knew he was flying missions, airlifts coded as *Baby Lift*, *New Life*, and *Frequent Wind*. The US was getting refugees out of Saigon as Ho Chin Min's vision of uniting North and South Vietnam became a reality.

Before the military had taken Finn from her life, he'd made a few visits to her dorm room in Tallahassee. Because her dorm had a curfew, they spent a good deal of their time in his Pontiac steaming up the windows. She was in love, madly so. They talked about the future, things they would do together after she graduated. Then came the war. When Finn's calls and letters became fewer and fewer, Leela blamed distance and their careers. He'd never said much about his time in 'Nam, though she knew he carried the ghosts of fallen comrades.

When he was discharged after the war, he took a job as a commercial pilot with American Airlines, headquartered in Ft. Worth. She'd bit her lip during his call to stem their tremble, the crushing disappointment. He could've taken a job with Delta headquartered in Atlanta where she lived. They both knew it. He never talked about his personal life, so neither did she. Though she'd had a few brief relationships, she remained unattached. She'd given her heart to Finn years ago, and until she knew for sure he didn't feel the same, well, she wasn't ready to let go.

She buried herself in her work and buried her feelings for him as well. Her career with the newspaper, with writing her book, kept her from dwelling on Finn. He was close with Ham; she knew that much. Leela had too much pride to ask Ham outright if Finn was involved with someone. He didn't volunteer, so she swallowed hard and held back the question she desperately wanted to ask.

When her mom and Brick moved to Atlanta to start a mail order business, the house stood empty. Sable and Sebastian, co-inheritors of Stone House, signed the deed over to Leela, Skeet and Ishmael. It was Skeet's idea to turn the six-bedroom house into a bed and breakfast. It was Leela's idea to hire Izzy; her degree in hotel and hospitality management was a perfect fit. Ishmael insisted on being the grounds keeper.

Leela presses her hands against the massive front door, hewn of heart of pine more than a century ago. The wood is warm, like a living thing. Eulie had crossed this threshold as a slave; she'd left it as a free and beloved woman by her descendants. Leela wonders if

327

they'd still have felt the same had they known who she really was. She wanted to believe it wouldn't have made a difference.

"I marked the words, Eulie," Leela whispers against the door, "just as you did. Your words live, Eulie; your story lives on in the hearts and minds of thousands. Your stars grace the newly built church in the piney woods. Your mural is admired by all who visit Stone House." Leela thinks back to the gathering, to Granme Delia's story of the bird who lost her song. The memory brings a smile to her lips and bittersweet joy to her heart. "I am your song, Eulie, we all are."

Voices from within call out to Leela. "I'm coming," she says, and opens to door.

Forty-Seven

ॐ REUNITED ॐ

Love follows many paths, all lead to the heart.
~ Delia Field-Dubois ~

When Leela steps inside, she's immediately surrounded by her friends. Izzy is first to wrap her arms around Leela. Skeet gives her a bear hug, squeezing the breath out of her. He's no longer the skinny kid with coke bottle glassed and freckles. He's tall, easily over six feet and filled out like a linebacker. Somewhere along the way, he must've joined a weightlifting gym. Ham, a big guy himself, shoves Skeet aside, giving Leela another bear hug.

At her feet, two little girls, twins, jump up and down with excitement. "Lelee," they shout in unison. They know her the from her infrequent visits with their father and mother. Ham beams proudly at his daughters. He hadn't wasted any time starting a family. He worked with Dr. King during Civil Rights, and now both he and his wife, Ruby, are teachers in Tallahassee. While Skeet, as his father predicted, is one hell of a lawyer in Washington, DC. He's a part time artist and a full-time advocate for voting rights. Leela's mom told her she believes he'll run for office one day.

A small, dark haired boy, Leela guesses he's around four or so, stands off to the side. He's dressed in a white shirt, tie and dark pants. He's hands are stuffed into his pants pockets.

"And who is this handsome young man," Leela says, moving forward to get a good look at him. The boy's eyes are quite dark, almost black. They have an upward sweep, tilted at the corners and almond shaped. His complexion is a creamy olive. He doesn't take after anyone she knows. So, not a relative. A friend of the children's, then.

"He's mine," says a deep voice Leela recognizes, causing her heart to jump. Finn steps out from the shadows.

"Hello, Leela. It's been too long, hasn't it?"

Leela's mouth forms an *Oh*. Her knees go weak. A wave of dizziness sweeps over her. Ham, his arm still around her, steadies her.

"Finn." Leela breathes out. *Finn has a child. Finn is married.* She doesn't think she can possibly face this now, yet what choice does she have. She pastes on a smile. She *will* be gracious to the woman who stole his heart, even as her own heart is breaking into a million pieces.

"Le-Leela." It's Ishmael, grinning from ear to ear. "Y-you see fa-flowers?"

"Oh, Ishmael, yes. They are so beautiful." She brings him in for a hug. He must feel her trembling because his eyes go wide with a question.

"Hey, y'all come on now," Izzy pipes up, breaking the tension. "I've been cooking for a week, so y'all better be hungry," she says, leading the way.

"Now you're talkin my language," Skeet laughs, sidling up to her. He sneaks a worried glance back at Leela.

The twins tug at Ham's pants, pulling him along. Ham glances back at Leela, offering her an encouraging look. Ishmael follows him.

Leela, left on her own, shifts her gaze to the little boy. She bends down to his level.

"I'm Leela. What's your name?"

"I know who you are. You're Leela, papa's friend. I'm Joshua."

"J-Joshua? That's, that's a wonderful name." Leela stammers, taken aback. Had Finn named his son after Eulie's Joshua? It has to be true; it's too much of a coincidence to be otherwise. Leela lifts a trembling smile to Finn. "He's so handsome. You and his mother must be incredibly proud."

"Yes. I am proud." Finn answers, his eyes are a darker green than she remembers." His mother hasn't seen him for some time now."

Leela raises her brows in a question, while noticing the deep etchings by Finn's eyes, by his mouth. He looks older than he should, she thinks. Yet the look he gives her burns, causes her chest to squeeze. Her throat tightens. She won't cry. She won't fall apart in front of him. Finn's son, Joshua tugs the hem of her skirt, pulling her attention from Finn.

"My mother had to go away. Papa Finn adopted me. He says that means I'm special."

"Yes, of course you are," Leela nods, though she's confused. Finn and his wife adopted?

She rises, thrusting out a hand to Finn. "Um, your wife, uh, she's not here?"

331

"Leela, I'm not married. She wasn't *my* wife. It's complicated." The warmth Leela feels from his hand races through her, causing her breath to hitch. *Not married? Never a husband? What does that mean?*

"We'll talk later, if that's okay with you?"

She nods, offering him a tight smile. "Of course, yes. Later."

Ham comes out from the kitchen. "Hey Josh, come on boy, the twins are waitin' on you. Let your pa and Leela catch-up. Their old friends."

"Okay, Uncle Ham. I'm coming." Joshua turns to Finn, grabs his hand, pulling his father down to his level. He whispers in his father's ear. Finn nods. "I will. I promise."

Joshua shifts to Leela, pulls her down to his level and whispers in her ear as well. Then he takes off running, eager to meet up with the twins.

Arching a brow, Leela asks Finn, "What am I to say *yes* about?"

Finn takes her hand, "Let's go out to the porch, Leela. I'll explain."

When they are on the porch, Finn leads her to one of the rockers, new ones painted a crisp white. They sit across from each other, knees touching, the way they had so many years before. Suddenly, the years fade away and she's that girl again. The girl who had no words, sitting with a boy who looked at her with his amazing green eyes. And as then, she finds she has no words.

"You haven't changed, Leela. Still the enigmatic girl from our childhood, and now a beautiful and quite accomplished woman. I've read your novel. You captured her, Leela. Eulie came alive in your words."

Leela smiles her thanks.

Finn looks out to the bay. The afternoon sun sends ripples of gold over the smooth blue waters. "We flew missions in 'Nam and Laos. Secret stuff. Hell, all of it was. My buddy, Wendel Vogel, we were friends, got to be the best of friends in training and during the war. We ran missions together. And later, Wink—his nickname, guys gave each other nicknames, all kinds. Don't ask for mine," Finn blushes. "Anyway, Wink, um, he fell in love with this girl. She was Eurasian, part white, part Vietnamese. It was in Bangkok during one of our layovers, he met her. She got pregnant. Wink, he loved her. He married her, which was against protocol. We were both flying F-4's. His went down. He was pretty messed up. His wife, Khai, gave birth to a boy. Wink begged me to bring them to the states if he didn't make it home. He didn't." Finn looks up, stares at her. His green eyes hold a plea, but for what? She stares back, dipping her chin for him to continue.

"There's no way to make this easy so I'll just say it. I brought her back. Her and the baby. She didn't speak much English. Didn't have any skills other than being a seamstress. She couldn't support herself, Leela. I got a two-bedroom apartment. She and the baby in one bedroom. Me in the other. There wasn't ever anything between us, Leela. Christ, she was my best friend's wife. I got her some training at a Tech School. She was young, just a kid really. When she turned nineteen, she got a job as a typist in a big company. She didn't want the baby. She wanted me to have the boy. He was three by then. He thought of me as his father. I, I couldn't let strangers have him, and I loved him too. So, there it is. I wanted to tell you so many times. I just, well, you have this amazing career, on a track to the big time. It didn't seem fair to put this on you. Understand?"

333

Leela let out a long breath. "I understand, Finn. I do. How could you think I wouldn't? And, hey, I won't lie, it's going to take a bit of doing to wrap my head around this, but I will. He's wonderful boy, and you, Finn, I know you of all people wouldn't let a good friend down. I'm proud you didn't."

"Thank you for understanding. I wouldn't have blamed you if you didn't."

"Okay," Leela smiles, her heart beating with relief. *He's single. He's not married. She still has a chance.* "So, what's this question I'm supposed to say *yes* to?" She's ready to say yes to almost anything as long as it keeps Finn in her life.

Finn ducks his head. When he lifts it, his eyes, blazing green the way she remembers, are filled with emotion. I love you Leela. I always have. I don't have a right to ask this, but I'm going to. Can we be close again? Resume where we left off years ago. I know my life is complicated. I don't expect…"

"No."

"What? I, Leela, please…" Finn's face crumbles.

"It's marriage or nothing. I've waited long enough. I love you, Finn. I always have."

All at once, she's in his arms. He's kissing her with all the passion held so long in both their hearts.

Loud clapping behind them breaks their kiss. Blushing, they cling together. Neither wants to let go.

"Damn, 'bout time you two got together," Skeet teases.

"I second that," Ham grins.

Izzy comes, throws her arms around them both. "I'm so happy for you. I knew the two of you would be together. Granme' Delia said so. And she was never wrong."

"Hey, you guys, I hate to break up this lovefest, but…" Skeet interjects. "There's a bunch of people waitin' on us at the church. The new one we had built in the piney woods. We got us a funeral service to get to. Delia said she wanted singing and dancing at her funeral. We can't keep her waiting."

And that's what they did, with joy and love in their hearts for Delia. It was one heck of a Gathering.

Delia was interred behind the church amid a beautiful landscape overflowing with masses of flowers, Ishmael's doing. Her modest sized granite marker is engraved with a bird ready to take flight. The inscription reads:

Delia Field-Dubois
Born 1882 Left this earth in 1977
Loving Mother and Devoted Friend to all who knew her.
"Raise your voices in song, so the children
can find their way home."

Epilogue

What is destined to be, will be.
~ Granme' Delia ~

MANHATTAN 1974

In a newly opened art gallery in Soho, the curator unwrapped a canvas he'd purchased at an obscure estate sale. His intention had been to purchase arcane pieces of furniture for the gallery, not the work of an unknown artist. His tastes ran toward minimalists like Dan Flavin, Carl Andre and Judd. Yet his eye had been repeatedly drawn to this 19th century landscape, signed by the artist, E. Carter. It was a stunning piece, vibrant with life, depicting an island sugar cane plantation. It was essentially of little value, yet he found he couldn't walk away from it. Landscapes were out of favor, picked up these days for pennies on the dollar. Even so, he thought it might complement his home library. If nothing else, it would certainly be a conversation starter. He smiled to himself, imagining the heated debates on style and trend that would ensue among his contemporaries.

He was taken aback several years later when a well-heeled investor offered a staggering sum for the landscape. The artist's life story, a former slave, he was told, happened to be the subject of a contemporary novel short listed for a prestigious book award. Turning down the offer, the gallery owner congratulated himself. He had stumbled across a valuable piece of work, which begged the question, where did the rest of E. Carter's work reside? For surely, an artist of this caliber had to have been commissioned for other works. His curiosity piqued, the gallery owner spent years scouring estate sales and auctions in search of the E. Carter's work. In time, he managed to collect several more of E. Carter's paintings. One was a stunning period piece depicting a harbor with tall masted ships where negros, bare chested, unloaded cargo. Barefoot children with shirt tails cresting their knees, clung to their mothers amid hog head barrels. His collection of E. Carter's work was displayed in a prominent section of his gallery.

Many years later, the gallery owner, elderly now and ready to retire, was in the process of selling off most of his collected works, when a middle-aged man entered his gallery. The man, exceedingly tall, whose eyes were of an unusual color, was interested only in the special collection by E. Carter. The gallery owner, unmarried and childless, was loathed to part with his precious collection until this man with the piercing eyes told his story.

He was Skeet Stone, a descendent of the artist, E. Carter and cousin to the author of *A Single Drop of Blood*, Leela Hawkins-Connell. He told the man the artist, whose given name was Eulie, had lived and died at his family's ancestral home, Stone House, and that it was now a registered Historical Landmark. Skeet invited the man to Stone House, still a fully operating bed and breakfast, to see Eulie's mural, which was still viewed behind velvet ropes. The gallery owner, shook Skeet's hand, smiling in relief. His precious collection would have a home, forever. Despite Skeet's generous offer to buy the collection, the owner donated the entirety of E. Carter's work to Stone House.

After the gallery owner retired, he made a trip to Bateaux Bay where he lodged at Stone House. There he spent hours spellbound by Eulie's mural, her bud and rose painting and the painting of the flowers and women. He was one of a special few allowed inside Eulie's room, filled now with the artwork he'd donated. He examined her stone bowl and pestle on the table where she'd made her paints. He leafed carefully through her journal of sketches, amazed at her ability to draw her beautiful sketches with nothing more than a stick of graphite.

Before he left to return to his home in New York, a Gathering was held in his honor by those who had known and loved, Granme´ Delia. He stamped his feet to beats of the singing wood, clapping and singing with the others. At the circle, Leela used her hands and voice to tell the story of the bird who lost her song. On his return home, he came to realize it had been much more than luck which had brought Skeet to his gallery that day.

Glossary of Gullah Words in Eulie's Song

Ain/are not **Bredder**/brother **Beke**/white massa

Buckra/white man **Chabine**/low caste **Chirren**/children

Dem/them, they **Demarra**/tomorrow **Dis/De**/this, the, that

Djok/strong **Eh**/he, her, it **Edder**/other

Enn/in or end **Ebil**/evil **Fer**/for

Fren/friend **Gii**/give **Gooly**/good

Gwine/going to **Haffer**/have to **Hab**/have done

Hoona/you **Isself**/himself, herself **Ketch**/catch, caught

Knod/knowed **Kum**/come **Luk**/like

Maanin/morning **Maroon**/ runaway slave **Nuf**/enough

Offer/of, off **Ooman**/woman **Pamoise**/crooked thumb

Pooty/pretty **Skade**/scared of **Tek**/take, taken

Titter/sister **Trute**/truth **Uh**/I

Waak/walk **Wile**/awhile **Wuh**/what

About the Author

Kathy Lauren Miller is a graduate of Florida State University. She holds a master's degree in Education. She is the author of The Magic Minute Reader, a series of interactive books for young children that facilitate basic sight words through American Sign Language. She was awarded a United States Intellectual patent for the process and content. In 2001, she was named Special Educator and Teacher of the year for Children and Families in Hillsborough County, Florida. She is the author of two young adult novels, The Starling and The Girl in Black. She lives in Georgia with her husband, Jay, and their beloved dachshund, Bunny. This is her third novel.

Made in the USA
Coppell, TX
07 April 2021